For keith,
Thanks for the years
of Tsing-Tao!

P9-EEN-654

THE
NeVeR
PRAYER

AARON MICHAEL RITCHEY

Aaron M Ritchey

Let us be the angels!

www.crescentmoonpress.com

The Never Prayer
Aaron Michael Ritchey

ISBN: 978-1-937254-41-4
E-ISBN: 978-1-937254-42-1

© Copyright Aaron Ritchey 2012. All rights reserved
Cover Art: Fran and Richard Weber
Editor: Lin Browne
Layout/Typesetting: jimandzetta.com

Crescent Moon Press
1385 Highway 35
Box 269
Middletown, NJ 07748

Ebooks/Books are not transferable. They cannot be sold, shared or given away as it is an infringement on the copyright of this work.

All Rights Are Reserved. No part of this book may be used or reproduced in any manner whatsoever without written permission, except in the case of brief quotations embodied in critical articles and reviews.

This book is a work of fiction. The names, characters, places and incidents are products of the writer's imagination or have been used fictitiously and are not to be construed as real. Any resemblance to persons, living or dead, actual events, locale or organizations is entirely coincidental.

Crescent Moon Press electronic publication/print publication:
February 2012 www.crescentmoonpress.com

For the Lauras and Andreas that made this book possible. And for all of those living on just this side of hopeless. Angels and demons alike.

dramatis personae

<u>family</u>
Lena Marquez
Jozey\Joziah
Aunt Mercedes

<u>friends</u>
Deirdre Dodson
Santiago Scarpetti
Gramma Scar

<u>paladins</u>
Rob Cutler
Avery Tyson
Parker Lee

<u>heretics</u>
Bruise\Bruce
Bramage\Dane
Emma Leon

<u>untouchables</u>
Pockets\Paulie
Tubitha\Tabitha
Remy Bach

<u>townspeople</u>
Sheriff Art Lancing
Principal Percy
Mrs. Weyland

<u>new boys</u>
Chael
Johnny Beels

COLD MONDAY

i
(the red purse)

"I'm not going to do it again," Lena Marquez whispered to the red purse across the hall from her nestle of blankets. "Never again."

All of her other purses, scarves, and belts were just shadows hanging from hooks on both sides of the bathroom door, but in the glow of the cracked Thomas the Train nightlight, the red purse glittered. Each sequin like a teardrop of blood.

The heater chugged on sending lukewarm air into the basement apartment, as cold as an icebox. In October, at ten thousand feet, Avalon, Colorado had no pity for the weak or poor. It killed both.

Through anorexic walls, Lena could hear her aunt's barking cough in the next room. But it wasn't the coughing that had Lena awake at 4:46 on a Monday morning. It was her three-year-old brother, Joziah, who would wake up any minute.

He was like an alarm clock, same time, every morning. So regular Lena was awake before he asked the questions she couldn't answer.

Already the work of the day felt like bricks on her chest. Her junior year homework continued to pile up among the dirty laundry around their mattress on the floor.

But first, Jozey, always Jozey, no matter what.

"Mama!" he called out, still caught in the clutches of sleep.

Lena smoothed his hair with dark purple fingernails, perfectly polished. "It's okay, Jozey. Lena's here. Lena'll

~ ☾ ~

always be here."

Only half awake, he struggled in his footed blue pajamas and asked the same question he asked every morning. "Where's my mama?"

"She's in heaven, Jozey." Her voice cracked.

"Where's Daddy?" He blinked as if he had forgotten everything.

Lena let go of her tears. She could only cry them with Jozey in the darkness of the morning, because once she had her mask of make-up on, she sealed up all emotion with base, blush, and mascara. Everyone was watching.

Jozey sobbed against her, soaking her father's t-shirt she wore as pajamas. "I want them, Weni, I want them." Weni, because he couldn't say Leni, what her parents had called her.

"I want them, too," she said through her tears, and she cried with her brother until he fell back asleep. She stayed with him, cradling his warm body, brushing the tears off his face.

The ritual of her morning continued. First, her orphaned brother, followed by a shower, then her equally orphaned aunt. Aunt Mercedes shuffled out of her room wearing the bathrobe she always wore at home, holding a cigarette that was always lit. She stopped in the narrow hallway to watch Lena apply her make-up.

Her aunt's voice came out in a slow scratch. "We need a hundred dollars. More if it don't snow and I don't get my real job at Copper Mountain."

An ever-so-slight tremor shook Lena's fingers as she fought the urge to throw her eyebrow pencil at her aunt. She forced herself to concentrate on her face in the mirror, but Aunt Mercedes was behind her, taking up most of the doorway, all sad eyes and dog face and bad square haircut. Next to her aunt, the red purse dangled on a hook tempting Lena to use it.

"End of the month, sure." She brushed on the eye-

~ ☾ ~

shadow with irritated strokes. "End of the month means we need a hundred extra dollars. I bet I could bring home a thousand and you'd still say the same thing." She changed her voice to mimic her aunt. "'End of the month, Lena, and we need a hundred dollars.'"

Aunt Mercedes took a long pull from her smoke. "If it don't snow, we won't make our rent. Then it'll only be a matter of time until the social workers come. Without me around, who you gonna hate?"

Lena froze. One of her eyes was made-up and gorgeous, the other was gaunt and haunted. Her dark hair, dyed platinum at the tips, stuck to her skin like snakes. In the mirror, she leveled a shotgun gaze at her aunt. "There's plenty of hate to go around, Auntie. You. God. The drunk psycho who killed my parents. Oops, he just killed my dad. We won't talk about who killed my mom."

Lena felt the words leave her mouth like bullets. She had gone too far this time.

Aunt Mercedes didn't move, didn't shout, didn't do anything for a moment.

Then the big woman reached her arm forward, cigarette first, and Lena thought her aunt was going to burn her. Lena didn't care. She deserved it with what she said.

Instead, her aunt ashed her cigarette into the sink and then withdrew. "I love you and Jozey. You're all I have left. Hate me all you want if it makes you feel better, but we need a hundred dollars."

Lena knew the bills and knew what she would have to do to pay them. Her aunt never asked where the money came from, which made her aunt really smart, or really dumb, or both.

An hour later, Aunt Mercedes was back in her room, and Lena emerged from the bathroom in her armor of beauty. Complete and flawless. She found the cleanest

~ ☾ ~

clothes she had, layers of black, red, purple skirts, black leggings, tight sweater, and her high-heel bitch boots, laced up to her knees.

Between six o'clock and seven-thirty, her world was Jozey. She laughed with him, threw cereal so he could catch it like a puppy, read him books, watched PBS Kids on the T.V. in the crumbling kitchen. He clung to her tightly the whole time, as if at any moment she would vanish and leave him alone.

Then it was out the door into the cold.

Lena's mind nagged at her as she car-seated her brother into the cab of her father's ancient Ford truck. Red purse, red purse, had to get the red purse and do what needed to be done.

If they lost the apartment, they would lose everything. The social workers would take Jozey and throw him into foster care, and her aunt would be locked away in an asylum because everyone knew she wasn't right. And Lena would be alone.

Feeling as numb as the frigid mountain peaks around her, Lena hurried back into her aunt's rat-hole basement apartment.

The red purse wasn't on the door to the bathroom where it should be. Where it had been for weeks. Aunt Mercedes hadn't left her room, and Jozey was too short to reach it. No, something else was going on.

"Not again," Lena whispered.

~ ☾ ~

ii
(the devil whispering despair)

Shattered-lung coughing came from behind Aunt Mercedes' door. Down the long hallway, Lena could see Jozey in the truck outside, smiling at her and waving. He had no idea they were late. Or that someone or something was playing tricks on her.

Lena waved back, then she dove into her room, throwing clothes. The red purse had been there on the door, she was sure of it. And now the purse was gone.

It had happened before. Whenever she got the courage to use it, the red purse would disappear right when she needed it. Most people would call that Murphy's Law, but Lena's mother had had another name for when things went wrong.

It was the devil whispering despair.

This felt like the devil shouting. She could work without the purse, but so far it had kept her safe and out of jail. With what she was doing, she needed all the luck she could get.

Lena finally found the purse on the last of her parent's boxes, stacked in the closet. She hadn't put it there, but there it was. A shadow seemed to pass through the room, and Lena felt the heat from the furnace keenly. Sweat trickled down her sides.

Her parents were long buried, but they whispered to her from the boxes, voices full of love. *Get rid of the purse. Find another way.*

"Easy for you to say." Lena closed her eyes. "You don't need a hundred dollars. Not much to buy when you're dead except for a coffin."

~ ☾ ~

She put the red purse next to her in the cab, then
started the rusted truck while Jozey sang sweet cartoon
songs. His words swirled into mists from the chill. Trying
to sort through her exhausted mind felt like digging a
hole in loose sand. Up too late again, doing nothing,
hoping Jozey would sleep longer.

The truck idled as she put her hand up to the heater,
waiting for the hot air to come. Her dad had always said
Ford heaters were the best.

Mountain Avenue was quiet. The Torres family in the
little gray house above them had the lights on, but they
weren't going to work. No work to be had with the snow
locked up in the cold sky. Every week it didn't snow, the
ski areas lost money. Which meant everyone lost.

Engine warm enough, Lena eased the truck onto the
street.

Avalon was crammed into a jagged valley, surrounded
by the Mosquito Range mountains too steep and wild to
ski. Mount Calibum and Ablach Peak rose like craggy
hands up to the dark lavender sky, the sparse snow like
vanishing white veins in gray skin.

Splitting the two peaks was Mountain Avenue, the
main drag of Avalon. Most people just knew it as
Highway 77 because there wasn't much for anyone to
stop for. Too many windows showed cardboard and for-
sale signs. Too many houses with broken windows,
tangled lawns, and siding so frazzled you could use it for
kindling.

In better days, back when the Climax Mine was open,
the little houses on the banks of Camlann Lake had been
filled with workers and their families. The little
neighborhood was still known as the miner houses.
Across the lake was the new housing development,
Lakeview, where Lena had lived for a short time in what
felt like a palace, every room filled with more windows
than wood.

~ ☾ ~

Of course that was before the accident. Before medical bills had taken everything.

Now the house sat empty on the slope of Ablach Peak, like a dog starved to death. Now some bank, somewhere, owned the property her parents had worked so hard to buy.

But the dark citadel of Avalon High School stood strong while everything around it crumbled. More than a century ago, they had hewn the stones out of the Rocky Mountains to make an ornate town hall. When the county seat moved to Leadville, the building became a school, housing everyone, K-12, from all over Lake County.

At a stoplight, Art Lancing's police SUV pulled up next to her. When he looked over and waved, fear swept through her like a blizzard wind.

In her old life, the sheriff had been a friend. Now, he was the enemy. She put up a trembling hand and breathed out a sigh of relief as he turned down the next street.

"Weni! Weni!"

Lena opened her mouth to snap at her brother, but she caught herself. It wasn't Jozey's fault they were poor. "What, Jozey, sweetie?"

In his cold, red fingers he held up a single, fluffy, black feather. "God birdies, Weni. The God birdies love us, Weni, right?" His face was still a little milk-drippy from breakfast. His wide, dark eyes with the baby-long eyelashes pleaded with her to agree. "God loves us, right Weni?"

"Right, Jozey. Just like Mama and Daddy in heaven." She said the words easily, as if she believed them, as if no one could ever doubt them.

She pulled the red purse close. She had her talisman. Now she just needed a cell phone so she could sell her soul one more time. Better to lose her soul than lose Jozey.

~ ☾ ~

iii
(heretics, paladins, untouchables)

With Jozey safely at his daycare and the drive to school done, Lena closed the cold out behind her and charged up the tiers to the top of the lunchroom. She needed a phone and she needed one fast, before the desperation dissolved into despair.

Their cafeteria was long and narrow with sectioned-off platforms rising from where the little kids sat by the door, all the way up to where the junior and senior Paladins ate looking down on their kingdom. The walls were the same smooth, gray stone of the school, covered with pictures of congressmen and town leaders from long ago, all trapped under thick glass, scratched and showing the graffiti of Heretics long past. Like all the rest of the school, the floors were polished hardwood.

Deirdre Dodson and several girls had spent a weekend decorating for Halloween, now just six days away. Black and orange crepe paper streamers hung about the halls, high enough so no one could rip them down. Hobby store spiders clung to the fakery of spray can spider webs. Plastic bats flapped lifeless on fishing wire, and round-mouthed ghosts served as a warning to the living that death was waiting for them, sometimes not very patiently.

Lena called Deirdre the best friend. Not her best friend. *The* best friend. As if her life required one, whether it was true or not.

Deirdre was tall, tight-jeans thin, and wore a blood

~ ☾ ~

silk blouse drooling down her shoulders. The other Paladin girls sat pretty and perfect around her, but Deirdre was too blonde not to rule them all.

Paladins because the school's basketball team was the Avalon Paladins.

Deirdre's face lit up when she saw Lena. "Why, Magdalena, we were just talking about you and your special gifts."

Lena raised a plucked eyebrow. With Deirdre, every conversation was a test of loyalty. Too many wrong answers meant exile. "My special gifts? Like how I can single-handedly have the most screwed-up life possible? Okay, I accept. Where's my reward?"

"No, my girl, this is Avalon. You have too much competition for the worst life. So no award for you." Deirdre poked out the last five words with a sharp, red fingernail. "We were talking about the caste system at Avalon, and your name came up."

"I am intrigued, D, but first, I need to borrow your cell phone."

Deirdre reached into her fur-collared coat and out came the bejeweled phone. "Not even a little curious?"

"Give me a minute."

Lena punched in the number and Santiago answered with a rasp and a cough. "Yeah." In the background, opera murmured and clashed.

The memories of Santiago's bed and kisses left her feeling nothing. Nothing was nice compared to what she usually felt: muddy sorrow oozing out of her heart. "You're going to be late for school," Lena said to the boyfriend. The best friend and the boyfriend, both requirements.

"Late for school? Whatever will I do?" Santiago feigned shock.

"I have my red purse," she said.

"*Bellisimo.* I'll have an address. Good timing, Lena,

~ ☾ ~

very good timing."

"For you." Lena hung up on him, then deleted the number from the log before giving the phone back to Deirdre.

"So, what's my special gift?" Lena asked.

Deirdre took her phone and smiled. "You are the only person at our little school able to straddle the castes."

"Sounds obscene."

Deirdre laughed and the others followed her lead. "I don't want the details of your love life. Straddle, as in you have one foot in the world of the Paladins and one in the cemetery the Heretics call their lives. No small feat to be both a Paladin and a Heretic."

"No award though," Lena said.

"No award. But maybe the best of both worlds? You get the bad boy Santiago, you get to experiment with fashion..." She emphasized the word "experiment" with a look of distaste. "And yet, you still get to hang out with us. You lucky, lucky girl."

Lena was taking fashion cues from a Heretic friend who made weekly pilgrimages to a thrift shop in Vail. Emma Leon crafted the used clothes into outfits as if they were art. Emma never came to school boring. But being a Heretic, sometimes she just didn't come to school at all.

"How come I don't feel lucky?" Lena asked. Going back and forth between the cliques was killing her, but she didn't see a way out. Deirdre was a necessary evil, a bit of normalcy in her otherwise ruined life, and Santiago was the dangerous paycheck she couldn't live without.

She was trapped.

Deirdre waved away her question. "Which brings us to our next topic of conversation. Since we have a miniscule school, a mini-school if you will, we don't have the castes other schools have—"

Lena interrupted with a question. "Don't you mean

~ ☾ ~

cliques?"

"Oh no. Clique is such a weak word. Castes are hereditary and forever. Like in India. No, Lena, we have castes in Avalon, forever and ever."

"Nothing is forever," Lena said, but she said it with too much force. It covered them all with an uncomfortable silence. At least with Santiago, Emma, and the other Heretics, she could never get too dark.

"Anyway," Deirdre continued, "since we don't have the castes other schools have, we think we should divvy out everyone, either Paladin or Heretic. For example, Pockets. He's too geeky to be a Heretic. And he's too psychotic to be Paladin. But if we had to choose…"

"Aren't we being a wee bit too catty for a Monday?" Lena asked. "We generally eat our classmates on Friday."

Deirdre shrugged. "Just idle conversation. It's perfectly normal for adolescents to categorize people. It's creating order out of chaos. Now, what about Pockets?"

He was sitting alone at a table down below them, talking to himself and laughing. His real name was Paulie, but Deirdre had started calling him Pockets because back in the eighth grade he had been caught with his hands in his pockets doing unfortunately private things in public.

Lena knew what they all expected her to say, but she was too frazzled and sleep-deprived to care.

"Pockets would be a Paladin," Lena said. "Not like a basketball player, but he's too smart for the Heretics."

"Please, Pockets would be a Heretic, of course."

Lena sighed. Got that one wrong, might as well get a few answers right. Pointing at the fat girl sitting alone. "And Tubitha would be a Heretic." Pointing at the only black guy in the school who was also sitting by himself. "And Remy would be a Paladin."

"I was thinking he would be a Heretic. I can see him going all ghetto." Deirdre put up her hands in fake gang

~ ☾ ~

signs.

"Racist," Lena said.

"Just kidding. Remy already is a Paladin. Why he left us, I have no idea."

Parker Lee struggled her way into the conversation. "It was after they cancelled football. That's when Remy totally changed."

"Be that as it may," Deirdre said, "he could still return to the fold if he wanted. The Paladins are a forgiving people, as long as you qualify."

"And how do I qualify?" Lena asked but didn't stop there. It was like she was taking her SAT's and marking every box black. Just because. "We all know the only reason I get to sit up here is because Deirdre and I have been friends for so long. And because I can still be pretty. But do you know what it really takes to be a Paladin?"

No one answered.

"How many Paladins live in the miner houses?"

Another question no one answered.

Lena marked in the last box black, failing the test by uttering the unspeakable. "It takes money to be a Paladin, pure and simple."

The morning bell saved Lena from her attempt at social suicide.

Deirdre only had smiles for her. Smiles with lots and lots of teeth. "Well, tell us how you really feel."

Lena lowered her head and attempted some damage control. She had already lost enough and wasn't ready to be cast into the darkness just yet. It was time to smile pretty like a good Paladin girl. "Sorry, D. It's Monday and I'm crazy."

Deirdre closed her eyes for a moment. Lena knew her friend hated that word, crazy, with good reason.

She heard Parker Lee grump and whisper, "Remy lived in the miner houses and he was a Paladin."

But by then Parker Lee and the other girls were

~ ☾ ~

drifting off to class.

Deirdre stayed and touched Lena's shoulder. "Was Jozey up early again?"

Lena nodded, shocked to find herself skirting tears. But she couldn't cry. Her mascara was too expensive.

"Did he ask where your parents were again?"

Another nod. Lena forced the tears down, forced the mud in her heart to harden into rock.

"You were right," Deirdre said. "It was an insipid conversation."

"Yet you do have such a nice vocabulary," Lena said, and they both fell against each other, laughing, almost like old times.

Almost.

"Why do you think your parents had Jozey so late?" Deirdre asked.

"I think they knew," Lena whispered. She searched Deirdre's blue eyes for something like doubt or hate or ridicule. "I think a part of them knew they were going to die early and they didn't want to leave me alone." Then she saw the flicker of amusement on Deirdre's face and recanted with a flip of her hair. "But he was probably an accident. I mean, really."

"Accidents do happen." Deirdre kissed her cheek and moved on.

All Lena could think about was Judas' kiss in the garden of Gethsemane.

~ ☾ ~

iv
(santiago's cold caring)

Before her parents were killed, Lena hadn't minded school. She had even liked some of her classes. But now school was just watching the clock tick.

The classrooms were frigid. The sun outside the window was a lie, worse than a lie, because it taunted them with no snow. No snow meant no skiing which meant no money. The mountain people called snow white gold, which was exactly what it was for Avalon.

Lena hadn't eaten and the hunger pestered her, but it was easier to worry than to eat. She chewed on her pens and wished for a cigarette. She had quit after the accident and the hospitals and doctors and darkness. She stayed quit by listening to her aunt wheeze and gag all night long. It was the best anti-smoking campaign ever created, and she thought sometimes about recording it and playing it over and over for Santiago to kick the nicotine.

Speak of the devil, the boyfriend showed up tardy, waltzed into the classroom, and lounged in the back row, black combat boots propped up on a broken desk in between Bruise and Dane Bramage. Bramage, as in brain damage, but not quite. Bruise as in Bruce, but not quite. Both equally combat-booted. The Heretics wore dark, baggy clothes to match the black circles around their eyes. They smelled like incense, cigarettes, and boozy King Soopers cologne.

Santiago smiled at her, and she smiled back and thought about Santiago's playlist on his MP3 player. Barking death metal and Italian operas, back to back,

~ ☾ ~

Scattershot and Giuseppe Bertoglio swirled together, and that was Santiago. Wicked sin and heaven-sweet.

Between morning classes, Santiago took her into his leather and cologne, kissing her while the halls emptied around them. The hallways were chiseled rock and hardwood floor, ridiculously wide, with tiny doll furniture lockers on either side of the chasm. Most of the lockers were empty and unused.

"You have got to get a cell phone, Lena," Santiago said. His dark hair was red-dyed and shot out all around his head, fashioned so it looked like he had just crawled out of bed. But Lena knew better.

"Pay me more, you cheap dime-store hood," Lena said. With Santiago, there were no landmines or traps. He threw his bombs the old-fashioned way, Molotov cocktails, overhand.

"What are you willing to do for it?" he asked. He murmured an opera line, his voice full and rich.

Both his words and the singing felt like a slap. She sighed and held out a hand.

He produced a broken pen and tried to write on frayed notebook paper. The pen scratched but didn't write.

"Pens hate me," Santiago said. "And I hate them."

"It's the devil whispering despair," Lena said. She found him a pen that worked.

"Hate pens, don't mind the devil." He smiled vacantly as he wrote down an address in Vail.

In her last period computer class, she could mapquest it and then erase it from the PC's memory.

He chattered away, casual, eyelids droopy. "This week's run is a big one, the last one for awhile. People I'm dealing with have a huge buyer from Buena Vista all lined up. The last thing I need is for you to screw the pooch."

"Yeah, I'm so incompetent. You might want to fire me."

~ ☾ ~

Droopy eyes squinted into red slits. "Nope. You're the best I got. But how come you don't come over no more? I have love in my heart."

"All you have is lust in your pants."

"It's like love, only harder," Santiago said, and again, sang in Italian, like he was onstage ready to give haircuts in Seville.

His fingers turned into metal hooks, but she didn't wince as he screwed his nails into her sweater to pull her close by a bra strap. She felt numb and wished she could always feel that way, dead and cold like winter stone. The halls were empty now and every word seemed to echo. So they talked in hushes.

"Seriously, Lena. This'll be my biggest score yet. New people, same dance."

"New people." Lena felt her heart shrink. The old ones had been bad enough.

"New people. And you know the song. You get snatched, you don't know me, you don't know them, you don't know you. I want you to be careful."

With his fingers still snagged in her sweater, she razored his face with a long stare. Her words were like ice on a coffin. "Because you care so much about my safety. Because you really love me."

Santiago cut her right back. "And you really love my money."

"Which makes me a slut."

Santiago twisted her bra strap harder. "No. It makes you a whore. Sluts do it for free." His kiss was as cold as handcuffs.

"And you think you're such a pimp," Lena said to him, pushing him away.

"Whatever. Just be careful. I do care about you, whether you know it or not." He was serious. There was concern in his hazel eyes, but there was also poison from the drugs. "The narcs are crazy for a bust in Lake County.

~ ☾ ~

Make sure they don't bust us. No one around here can afford that."

She took a step toward class, but he caught her by the arm. She glanced down at his chipped, black fingernail polish. So much drama in his make-up.

"Lena, you know I don't have a choice, right? It's not like I grew up wanting to be a drug dealer. If I didn't deal—"

Lena closed her eyes and cut him off. "Shut up. I know the score. So just shut up."

He softened. "Look, I can get Bruise to go. I mean, he was already planning on it. You don't have to do this."

"I'm doing it. Don't get all weepy on me and don't pity me." Lena felt hot again. Sweat tickled her scalp.

"It's not pity," he whispered, picking a black feather off her sleeve, like the one Jozey had found. "Not pity at all."

She left with Santiago's cigarette taste in her mouth. She had quit cigarettes. Now if she could only quit Santiago and stop playing his red purse games.

~ ☾ ~

V
(the dog men)

After her last class, Lena stopped at Jozey's school on her way out of town, the adrenaline already wrecking her. The Cherubim Daycare Center was past the miner houses, on the banks of Camlann Lake where the pale water looked like liquid cold.

Usually she picked up Jozey right after school at three, but she paid Mrs. Weyland to keep him until six and thought to duck out before Jozey saw her. Too late. All smiles, he ran over and threw his body against her. "Weni! Can we play?"

"No, sweetness. I have some work to do." She wasn't able to look him in the eye and had to kiss away his complaining.

Lena trudged back to her truck, got in, but when she turned the key, nothing happened. She struck the steering wheel with her palm. The truck had been running fine. It wasn't fair. More of the devil whispering despair.

She dabbed at the sweat on her forehead, careful of her make-up, and twisted the key again. Nothing. It was too hot in the cab, maybe from the engine, so she had to check.

She banged out of the truck to unlock the hood. The sound brought back memories of her father. He had loved his truck as much as he had loved his daughter, and all three of them had spent a lot of time together.

She saw the problem right away. A spark plug connection had slipped off. She carefully pushed the cable back in place. When she tried the key again, the

~ ☾ ~

truck rumbled up, and she was gone.

With her father's old cassette tapes scattered around the cab, it was like he was right there, talking to her about the glory of 80's music. The Crutches, Curious Religion, Burning Wheel, the Sympathies. She liked the Sympathies the best, the slow guitar, the moody lyrics, the drum beating like a dirge.

Same music they had been listening to that night.

She and Jozey in the backseat of the new SUV. The windshield wipers thwacked along cleaning away the fat snowflakes and draining the residual off the glass. They approached the car parked on the side of the road slowly. Lena remembered the brake lights glimmering like red demon eyes winking.

"Watch out for that car," her father had said.

Her father had warned them but of the wrong thing. The car hadn't been dangerous. It wasn't an accident that had killed her parents.

"Should we stop?" her mom had asked.

That one question still echoed in Lena's mind.

No, they shouldn't have stopped.

And in Lena's fantasies, her mother had asked the echoing question and they had all said no, like in a cartoon, and they kept on driving and it was all okay.

At Highway 91, Lena paused and realized the tape had shut off. She had been barely listening. On her right was the Gas 'n Sip, where her aunt had a nothing little job that barely fed them.

Lena sighed, thinking of her aunt, and turned right, going north to I-70. The Sympathies weren't touching her right, so she slid in Scattershot.

The infuriated guitars and demon screaming slammed her all the way into Vail.

The condos behind the Safeway were nothing but peeling paint, splintered wood, and stained windows. She parked, grabbed the red purse, and walked past a

~ ☾ ~

mashed-in, mustard-colored Ford Bronco to the door. A chill wind brushed her face and tried to steal her breath, but she wasn't breathing.

Her heart had hammered her lungs empty.

Dizzy, she rang the doorbell.

"Who is it?" the gravel of a hard man's voice asked.

"Santiago sent me."

The door clicked open. It was dark inside, the curtains drawn. The smell of smoke, dogs, and drugs gagged her.

She didn't want to go into that darkness and stink.

"For God's sakes, get in here."

Seized by the wrist, she was dragged inside. The touch threw iron into her soul. "Hands off!"

The man showed her his palms, grinned, and backed up. "Sorry, princess." He was tall and thick, a scraggle of a beard on his face. He had too many teeth, too big for his mouth. Three other men as hairy, big, and leathered were clustered around a table in the kitchenette, smoking and drinking under an orange light as if the bulb was swimming in rancid oil.

Once her eyes adjusted, she saw the dogs all around, eyes gleaming hateful, maws full of yellow fangs and black tongues.

Four men and a roomful of dogs. Every eye, both man and dog, on her.

"I haven't seen you before. Where's Bruise?"

Lena didn't know where to focus her eyes. Which were more dangerous? The dogs or the men?

"We take turns," she said.

"You take turns."

"Yeah, we take turns."

"When do I get a turn?" he asked.

Lena could feel how far away she was from the door and sunlight. The stink was overwhelming, but worse were the eyes, all those eyes, caressing her. She clenched her jaws against the rabbiting of her heart. "If we're just

~ ☾ ~

going to chit-chat, I'm going to leave. Or are you going to give me the package?"

"You wanna drink? How 'bout a smoke? Or how 'bout you take home one of these goddamn dogs?"

"No. Just the package."

The leader man left and the other dog men were silent. One of the dogs gruffed and was backhanded for it. Another dog growled but movement from the table brought obsequious whimpering.

Lena stood frozen, every muscle tightened so she wouldn't shake.

One of the men poured fingers of whisky into his red, plastic cup. The booze chugged out in slow motion.

Then the leader came back and things got worse.

He had the drugs wrapped in a Safeway plastic bag. Lena opened her red purse to put it inside, but he just gave her a wet, toothy grin.

"Oh no," the dog man said. "Bark first. You gotta bark for your dope."

"You've got to be kidding me," Lena said.

"Everyone has to do it. Santiago should have told you. And from what I understand, he needs this last drop pretty bad."

Lena glanced at the men, as if asking for help. Dead eyes answered her unuttered pleas. All the dogs were up, muscles tense.

There was nothing she could do. She barked. A few of the dogs barked with her.

"Louder!" the dog man shouted.

Lena gritted her teeth and barked just that much louder.

And then the condo fell into a hell of howling.

The man with too many teeth dropped the package into her purse and Lena fled to the door. The other men got up, cursing and beating the dogs to shut them up. Lena hurried outside to her truck.

~ ☾ ~

As she pulled onto I-70, Scattershot screamed murder from the speakers and she screamed with it, pounding on the steering wheel, stomping the gas pedal to the floor. All of that torment and humiliation for a hundred dollars. Her skirt cost more.

She saw the lights from the police car but never heard the sirens. She had no idea how long he'd been behind her only that her speedometer was reaching for ninety.

Highway 91 was just ahead. Might as well have her life destroyed on the same stretch of pavement that killed her parents.

~ ☾ ~

vi
(on the side of the road)

Lena's rage melted into sharp panic, like she had eaten sheet metal and could feel every edge. Pulling the truck off the highway, she crunched onto a wide patch of gravel next to the Copper Mountain ski area.

The cop drove up behind her, sirens wheeling madly in the dimming light.

Bad enough to be stopped for speeding, but her purse was full of drugs. Lena didn't know what kind because she never looked and didn't care.

Wind rocked the truck and she felt the stone inside her heart crumble to dust, broken by the weight of the past months. A chill had gotten into her, and despite the heat, she was shivering. She couldn't do another day.

She was going to hand him the red purse. She was going to throw gasoline on the fires burning in her life and then watch the flames devour it all. She'd get locked up, Jozey thrown in foster care, and the darkness eating Aunt Mercedes would finish the job until she faded away.

Swallowing made Lena feel like she would puke.

Just one cop. Highway patrol. He motioned for her to roll down the window.

Her hands shook, but she did it.

"License, registration, insurance."

It felt like a bad juggling act, trying to get all her paperwork to him. And then she held up the red purse.

"What's that?" the cop asked.

"Take it." She choked out the words. It was her voice, it was her breath, but it felt like someone else talking. Someone without a heart. The devil could whisper all he

~ ☾ ~

wanted now.

The cop reached for the purse, then turned, his attention caught by the grind of footsteps in the gravel.

One of Jozey's black feathers slowly floated through the cab of the truck. "Hey, Officer."

The sudden voice made her look in the rearview mirror. A boy her age with black hair, olive-dark skin, and midnight eyes stood between the cop car and her truck. He was staring right at her. Lena's dusty heart trembled back to life. She dug her fingernails into the scratched red upholstery.

He scared her.

The cop put a hand on his holster. "What do you want?"

"Can I talk to you for a minute?" the dark boy asked. "It's important."

The cop walked away, and Lena watched in the mirror as they huddled together, urgently whispering.

"Thank you! Jesus, thank you!" the cop suddenly shouted and hugged the dark boy, then pushed Lena's documents into the stranger's hands and ran back to his car. The policeman took off speeding without lights or sirens, tires throwing roadside dirt.

Lena sat, mouth open.

The dark boy tramped up to her window. She was about to thank him when he hurled the bits of paper at her. His dark eyes boiled, his narrow nose flared, his mouth sneered, and then with a quick motion, he drew his white hood over his head and stormed away toward the ski area.

Lena dashed out of the truck after him. "Hey! What did you tell that cop?"

The dark boy's black coat was like spilled oil against the white hoodie. His jeans were aged white, the cuffs frayed and feathery, brushing over scuffed cowboy boots.

He didn't stop walking, but she did.

~ ☾ ~

"Who are you?" she called after him.

Wind blasted Lena with fistfuls of frigid razor blades. A glance up showed her a swirl of arctic clouds drowning the tops of the purple-shadowed mountains nearly black with night. When she looked back, he was gone.

"I'm pathetic," she whispered, still trembling. Seconds before, she had almost thrown her life away. She had to get out. She was going to give Santiago his drugs and never, ever deal with him or his Heretics or their crimes ever again.

But a part of her knew getting out wouldn't be easy, just as she knew the milky, cold clouds would settle in like a funeral shroud in the valleys of the mountains and do their best to freeze them all to death.

~ ☽ ~

vii
(gramma scar)

Having Jozey in the truck was better than eating ice cream. He was smiles and songs and talk about school and his friends and the clouds and the snow and skiing and feathers and the God birdies.

"So you had a good day?"

He nodded. "But you sad, Weni. Why you sad?"

"I'm not sad," she said.

"You always so sad, Weni."

"Not always."

"Always."

Lena had to smile. "If I wasn't sad before, this certainly is depressing. I'm losing an argument to a three-year-old."

"Did you see a God birdie today, Weni?"

"Sure did." She picked up a black feather and handed it to him. "You know they're called angels, right?"

"Angels are in heaven. The God birdies are here and all around us."

His face was solemn, and those dark eyes with the long eyelashes sprinkled love into her heart. She smoothed his hair and drove home.

Lena left the red purse in the truck. She didn't want the evil thing anywhere near her brother.

Jozey book-ended each day. She washed him, brushed his teeth, and held him as he went to sleep in the nest of blankets and sheets on their bed. Too many sheets because she hadn't folded and put them away like she should have, but sleeping in the pile was nice, like crawling into a soft mouse nest.

~ ☾ ~

Lena felt herself drifting off with Jozey, but her day wasn't over. The bedroom door down the hall opened and Aunt Mercedes shuffled past.

There was the creak of a chair in the kitchen, the click of a lighter, and then the smell of smoke.

Out of bed, Lena grabbed another purse, her black leather one, and then stopped at the front door. "Can you listen for Jozey? I have to go out for a bit."

Her aunt exhaled smoke. "What time will you be back?"

"Too late for you to be my mom, Auntie. Too bad my real mom's not still alive to take some of the pressure off you."

Aunt Mercedes' droopy face showed no emotion. "You're asking me to watch Jozey. I need to know when you'll be back. I'm not being unreasonable. It's just common courtesy."

"Fine. I'll be back before eleven."

Outside her basement apartment, Avalon had turned into a ghost world. The cloud bank hovering over the mountain tops had settled into the valleys and everything was veiled in mist. Not fog. A frozen, freezing cloud.

She drove to the miner houses where Santiago lived with his mom, but his house was deserted, every window dark and muted in the mist. The memories here were thick. Driving to the house on nights where she danced with despair, letting Jozey watch T.V. while she and Santiago talked and kissed in his basement room.

Santiago understood her pain. He had lost his father. And he didn't want to help Lena. No, what Santiago had wanted was simple, and it made Lena forget about her life for a while. But never long enough.

The connections in a small town were easy enough to draw. Lena was friends with Santiago's grandmother, which led her to Santiago, which led her into the drug

~ ☾ ~

muling business. A to B to a dark little C, but only when Lena had to. "Had to" had turned into the end of every month when Aunt Mercedes ran out of money.

It was only a little after eight. Santiago should have been home. Or his mom should have. Santiago missing meant something was wrong. Bruise, Dane Bramage, and the other Heretics always clustered around the house, especially at night.

The red purse glittered in the muffled streetlights as she drove by the St. Michael's Catholic Church with the Bearly Inn, more bar than grill, across the street, then on past Luther Pem's general store, past scattered storefronts pretending to be gravestones, and on to the restaurant owned by Santiago's grandmother. Even though Lena's basement apartment was only a hundred yards away, she pulled around back into the empty parking lot. She walked through cloud to knock on the door.

Gramma Scar would be on her stool watching T.V. behind the cash register. On busy nights, her daughter-in-law helped, but most of the time it was just Gramma Scar who did everything, waitressed, cooked, cleaned. If Santiago had a soul, it was Gramma Scar who had given it to him.

The old woman waddled to the back door and took Lena inside. "What a night to be driving around. Come in, come in. The weather people say it's too cold to snow. I can never believe that, but that's what they say."

Gramma Scar wore a bad wig the color of autumn grass to cover up her bald patches. But the make-up on her face and the dresses she wore made up for the wig. She insisted she would not become a frumpy, fat, old woman. Just because she was already old and fat, didn't mean she also had to be frumpy.

Inside the tiny restaurant, the red booths were empty but everything was in its place: the checkered

~ ☾ ~

tablecloths, the pictures of Italian basilicas on the walls, the fake grapevines, the wax-baptized bottles holding candles.

"I'm trying to find Santiago."

Gramma Scar looked at her closely. "You eat today, Lena?"

Lena shook her head. She felt too tangled to eat. "But I promise I'll eat once I get home. What about Santiago?"

Gramma Scar threw up her hands. The bright orange dress she wore tugged on her plump arms. "Oh, my precious beauty, you have to eat. You're taking care of that little boy and that's hungry work. Let me fix you something. Please. Please, let me. Please."

"Okay, but I'll pay."

"You being friends with my grandson is payment enough. I don't know where that scoundrel is, but his mother is in Denver, doing what, I don't even want to know." Gramma Scar banged her way into the the kitchen orchestrating pots and pans, pasta and meatballs.

"Can I use your phone to call him?"

"Be my guest."

The phone was a cracked yellow antique with sticky buttons and a cord. Lena had to dial Santiago's cell twice.

He picked up, voice low and tight. Santiago's voice, but not Santiago. "Gramma, I can't talk now."

"It's Lena. Where are you? You said you wanted my red purse to wear with your new pumps."

"Tomorrow after school. Bye."

And Santiago was gone. No opera, no jokes, nothing. Lena sat down at a booth, wondering if he had been picked up by the police. And if he was telling them all about her.

A loud voice sounded from the kitchen. "But as far as Santiago goes, I can't blame his mother, though she certainly doesn't help things. No, he gets all his bad from

~ ☾ ~

my side of the family. My father came out here mafia, but
Denver mafia, how can you take that so seriously?" With
a meal in hand, Gramma Scar came out swathed in
aprons. The top one said, "If you loved me, you'd eat
more."

She sat down and drank decaf coffee across from Lena
while she ate. The meatballs were spicy and greasy, the
sauce was full of seasoned love, and the pasta was thick
and doughy. It was the best thing she had ever eaten, but
she said that about every one of Gramma Scar's meals.

Between the food, the warm room, and Gramma
Scar's smiles and bright eyes, Lena felt her heart melt
back into mud. Before she knew it, she was struggling
against the tears, but the old woman saw everything.
Lena was unmasked.

"Oh, my little girl. Oh, my precious beauty."

The woman got up and hugged Lena to her, and Lena
fell into the smell of perfume and spices and cooking.
She cried harder and Gramma Scar whispered soothing
words until Lena pulled away.

"Well, might as well cry now," she said, grinning shy
through her tears. "Don't need to worry about my
mascara this late in the day."

"It's not about Santiago, is it?" Gramma Scar asked.

"Kind of."

"You're involved in his bad business."

Lena nodded and wiped away her tears.

The old woman patted her and went back to her
kitchen. "Lena, you make bad choices for the right
reasons. But they're still bad choices. Time to start
making good choices no matter what."

Lena ate a little more, but eating reminded her of her
mom, and so it was just easier to stop eating than to be
tortured by the memories.

Gramma Scar came back with a little brown bag.
"Meatballs for Jozey. I know how he loves them." She

~ ☾ ~

touched Lena's cheek. "Come and work at the restaurant with me. I might not be open in a month, but I'm open now."

"Is it that bad?" Lena asked.

Gramma Scar shrugged and tilted her head in one motion that said no big deal. "Once it starts to snow, business will pick up. Dodson is coming up with some scheme to open ski condos and who knows? It might work. Please."

Dodson. Deirdre's father.

Lena stood up. "Thanks, Gramma."

"Please, come and work for me while I still have a place for you to work. Santiago is useless in the kitchen, and his mother is only getting worse."

"I'll think about it." She kissed the old woman's cheek. "Thanks so much. I feel better."

Lena left through the back door and cold cloud swallowed her.

From behind her, a footstep echoed in the mist. It was too dark and hazy for her to see anything. A garbage dump's stench thrashed her nose. Something brushed against her and she yelled and threw punches, but nothing was there. Just mist.

"You okay, Lena?" Gramma Scar stood at the door, a broom in her thick hands.

"Yeah, fine. Just the fog scaring me."

"Be careful. And think about what I said. Make the good choices."

"You sound like a commercial."

"Yeah, well, you don't know everything, my precious beauty."

Lena drove the short distance to her apartment. Working at La Rosa Calda would be convenient, but who would watch Jozey? Once it snowed, Aunt Mercedes would be at Copper Mountain during the day and the convenience store at night.

~ ☾ ~

Getting out of the truck, Lena stuffed the red purse full of drugs behind the seat.

At the kitchen table, she spread out her homework but ended up sleeping on it. She took off the rest of her make-up, then crawled through the dirty laundry and into the piles of sheets and blankets next to Jozey. She slept only a few more hours until her little brother woke up, asking for their mother and father.

That Tuesday morning, Lena didn't cry. She just held her weeping little brother and told him lies about heaven.

Hell held the only truth she could believe in.

~ ☾ ~

DESPERATION
TUESDAY

i
(lunch with the heretics)

The Paladins owned Lena before school, but at lunchtime, the Heretics had their hooks in her. Santiago was back to his old stoned self, not talking about what he had done the night before. Lena wanted to get rid of the purse, but Santiago said he would deal with it after school, and it was safer not to talk about it until then.

The Heretics pretended to eat lunch near the courtyard that cut a square out of the school. On warm days they would sit among the skeletal trees and yellow grasses, but now with the frigid clouds, they were forced inside to sit on benches right next to the principal's office. Santiago said you should keep your friends close but your enemies closer. Funny, but Mr. Percy, the principal, said the same thing.

From where they sat, Lena and the Heretic girls watched the boys beat on each other, either with words or fists, as if they were puppies. Except for Dane Bramage. He didn't play. He just sat with a safety pin, scratching patterns into the dry skin on his arm. His real name was Dane Johnson, but Dane Bramage fit him snug. Surrounding him like mosquitoes were stories of mental institutions, straitjackets, and shock therapy. With his parents gone, Bramage had been cast into the forest to live with an aunt and a sister no one ever saw.

Lena didn't know what to believe, but Bramage looked the part. He cut his own hair with a straight razor, hacked it down to the roots in some parts, left it sprouting like a bush in others. He finished off the safety pin fun by running it between the piercings in his nose

~ ☾ ~

and lip. It left him with a snarl.

He called out through the safety pin. "And I say unto thee, there will be Armageddon visited upon Avalon. No stone untouched. No soul unscorched. Apocalypse now."

"The horror, the horror." Santiago brayed laughter.

Yes, back to his old self. After school, Lena would give him the red purse, he would give her the money, and she would be free again. For now, she would just have to listen to his stupid laughing.

"Avalon don't need no snow," Bramage whispered through his snarl. "Avalon needs a cleansing fire."

Bruise grunted and shook his head. "He ain't right. Living out in the woods has finally gotten to him."

Lena wondered, like she did every day, what she was doing there. The thrill of Santiago and the evil that men do had worn thin. But it was easier than navigating Deirdre's minefields.

Emma, the dress sculptor, with midnight make-up and facial piercings, chewed a fingernail. She wore a pink princess dress, a scarred ballerina tutu, and a Scattershot concert t-shirt. All under a daisy-painted leather jacket. "How is Jozey doing?" she asked.

It was no secret why Emma was interested in Jozey. She had a half-brother Jozey's age who had been taken into foster care after her stepmom nearly beat him to death. Emma's dad left the woman, got a job down in Beaver Creek, and now Emma hardly ever saw him and was alone with her clothes most of the time.

"Jozey's okay," Lena said. "Up early again."

"You're so lucky to have him."

Lena wanted to shrug her words away, but she didn't want to add to Emma's wounds. Nice thing about the Heretics though, Lena didn't have to hide an ounce of her tragedy. They all lived on just this side of hopeless.

"Yeah, he's the best part of my life," Lena said, and found to her surprise that she meant it. Four o'clock

~ ☾ ~

questions, the hassle of bathing a three-year-old, the whole package.

"So lucky," Emma murmured.

"Yeah, she is!" Santiago howled. "She gets to be with me. Grand freakin' prize 'round these parts! *Lei e la mia dolce rosa, mia dolce, bellissima rosa rossa.*" He sang the last words and his voice echoed in the hall.

The principal's secretary leaned back in her chair and yelled through the open door. "No opera today, Santiago. Not today."

"But it is not opera! It is Giuseppe Bertoglio!"

"Not today!"

Santiago just grinned and sang it all anyway until the secretary slammed the door closed.

"Some people have no taste in music." Santiago brushed a hand past his lips, as if he had a cigarette dangling there.

"Opera sucks, man," Bruise grunted. "If it don't have guitars, it ain't music."

"Gotta agree with Bruce on that one."

Avery Tyson, Rob Cutler, and the rest of the basketball players ambled out of the corridor.

"Oh deary me," Santiago whispered. "The Paladins have come to darken our doorstep. You bring swords?"

"Wouldn't need a sword to cut you down. Just wanted to see how the other half lives," Cutler said. He fully and completely embraced his buzz-cut hair and sports apparel. Lena wouldn't be surprised if he had a Nike swoosh birthmark on his butt.

"To live is to die, my friend," Santiago said. He walked into Cutler's face.

"How come you guys never eat?" The Paladin smirked the question.

"Who needs to eat when you got drugs?"

Lena rose up and pushed herself between the kings of the school, her hands on their chests. "That's enough,

~ ☾ ~

boys. Us girls are getting all woozy with your displaying."

Avery stood behind Cutler, shaking his head. Avery was quiet and handsome, but a Paladin to the bone. Or so Lena thought.

"What happened to you, Santiago?" Avery asked. "You were the best shortstop I ever saw, like a vacuum."

"Yeah, well, things change," Santiago droned with a stoned smile but didn't look at him. His eyes still roasted Cutler. "But you don't change, huh, Avery? You and your old man and Deirdre's pop gonna save Avalon with ski condos?"

Cutler pushed against Lena's hand. She felt the muscles in his chest harden. "Maybe. At least we're not trying to tear it down."

Avery shook his head and walked away. "It's just sad to see you ruin your life."

Santiago reeled and sang. "*Il mondo e molto fragile.*"

Lena thought she might have seen tears in his eyes. Then he was right up against her, his body as tense as Cutler's.

"Go back to your throne, your highness, and leave us poor serfs alone."

A smatter of laughter erupted out of Cutler. "You and your dirtbag friends are such a joke, Santiago. How can you wake up every morning and not kill yourselves? Being poor is one thing, but being pathetic is another."

Cutler followed the other Paladins down the hall as Santiago sang tragic Italian, his eyes closed, his voice full. Lena recognized the words and she couldn't help but be moved by them.

I am a poor, poor man in a rich man's world.

Forty-five minutes later, the police descended upon them.

~ ☽ ~

ii
(the text message)

Math class after lunch and Lena sat gazing out the window at a world lost in cotton ball clouds hiding away the familiar hands of the mountain peaks in swirls of mist. Normally, she could look out at Mount Calibum and dream of flying to the very top, seeing a world of mountains and valleys, standing so close to heaven she could touch the hand of God.

Instead, it was just school. Deirdre texted the other Paladin girls, the Heretics were in the back, specters in black, and the Untouchables—Pockets, Tubitha and Remy—were spread about, alone in their outcast lives.

Then a knock on the door killed all normalcy. The teacher went over and opened the door. Art Lancing, Avalon's sheriff, huge belly and bigger beard, filled up the doorway. Behind him were more police.

Lena froze, wondering if they had searched her truck and found the red purse behind the seat. But then it was clear they weren't there for her.

"Santiago Scarpetti, can you come with us?"

He stood up, swaying, a sloppy grin on his face but tears in his eyes. "Howdy, Sheriff. You got a problem?"

"Just come with us, son."

"Ain't your son, Art," Santiago said and then spread his arms wide. "Well, my friends. All good things must come to an end."

Every eye was glued to him, and when Santiago had an audience, he sang. He was blasting through a Bertoglio aria when they dragged him out in handcuffs.

The door slammed shut. In the silence that followed,

~ ☾ ~

the teacher attempted math again, but no one was listening. Lena's mind whirled. She still had the drugs, her connection just got arrested, and she was without her hundred dollars.

She was chewing through her options when her black leather purse buzzed. Inside was a cell phone vibrating like a writhing scorpion. But she didn't own a cell phone.

Keeping it hidden under her desk, she read a text message.

I'd like 2 c yer red purse after school. Meet me in rm 7 upper halls.

The picture on the welcome screen was an eclipsed sun, the red of the muted light the color of dried blood. Questions flooded her. Whose phone was it and how did it get in her purse? Who would text her just minutes after Santiago's arrest?

After class, she latched onto a very pale Bruise in the hallway. "You or Santiago stick a phone in my purse? I got a text message. Was it from you?"

Bruise shook his head. He was massive, with a full beard and a shaved head. Well, mostly shaved. There was still some stubble, and Lena had spent one smoky night trying to figure out what the patterns on his skull might mean. Like some sort of Rorschach test for the criminally insane.

Cutler shouldered into Bruise. "Too bad your boy got picked up. Santiago is probably turning all you dirtbags in. Gonna need the paddywagon to haul you all off."

Avery pulled him away. "Come off it, Rob. Let's get to study hall."

Bruise glared them down the hall, then turned back to Lena.

Who was nearly spitting from frustration. "Bruise, don't worry about them. What about the phone?"

He shrugged. "Dude, I don't know what's going on. You see Santiago last night?"

~ ☾ ~

"No, I called him, and it was weird. He wasn't singing for once. Did Santiago talk about someone else coming in on the red purse thing?"

Bruise shook his head, eyes dull.

Lena pulled him toward their next class. "Listen, the text message said to come to the upper halls after school. Would you come with me?"

"All them rooms are shut down and there's that gate thing blocking them. No way to get up there."

Half the school was in shadows, too expensive to heat.

Bruise went on. "And this could be a trap or a sting or whatever you call it. The cops—"

"I know. But would you help me?"

Bruise nodded, but his face was uncertain. "Sure. After school."

"Right at the third floor gate. I'll have to hurry. I can't be late to pick up Jozey."

They hit the classroom just as the bell rang.

And there, sitting next to Pockets, was the dark boy from the side of the road. Same hooded white sweatshirt. Same coal-black coat. Same vicious stare.

~ ☽ ~

iii
(the new outcast)

After the teacher introduced the dark boy, whose name Lena didn't quite hear, Deirdre plunked herself down next to Lena. "So sorry about the tenor getting arrested, but I hope the new boy hasn't caught your interest."

"Heretic or Paladin?" Lena asked in a whisper over her open, unread book.

Deirdre smiled like a she-wolf. "You see how intense his eyes are? It's like he looks right through you, but not in a good way. I think he's even too creepy for the Heretics. No way he could be a Paladin. Look at how old his clothes are. And on his first day he sits with Pockets? Such recklessness brands him an Untouchable, forever and ever, amen."

"Did you hear his name?"

"Something odd, I believe. It sounded harsh, whatever it was, but we don't need to concern ourselves, since he is obviously of very little consequence."

Lena sat at the desk, thoughts grinding through her head. All the things she wanted to talk about were beyond Deirdre. The dark boy saving her, the phone mystery, the red purse.

They went to study, but Lena's gaze kept traveling to the dark boy's face. Every time the dark boy caught her peeking, she had to glance away, flushed and unnerved by the heat in his inky stare. Like too much summer sun on bare flesh.

The bell rang and it was computer class, last class of the day. Only fifty minutes until the rendezvous in room

~ ☾ ~

seven.

Lena moved toward the door on quaking legs. Fear and hunger were wrestling around inside her, leaving a gaping hole. Probably shouldn't have skipped both breakfast and lunch.

Out in the hallway, she bumped into the dark boy. He spun, and Lena thought he was going to hit her. Pockets was further up the hall.

Where she had brushed the new boy burned.

"What were you doing on the highway last night?" she asked, rubbing her shoulder like she could wipe his hot touch away.

"Someone had to save you," the dark boy said. His black eyes never wavered.

"What did you tell the cop?"

He shrugged. "Does it matter? I'm just wondering how you're going to screw up the chance I gave you. We both know you will."

Lena snarled. Her hands hooked into claws. "What do you care? You don't know me."

"I do know you." He said the words as if he had witnessed her birth and could see her death. "I know you're too stupid to change, no matter how bad things get. I know you are chaff when you should be wheat. And you say you love your brother, but all you do is risk his life every minute of every day. I know—"

"Stay away from me." She couldn't listen to any more. She cut him off and clacked past Pockets, her boots on the hardwood floor echoing like gunshots.

"What did you say to her?" Pockets asked from behind her.

Lena didn't hear the response. She didn't care. All that mattered was getting rid of the red purse and getting her money.

~ ☾ ~

iv
(the blond boy in the cold room)

The steps to the third floor ended at a gate that was always sealed shut with a big padlock. Not always, it seemed. The lock wasn't there and the accordion steel mesh was open. The walls beyond were frigid and dark. Lena exhaled and her breath came out in a mist. She had ten minutes. No time to wait for the chronically unreliable Bruise. If it was a trap, at least the police wouldn't find the drugs on her. They were still in her truck, hopefully safe.

Shadows drank up the clouded light from the narrow windows, but she could see the footprints she left in the dust of the wide corridor. She turned the corner and there was room seven, the door open.

Inside was a large room facing a window that should have shown Ablach Peak but only showed clouds strangling Avalon. Bookshelves lined the walls, but it was more graveyard than library. Only stained, torn books and the shredded corpses of magazines had been left behind.

There were two fireplaces on either side of the cold room. At one was a blond boy, Lena's age, wearing dark jeans and a loose white shirt, crouching before a small fire. His cowboy boots were new, black and polished.

When he turned to her, his hair hung in his face for a moment, but then he swept it away. His eyes were desert-sky blue. A blond beard covered his chin.

She grew weak at the sight of him, wondering if the

~ ☾ ~

cell phone in her purse had a camera because she had the silly idea of taking a picture of him. "I'm here," she said, trying to breathe.

He smiled with white, clean teeth. "Hey, I'm glad. Just got a fire going, but it took me awhile. I'm not too good with flames." The words had the lilt of a Southern accent.

Lena couldn't get a breath in to speak. The air seemed to grow colder. And then she thought of Jozey. No time for romance or lust or awe or whatever she was feeling. "How come I have a cell phone in my purse?"

"Just how life works sometimes. The world'll give ya gifts if yer smart enough to grab 'em with both hands."

"Yeah, well, you could have fooled me," Lena said. "No wonder they closed these rooms off. It's sub-zero in here."

"Yeah, it sure ain't Louisiana." He ripped some pages from a book and fed them into the fire before throwing the whole book in. He then pulled a chair over for her. "Now, sit down and let me get ya somethin' to eat."

From a King Soopers bag, he pulled out an apple, some cheese and crackers, and some chocolate kisses. With a pocket knife, he cut her off a hunk of apple and handed it to her. "So, Leni, I'm the new guy."

She took the apple but didn't eat it. Her heart was floating around inside of her. "My parents called me Leni. And my brother, kind of. I mean, my real name is Magdalena, but everyone calls me Lena." Inside, she cringed. Why had she rattled all that off? Normally, she could handle the drama, but something about the blond boy had knocked her off center.

"Well, Leni, I'm Johnny Beels. But y'all can call me Beels. Everyone else will." He smiled warmly at her for a moment before continuing. "From talking with Santiago, yer quite something."

"Why do you say that?" She unconsciously took a bite of the apple, crisp and sweet with autumn sunshine.

~ ☾ ~

Beels crouched by the fireplace in front of her. "You got a lot on yer plate with a little brother, no parents, the thing with Santiago. And yet ya manage. Lotta folks would have snapped by now."

"Well, there are days I think about snapping, but I don't have time." With the blond boy there, with the fire and the food, she never wanted to leave. But Jozey and responsibility called. "Listen, this is great, but I have to get going."

"Sure. Sure." He unwrapped a chocolate kiss and took a bite. "Well, Santiago is gettin' locked up, and all ya got for yer troubles is a red purse overflowin' and no cash. But I can help."

Lena laughed. "If you want to help, tell me the truth. Who are you? How did you get up here? And what about the phone in my purse?"

Beels shrugged. "I'm just taking over for Santiago. We knew he was going to get picked up today, and we didn't want to leave ya hangin'." He stopped to chew more chocolate. "And as far as the room, it's cool. Good view on clear days I'm sure. As for the locks, easy when you know a locksmith and the head janitor ain't too careful about where he leaves the master key. And the cell phone, well, Santiago always said ya needed one. He was too cheap and didn't follow the one rule that is required in this red purse racket."

"Which is?" Lena asked.

"Never get high on your own supply." He handed her a chocolate. "So instead of a toke, I bought you a present. Had someone slip the phone into yer purse this morning. There. All questions answered. No mysteries."

She bit into the chocolate, which was more bitter than sweet. She liked that. "So are you going to come to school here?"

"Eventually," he said with smiles and dimples and shining eyes.

~ ☾ ~

Quick peek at her watch. "I hate it, but I gotta go." She stood. "About my red purse..."

"Hope it has sequins. I love me some sequins." He stood with her.

"Yeah, sequins." She found herself grinning like a fool. Next to him she felt like a clown in floppy shoes.

"Tomorrow night I'll take the purse and pay you yer money. Then ya can get out of the business. It don't suit ya, Leni, and there are better ways to make money. But ya can keep the phone. It's paid up through the month."

Lena felt surprised at being dropped, but a part of her glowed. Santiago had always said he wanted to get her out of the game but never did anything about it. In just fifteen minutes, Beels was sending her on her way.

"Hey, Leni, I'm throwin' a welcome-me party on Thursday night and I'd like y'all to come with me. How 'bout it?"

"Oh yes," Lena said too quickly, too eagerly. Another internal cringe.

From his pocket, Beels pulled out a key and gently gave it to her. His hand was cold, but his skin was soft. "Keys to the kingdom. It'll work on every lock in this place. Might come in handy the next few days until we can get ya out. I'll be in touch."

The way he said "touch" sent tingles over her skin.

"Okay, I got the phone." She grinned, backing toward the door.

"I'll ring you," he said.

Oh, I bet you will. She shivered at the thought, but she kept her face straight.

She backed out into the hallway and closed the door. It shut with a click that echoed in the empty chill of the dusty hall.

Lena moved as fast as her heels let her. On the third floor gate, she found a white feather stuck in the metal. She took it and shoved it into her pocket. For Jozey. Her

~ ☾ ~

fingers brushed the key Beels had given her. It felt like a promise ring for some strange reason.

Who was Johnny Beels? Really.

She would have to pry Deirdre off him if her friend caught sight of the new blond boy.

Back in her truck, after checking her hair and make-up, Lena let go of the excitement of her new connection and steeled herself for a battle with Mrs. Weyland, the woman who ran the Cherubim. Mrs. Weyland hated late parents.

But Lena didn't have to worry because when she walked through the door of the daycare center, the dark boy was there playing with Jozey.

~ ☾ ~

v
(the cherubim day school)

The dark boy played with Jozey as if he was the sun and everything else was darkness and cold. Lena knew how that felt, and it sent her storming through the toys and clutter of the daycare center to get to her brother. She snatched him away from the dark boy, mid-play.

His eyes met Lena's and it was as if he could read each minute of her life like pages in a book. His eyes filled with tears.

She expected a different reaction, more hatred, more criticism, more vitriol, but instead, he cried at her life.

Which made her want to weep along with him. She shed fury instead of tears. "What are you doing here?" she razored out the question, clutching Jozey's squirming body against her.

"Weni, let me go!"

A few children started to cry before Mrs. Weyland hustled into the room to comfort everyone. "It's okay, it's all okay." She turned on Lena. "What is your problem?"

"Him!" Her finger crucified the dark boy. "He's too stupid to know I'm not rich enough or famous enough for a stalker."

"I'm not stalking you." A bare whisper from the dark boy.

Mrs. Weyland sighed and shook her head. "Please, Lena, settle down. It's all very simple. Miss Terri called me out of the blue this afternoon and said she's moving away and not coming back even though she knows I can't run this place by myself. Then Chael shows up right when I needed him."

"Chael?" Lena blinked at the odd name.

~ ☾ ~

Jozey jumped away from Lena, escaping her arms.

"Chael," the dark boy repeated, the tears gone.

"What kind of a name is that?" she challenged.

"What kind of a name is Magdalena?" he challenged right back.

Jozey stood between them, his fists clenched, an innocent child caught between warriors on a battlefield.

"Magdalena's an old name, from Greece, from the Bible."

"Then it's like my name," Chael said, his eyes like obsidian, "but that is the only thing we have in common."

"Yeah, it is." Lena matched his glare. "Certainly we don't share fashion sense."

His next words were brittle. "Hide all you want behind your clothes and make-up, but ugly is ugly when it comes to what we do and say."

If she had been closer to him, she would have slapped him. "Well, you must be hideous then because every time you open your mouth, it's to judge me."

"Some people need judging," he said.

"Start with yourself then."

"Weni! Don't be mean!" Jozey shrieked and started to cry. He didn't reach out for her. He reached for the dark boy, and Chael picked him up.

Seeing the two together again was a knife in Lena's chest. She whirled on Mrs. Weyland. "How can you let a stranger work for you?"

Mrs. Weyland blushed. "I told you. I need the help. If you're so worried, you should come and work for me. God knows I've asked." She nodded toward Chael. "But see how good he is with Jozey?"

Lena didn't want to see. She seized Jozey and tore him away from Chael. Her brother fought her, but Lena pulled him hard and forced him to release his grip. She drew him close, then snarled at the dark boy. "Stay away.

~ ☾ ~

You're not welcome around us."

"I know," Chael said. "But I had to come anyway. I had to."

The force of his words stole away every other thought from Lena, silencing her. He wasn't just talking about working at the Cherubim or showing up at Avalon High School. He was talking about something else, Lena could feel it, but she didn't want to care.

"Weni, why you so mean?" Jozey howled, then twisted to reach out for Chael. "Help me, Chael. Help me!"

"It's okay, Joziah, it's okay. Remember, I love you." Chael's tears returned. "And Lena loves you, too." He turned his attention to her, studying her with a steady gaze. "You have to change. Every time you risk yourself, you risk your brother. The police will catch you eventually, no matter how careful or tough you think you are."

"We're fine," she said. "Leave us alone."

With Jozey in her arms, she rushed outside, covered with sweat. The cold clouds swirling around her felt like the lick of an icy dragon. She shoved Jozey into his car seat, wrestling with the straps and cursing, then slammed the door shut and stomped over to the driver's side of the truck.

Jozey yelled at her when she got in. "You're mean, Weni. Chael's my friend forever. Forever and ever, just like Mama and Daddy in heaven."

"You can't trust people like that," she snapped as she sped onto the highway. "We don't know a thing about him. And the way he said he loved you, it was creepy."

But it wasn't. The words, his tears, the way he held Jozey, it was the way their mother had held him.

Jozey screeched tears and snot. "You don't know anything! He loves me! He's my friend!"

"Well, he's not my friend, Jozey. So you'll have to choose." She wanted to take the words back, but it was

~ ☾ ~

too late.

"But I love you both!" More tears trailed down his red face.

"I'm so sorry, Jozey, you don't have to choose. It's okay. You can love us both." But it took the whole drive home to convince him of that. Her brother always brought out either the very best in her or the very worst.

Dinner, bath, books, and Jozey slept against her in bed while she tried to read a book for school, some Shakespeare thing. The book was marked up with curses, and it smelled sour like someone had dunked it in milk.

Her new cell phone lay mute by Jozey's sippy cup on the floor. She hoped it would ring with Johnny Beels on the other end, but instead, there was a knock on the door. Late on Tuesday night no one should be knocking.

Wading through the sheets, she walked the cold floor and cautiously opened the door. There in the clouds was Art Lancing, Avalon's sheriff.

Lena's heart shuddered to a stop.

~ ☾ ~

vi
(lancing at the door)

The sheriff stood in the doorway with his hat in his hands. "Sorry to bother you, Lena, but I wanted to ask you a few questions."

She drew the door open further and he shambled forward in snow boots. In the kitchen, he sat down in a wire chair, the leather of his belt and holster creaking as he settled in.

Lena winced, hoping the little chair wouldn't break. With his bushy beard and swelling belly, it was like a bear had walked out of the mountains and into her home. She stood by the humming refrigerator feeling like she was in a line-up.

"Can I get you some water?" she asked.

He shook his head. "I won't bother you longer than I have to. You're friends with Santiago Scarpetti, and you know about the drugs he was dealing. I'm here to find out how much."

Time stopped. The world ended. Lena ignored all that. "I don't know what you mean. I knew he did drugs. I mean, he's a Heretic after all, but I didn't know he was dealing."

Lancing squinted at her lies. "It's a shame what happened to your parents. I mean a real shame. But that little boy in there, what would happen if you was to get arrested?"

Sheriff or not, people who talked about her parents dying like they understood made her rattlesnake-crazy mad.

Crossing her arms, she spat venom. "Well, I won't get

~ ☾ ~

arrested because I didn't do anything. I never used drugs. You want to drug test me? I'll pee in any cup you got."

He stood up and put his hat back on his head like it was a helmet and he was ducking bullets. "Fine, Lena. I wanted to give you a chance. Next time we talk, you won't get no more chances. Just because the world hurt you, don't mean you gotta hurt it back. Not when there's a youngster in there who needs you."

"Yeah, well, he has me. Now go."

He handed her his card. His eyes were muddy brown and as mild as a summer picnic. "You change your mind, maybe I could spare another chance. Out of respect."

"Yeah, sure, whatever."

"You know, I've been thinking…" The sheriff paused and took in a deep breath. "Taking care of that little guy and keeping up with school and your friends, well, we all know it's hard on you. Especially with how your aunt is."

"What are you saying?" Lena didn't like where he was heading.

"I got a sister in Alamosa who can't have kids. Maybe Jozey, or both of you, would want to—"

She laughed, but she heard how shrill it was, how crazy. "Well, I'm sorry for her, but Jozey and I aren't going anywhere. You were thinking you could save me? Well, take a ticket, stand in line. Whole damn town is all about saving me, but maybe I don't need saving, did you ever think of that?"

"We all need a bit of helping," Lancing said. "Seems to me you're the one who needs to do a little thinking." He tipped his hat and was out the door.

All she could do was growl. First Chael, now Lancing. Were there special town meetings to discuss her every move?

Lena waited until she heard his SUV drive away before snatching up the kitchen phone and punching in

~ ☽ ~

Deirdre's number to ask for a favor, a huge favor.

It was like Deirdre came on mid-sentence, talking non-stop. "I spoke with Beels and he said he gave you a cell phone and he gave me your new number. About time. Anyway, we're on the same network, so the minutes are gratis, which is so nice for me since my father tracks my phone to the second. But anyway, I digress. Beels slays me. Good-looking and smart. All that and a bag of chips."

Of course, Deirdre would sniff out the blond boy. Lena closed her eyes and rubbed her forehead.

Deirdre kept on the chatter. "So we're conversing, Beels and I, and we start discussing the other new guy. Did you know he has no parents and no one knows where he's living? How he got into school, I have no idea. And rumor has it he was the one who turned in Santiago."

"Yeah, his name is Chael," Lena said, but he was the last person she wanted to talk about. "Listen, D—"

Deirdre cut her off. "Chael? Odd name for an odd guy. Well, I think we can safely shelve Mr. Chael under Untouchable. Next, he'll be dating Tubitha."

Lena persisted. "D, I gotta ask a favor."

"Yeah, sure, anything. What?"

Lena let out a long breath. "I have this red purse. I need you to hold on to it for a while."

Silence on the other end of the phone.

"I would imagine it's not just a fashion accessory you want me to safeguard for you, huh?" Deirdre asked the question slowly.

"It's not. Sheriff Lancing was just here. Look, I wouldn't ask if I wasn't desperate."

"God, Lena, can't we just be catty and gossip? I wouldn't last ten seconds in a woman's correctional facility. I'm a Paladin."

Lena closed her eyes but kept herself from sighing.

~ ☾ ~

Deirdre was nestled in her perfect rich girl's world with a good father, a mother in Switzerland, and an older brother in a college on the East Coast. She was the queen of the school. Why should she help Lena?

"Yeah, I shouldn't have asked, D. I'm sorry. Forget I said anything."

"Just get rid of it," Deirdre said. "Flush it down the toilet."

Lena needed the money for the delivery, but more than that, if she lost it, Beels and whoever he worked for would come collecting, looking for a return on their investment.

"Yeah, maybe," Lena said. "I gotta go."

"Lena, please—"

Lena hung up on her, then texted Beels. *Can't wait - need 2 get rid of my purse tonight.*

She waited until there was a buzz back.

tonight then. same place. rm 7.

She typed in a response. *Leaving now.*

But Aunt Mercedes wouldn't be back until midnight. Tuesdays and Thursdays were her late nights at the Gas 'n Sip. Which meant Lena would have to leave Jozey alone.

Most likely he wouldn't wake up, but what if he did?

"You can't leave him," she said to herself.

"I have to," she whispered back.

"Just wait."

But how long would Beels be at the school?

She texted him back, seeing where he would be after midnight, but there was no response.

She paced around the apartment, but every time she went past her closet, she put on one more piece of dark clothing. Back and forth, until she was dressed in black jeans, a long black sweater, black Skechers. She found a hat and stuffed her platinum tips underneath.

"Sorry, Jozey," she whispered to her brother. "Don't

~ ☾ ~

wake up. Please, don't wake up."

She kissed him and locked the front door behind her.

It was like there were eyes in the night, watching her every move, waiting to swallow her whole.

~ ☾ ~

vii
(chael's hell)

Lena sneaked to her truck, glad for the swirling clouds and darkness, but her soul ached.

She imagined Jozey waking up, calling out for her, clutching his special stuffed lion to his chest while he cried.

This was what drug dealers did: abandon their families, lie to the police, live secret lives of deceit. The money wasn't worth it. Nothing was worth it.

She prayed to her mother and father, asking them to keep Jozey asleep.

In minutes, she had pulled the red purse from the truck, closed the door, and was walking down the back alley past the empty stores and cramped houses on Mountain Avenue. Walking, because if the police were watching her, they would expect her to drive to do a drop. On foot, she had a better chance of going undetected. And her school was so close.

The blurred eyes of a car in the clouds drove down the alley toward her. She ducked behind a dumpster and waited for Mrs. Clarkson's Honda to pass.

Just Mrs. Clarkson. Nothing police about her.

Lena made it through the fog to the school and used Beels' key to crack open the door. Inside were the tangled back hallways that twisted through the stone like intestines. She heard voices and footsteps coming toward her and slid into the rank darkness of a utility closet.

Art Lancing and Mr. Percy walked by.

"Let's just see if anything is in his locker," Lancing was saying.

"At ten o'clock at night? I still don't know why you had to drag me down here right when I was winding down."

"We want to get this over with quick. Don't need Avalon in the news for drugs. Not where we are, not without snow."

"The Scarpettis will probably lose their house. The kid was bringing in the cash to pay for it. Helluva thing. Too bad we can't get to the bastard Santiago is working for. Gotta give that kid some credit. He's loyal."

"Loyal to the wrong cause. Poor Gramma Scar. That restaurant is her everything. You know she'll sell it for the legal fees. Last thing we need is one more business to close on Mountain Avenue."

"At least the kid is willing to try treatment."

The men walked off. Their voices faded into silence.

Lena tip-toed out of the closet and into the glow of emergency lights. With Lancing around, no way could she get to Beels for the drop.

Out of the corner of her eye, she saw something white smearing the darkness, and she jerked her head just in time to see Chael turning a corner, headed downstairs.

What was he doing in the school after hours? She couldn't help it. She followed him down the steps, moving noiselessly over the polished hardwood, hands tracing the jagged, rocky surface of the walls.

She had to hurry, figure out what he was doing, and get to room seven. How long would Beels wait? What if Jozey was already awake?

The basement furnace was blasting. Red, flickering fire threw bloody, dancing shadows across the pipes that criss-crossed the ceiling in a spider web, some dipping low, like the bars of a prison. The floor was dusty dark, filthy splotches marking the concrete. Cast-off school desks were stacked around like teetering stalagmites.

Chael stood in the middle of the room, unsure of himself, like he didn't want to break any rules and was

~ ☾ ~

searching for a teacher for help.

Yet when he saw her, he stormed over and pulled her close, only to let her go.

His touch, even with the layers of clothes, burned her. Burned him, too. She saw him wince. They both glowed with sweat.

His words came out in an angry torrent. "What are you doing here? Have you completely lost your mind? Is Joziah home alone?"

She clutched the red purse like Jozey held his stuffed lion, right next to her heart. "What are you doing here?"

She could see him trip over the question. He teetered, then he was right back on her. "I came to help, but I shouldn't have." His eyes went to her bag. "I know what you are doing here. You have the red purse."

"Okay, so bust me. Turn me in. That's why you're here, right? You narced on Santiago, and now I'm next."

He closed his eyes and shook his head at her like she was a naughty child. "I didn't turn in Santiago. I talked to him, but that was before the police picked him up. I knew it would happen. I warned him. Like I'm warning you."

She laughed. "Yeah, you know everything. What are the lottery numbers this week?"

"A million dollars wouldn't solve your problems."

"What would?"

"Stop being so stupid," he said, those intense eyes scorching her. "Stop trying to do everything yourself."

"God, don't you have any new material? How about we not talk about me for a minute? Let's talk about you since you're so perfect. What is your story?"

His face turned hard. "I would tell you the truth, but I don't trust you, Lena. Look at you. Would you trust you?"

She didn't have time for this, not with Beels waiting, not with Jozey back at home alone. Just three years old.

~ ☾ ~

Lena went to run, but Chael caught her arm. Burned, she pushed him away. "Hands off!"

"Lena, wait. You don't understand."

"I understand perfectly." Her voice was ragged and low. She had to end this, but he wouldn't let her go, so she hit him with everything she had. "You think I'm some dope dealing whore. I'm not. You're here five minutes and you've already judged me and you're itching to follow through with the execution. Who are you really? Where are you from?"

Chael opened his mouth, then closed it. "I'm no one from nowhere."

"And then one day you move to Avalon, Colorado, where you just happen to save me from getting busted. What did you tell the cop that pulled me over?" God, why was she still asking him questions?

"I told him his wife was better. She was down at Denver Health in a coma, and she had just woken up."

Lena shook her head at his lies. "And how could you possibly know that?"

"I just know things," he said. "Like I knew Santiago would get arrested. And you'll get arrested. And Jozey will be taken into foster care."

"That's not going to happen," Lena said, her hands fists.

"Why, because you say it won't?"

"I can handle this."

"You can't. The prayers you are praying will never be answered."

Lena went to lash out, but the phone buzzed in her purse.

Chael put up both hands. "Don't answer it."

But she had already pressed the talk button.

"Leni! Is that you? Hope I caught ya sinnin'." It was Beels.

"No," she said, eyes down, avoiding Chael.

~ ☾ ~

Beels spun his words on the silk of his accent. "Cops're everywhere, girl. Not a good time for red purse fun tonight. Gonna have to wait for the big party. Hey, I was lookin' for the other new kid. Ya seen him around?"

Lena looked up and Chael was gone. Again.

"No, I have no idea."

"Just be cool, Leni. As long as I'm around, yer safe. Ya got that?"

Hunting for Chael, Lena held the phone to her ear as she walked further into the basement, further into the heat, the hellish hot glow, the furniture a junkyard around her. She stopped when she walked through a spider web, sticky on her skin. She drew some of the cottony web off her hat and hurried toward the steps.

"Leni? Y'all there, girl?" Beels' voice resonated from the phone.

"Yeah, right here, but I gotta go."

"Sure ya do. Just be cool. Lancing is just thrashing around like a catfish lookin' for a hook. We're safe. Just hang on to that red purse for a couple more days. Just a couple more days."

She hung up on Beels and his bad news.

Back home, Jozey was asleep, had most likely slept the whole time.

Or so she thought.

~ ☾ ~

BROKEN WEDNESDAY

i
(questions and blood)

Lena was asleep and climbing through dark dreams where faces were either too big or too small for her to see.

Jozey called her from the dreams at five o'clock in the morning asking a new question. "Where'd you go last night, Weni?"

It shocked her fully awake but not awake enough to tell the truth. "I was here. What are you talking about?"

Jozey's shook his head. "Uh-huh. I looked. You and Auntie weren't here. I looked."

Their room was as dark and cold as a cave. Only the nightlight from the bathroom gave any light. It was too dark for Lena to see Jozey's face. "I'm so, so sorry. I had no choice." She could almost hear Chael in her head disagreeing with her. "Were you scared?" she asked.

"Yeah, I thought you were deaded. Then Chael came and he said it was okay. Then you came home."

Chael, always disappearing, always so mysterious, but it was impossible. It would have taken him too long to get to her apartment, the doors were locked, and no way would Jozey have let anyone in that late at night. Her brother was just telling a three-year-old's version of reality, but it still didn't make his words any easier to hear.

"Where were you?" Jozey asked.

Lena swallowed hard. "Just with friends. I was only gone a minute."

"See my feather?" The edges of the black feather glowed from the nightlight as Jozey held it up in his tiny

~ ☾ ~

fingers.

"Yeah, I see it." But Lena had her eyes closed. With only four hours of sleep, she felt crumbled. At least these questions were better than Jozey's usual routine. These she could attempt to answer. "Let's try and sleep some more."

Jozey tried, but his wrestling around and his little songs pulled all the sleep out of her.

So the day began. A long morning with her brother, and while she had time to eat, she didn't. Out of habit. Or because eating felt too much like being with her mom.

Backpack over his shoulder, Jozey waited for her at the door. "Weni, I wanna be an angel for Halloween. Angels are in heaven. Not like God birdies."

She stumbled out of their room, the last of her wardrobe in place, and nodded wearily. "Yeah, tonight we'll work on your costume. With all the feathers you have, it will be easy."

He smiled at her with so much love it hurt.

The clouds were still suffocating the valley, but it was colder than it had been before, colder and getting worse. A kiss, a hug and Jozey was safe in the Cherubim and Lena was back in her truck, stopped at a traffic light.

She could feel the red purse behind her seat, like she was a princess and the drugs were a pea buried beneath a hundred mattresses with her on top of the swaying pile trying not to fall.

If they still had their SUV, she could have hidden the drugs way in the back, but she and Aunt Mercedes had sold it. The cleaners had said they could get the blood out of the upholstery and fix the bullet holes in the glass, but they couldn't clean or fix the memories. Being in her dad's truck was bad enough.

Should we stop?

"No," Lena whispered. But she needed to yell it, to get her dead mom to stop asking the questions that had

~ ☾ ~

nearly killed them all. "No! We shouldn't have stopped! No!"

But her dad had said, "Sure, let's stop and see if they need any help."

The gunshots had been so different than the movies. Louder in some ways, softer in others. Simple. No drama. Just simple noise.

The light pock of the bullets through the glass.

Jozey screaming.

Memories clinging, Lena found herself in the parking lot at school, too jagged inside to cry. Sweat itched through her hair. "Stop thinking about it, Lena. Just stop. It's over."

Her mother in the hospital, the doctors, the nurses, the blood. Her aunt crying and trying to hug her, but Lena too cold to let her. Her father was dead.

Should we stop?

That's what her mother kept asking her, but her aunt had a different question. *What should we do, Lena?*

The click and wheeze of the respirator breathing for her mom.

What should we do, Lena?

Lena took her right hand, pushed her coat up her left arm and pushed her long fingernails into the flesh of her wrist. "Stop it. Stop this."

Her aunt's droopy dog face, ashen.

What should we do?

Click. Wheeze. Click. And the doctors giving them a choice.

Lena gripped her arm harder, but the pain felt distant. Then she remembered people would be looking for wounds, for scratches, for razorblade marks. She wasn't going to give them anything to talk about.

She tore herself out of her truck to go sit with the Paladins and pretend she wasn't bleeding.

~ ☾ ~

ii
(damaged)

Pretty Paladin princesses, all in a row. Lena, Deirdre, Parker Lee, and the rest of the girls.

"Hard morning, darling?" Deirdre asked.

"No, just peaches, sweetie." Lena smiled through the mask of faultless beauty and feigned money. She smoothed a hand over her arm, pushing the coat against her wounds.

"What did you end up doing?" Deirdre asked.

"With my red purse?"

"I guess," Deirdre said, shrugging.

All eyes on Lena, she lied and grinned and lied some more. "Got rid of it. Just one more useless purse, cluttering up my closet."

Deirdre shined with a smile. "Good. I guess you'll be sitting with us at lunch again."

"I was thinking about sitting with Tubitha," Lena said.

It brought laughter, and while she laughed too, Lena felt a hole open up inside her, big, wide, and empty.

Deirdre leaned in close. "Come over tonight. We can pretend to do homework. And bring Jozey, since it has been far too long since I have gazed on him. You need the calming influence of the Paladins at this stage of your life."

Lena nodded. A night with Deirdre sounded nice and normal.

Not nice, not normal, Dane Bramage came marching through the lunchroom with an empty backpack flapping against his scorched trench coat. He had burned it into patterns as wild as his hair.

~ ☾ ~

Lena thought he was going to keep going, but instead, he stopped in front of the Paladin girls and stared at each of them.

Deirdre stared back. "What do you want?"

He stood there, motionless, no expression on his face.

What he was doing was strange, but three things were stranger to Lena. First, that he was at school that early. Second, that he appeared sober. And third, he had a backpack. Bramage wasn't much for homework. And why was it empty?

"God, it's such a psycho," Parker Lee said. "Can you say something to make it go away, Lena?"

The Paladin boys were beginning to grumble at another table.

Bramage stuck out a finger. "You." He pointed at Parker Lee. Then he switched to Deirdre. "You." Then at Diane Cassidy. "You." And he did this until he got to Lena.

He gazed at her, dropped his arm, and said blankly, "Not you."

Lena thought he was going to move off, but he didn't. He continued to stand there, dead eyes fixed on her.

"That's it!" Cutler jumped down from the top tier and grabbed Bramage.

Bramage let himself be grabbed, and in a lifeless whisper, said, "You. Definitely you. You most of all."

"Me what?" Cutler had his fist raised.

From a whisper to a scream, Bramage howled out his mantra. "No stone untouched! No soul unscorched! Apocalypse now!"

"What's wrong with him, Lena?" Deirdre asked, like they were watching a nature documentary.

Lena shook her head. "I would guess he's off his meds, but I don't know."

"Yeah," Deirdre agreed, "he does seem like a boy who needs his morning vodka."

~ ☾ ~

"He needs some sense beaten into him," Cutler hissed and was about to do just that, when Johnny Beels strolled between them, chewing on a candy bar.

"Now, boys, I'm sure y'all don't need to be fightin' this early in the mornin'." He put out a fist to Cutler. "I'm Johnny Beels, but you can call me Beels, 'cause everyone else will."

Cutler let go of Bramage to bump fists with Beels. "Rob Cutler. You new?"

"New, yeah." Beels said it with a smile, as if it weren't true. He was munching on his chocolate when he turned to Bramage. "Are we okay here?"

Bramage tilted his head. "Okay? We live in a fallen world. Nothing is okay. You know that."

Beels grinned. "Don't mean we can't have fun, though, right? It bein' a fallen world and all, might as well enjoy ourselves."

Bramage squinted up his face and broke away with a shout. "Johnny Beels! Johnny Beels! Johnny Beels! No stone untouched. No soul unscorched. Apocalypse now!"

And then he was gone through the corridor with little kids scrambling out of his way.

Lena couldn't believe her eyes. Beels and Bramage knew each other, but how? One was insane and damaged, the other as cool as summertime lemonade.

Beels raised an eyebrow. "Now there goes one interestin' feller."

"You wanna sit with us?" Cutler asked.

Beels finished off his candy, crumbled up the wrapper, and stuffed it into Cutler's hand. "Thanks, Cutler, but not today, though I do like where y'all sit. Looks comfy. I gotta talk with Leni. You understand, right?"

Cutler frowned, obviously trying to figure out if he had been slighted or not.

Beels bent over the wall and offered Lena his hand. "Hey, Leni, can we chat?"

~ ☾ ~

She felt all the girls and their jealousy as she let the blond boy lead her away from the Paladin tables.

Out in the hall, Beels' face shone on her. "Listen, Leni, I'm so sorry about last night. I was going to meet up with ya, but well, ya know how it goes. We gotta be careful, yeah?"

He brushed a lock of hair behind her ear with a cold hand. Lena felt all breath leave her body, and she couldn't get another in because of the jangle of her heart. She could only nod.

"Good," Beels said. "Let's just give it a bit. Tomorrow night at my party, I promise, I'll take that ol' red purse off yer hands. Okay?"

"Yeah, sure," she said, even though holding onto the drugs was killing her. Usually, Santiago took them away from her right away, right after she picked them up.

Beels touched her arm. "Don't worry. Cops ain't got no clue about what's really goin' on. And I know yer one careful, capable girl, so we ain't got no worries. Ya got it safe, right?"

"It's safe," Lena said.

"Good, good."

"Where are you sitting at lunch?" Lena asked.

He smiled. "Not in there. Not sure I'm ready for Avalon High School lunchtime politics just yet. Maybe tomorrow."

He left her just as the bell rang. He wasn't in any of her classes, and at lunchtime, Lena sat with the Paladins, wishing he was there, charming them all and just being Johnny Beels.

Chael was alone with Pockets until Tabitha moved over to sit next to them, and then Remmy Bach. All four of them talked intently about something. Lena could see it on their faces.

Pockets suddenly yelled, "Free will? God kills us with free will. Most of us are slaves to one thing or another

~ ☾ ~

anyway."

Tabitha blushed, Remmy rolled his eyes, but Chael just said something back to Pockets, then glanced up and caught Lena looking. She pretended to be interested in Parker Lee's recent shopping trip in Aspen and didn't dare look back. Everyone else ignored the outburst.

After lunch, Lena was on her way to class when Chael stopped her. "I want to talk with you after school."

"We don't have anything to talk about," she said.

"We do. Can you drive me to the Cherubim?"

"No," Lena said. "All we do is argue, and you look too tired to fight."

Wounded shadows circled Chael's eyes and his skin appeared papery, like an argument would torch him up, a match to brittle autumn leaves.

"God," she said, "you look like how I feel."

Chael nodded, eyes closed. "I forget I need sleep. Maybe like you. But Lena, you were right when you said I don't treat you right. I want that to change. Can we please talk after school? It's important."

"Fine." She sighed. "But just so I can see you act nice."

He breathed out an exhausted chuckle. "Act nice. I've been acting nice forever now."

"Not to me," she said.

"Not with you," he agreed.

And then she was hurrying through the halls, wondering at the change in Chael, worrying a little over what he wanted to talk to her about.

When she reached class, though, she came face-to-face with other things to worry about.

Mr. Percy stood waiting for her. "You'll need to come with me," he said. "Your aunt is here to talk to you."

~ ☾ ~

iii
(threatened)

Lena felt like someone had hooked her up to a car battery with an electric current running from the top of her head down to her boots, rattling her soul, making the fillings in her teeth spark.

Her aunt never came to school, only left her room to work, was too destroyed to function.

Yet she was there to see Lena.

Mr. Percy's office was stuffed with paper and gloom, like a dungeon for secretaries. Aunt Mercedes sat by a dusky lamp with darkness on her face.

"I'll leave you two alone to talk," Mr. Percy murmured and closed the door.

Her aunt's voice was as shadowy as everything else. "Lena, Child Protective Services stopped by this morning. Someone called them."

The thread holding Lena together snapped. "Perfect timing! Such wonderful news you have for me, Auntie! And Merry Christmas to you. Did they say who called them?"

Aunt Mercedes shrugged. "I don't know. They just said it was anonymous. And they have to check, but they'll be back. They didn't say when."

Lena knew it was because she had left Jozey alone. And only two people knew about that. Johnny Beels and Chael. And Beels wouldn't be making those kinds of phone calls.

Lena ground her teeth. Chael wouldn't leave her truck alive.

"Okay, so what does this mean?" Lena crunched out

~ ☾ ~

the question.

Aunt Mercedes' chin fell to her chest and stayed there. "I don't know."

Lena had seen her look like that before, at the hospital, next to the wheezing respirator. Lena would never forget the sound of the machine that kept her mother breathing, like a little bird was caught in her mother's chest, fluttering to live in the wind of the machine.

What should we do, Lena?

Lena squeezed her eyes shut. "Okay, so we don't freak. We take good care of Jozey. We'll be fine."

"Art Lancing called me as well," her aunt whispered. "What kind of trouble are you in, Lena?"

"I'm not in any trouble, Auntie," Lena said in a firm voice. But she would be once she murdered Chael.

"Santiago was your boyfriend. He was a drug dealer. We all think you were helping him."

Lena laughed. It was the sound of icicles shattering. "Oh yeah, that's me. I'm such a criminal. What's your proof?"

Aunt Mercedes shrugged.

"Yeah, that's what I thought. I have nothing to hide."

Her aunt sighed. "Well, Lena, with Art Lancing and the CPS people looking for problems, you can't hide anything. They'll find out the truth."

Lena felt her heart harden into solid concrete. "Well, Auntie, raising teenagers is a real bitch, huh? I bet you didn't think there would be this much drama when you pulled the plug on my mom. Probably shouldn't have done that, huh?"

Aunt Mercedes lifted her head. Lena wanted desperately to see hatred in her face, but there was none. Just a crushing sadness.

"I pray to God, Lena, you never, ever have to make the choice I had to make. I pray to God."

~ ☾ ~

Her aunt had asked her what they should do. Turn off the machines which kept the little bird of breath inside her mother alive, or let her fly free.

What should we do, Lena?

Lena hadn't answered. She hadn't cried, hadn't said a word; she just let her aunt make the decision to turn off the machines. And now she hated her for it.

It wasn't fair. Lena knew that, but she couldn't help it. The hate inside her had a life all its own. "I'm sorry for what I said."

Aunt Mercedes dropped her head again. A tear fell to the floor. "It's okay. It's okay."

But it wasn't. "I'll be nicer to you, Auntie, I promise."

"No, you won't."

Lena left the room and sat in the classroom, numb. If she went to the police with the red purse, they would arrest her and the CPS people would take her brother away. Losing Jozey would kill her.

The only solution was to give the red purse to Beels and get out. Get out and stay out. Better to be homeless than to lose Jozey.

And it had to snow. Things had to change.

Outside her classroom window, Lena watched the cold clouds swirl. For a moment, she felt herself drowning in the whiteness, then she thought of Chael. She was going to destroy him for threatening her and Jozey.

The thought made her feel better. For a moment.

But the memory of her aunt's words brushed all the anger away, and sadness, like snowflakes, drifted down to cover Lena's soul.

~ ☾ ~

iv
(chael and lena)

After school, in the parking lot, Chael walked through the cloud in his dark coat and his white hoodie. When he saw her, his face warmed into a small, kind smile, soft and open.

Until Lena shot him down. "You get into my business again, I'll kill you."

His face closed. "You have no idea what you are saying. Not a clue."

Before she knew it, she had his white hoodie balled up in her fists, and she was in his face. "You called Child Protective Services on me. You say you care so much about Jozey, but what will happen to him if they take him?"

"I know what will happen," he whispered. "I know because I grew up alone. My parents were killed, and there was no one to take care of me after I lost Darlita. I was just another orphan from the war. I slept with pigs."

Lena relaxed her hands. He had to be joking. "Pigs?"

"At least it was warm."

Everything about him was wrong. As if he played by a completely different set of rules. Or she did.

He continued to talk in a low voice. "A funny thing happens when you're alone and no one loves you. You stop caring about life. It's all just cold. It's all just gray. It's all just stone. That will happen to Jozey if he loses you."

At the name of her brother, she lashed out. "Then why did you report me? I was only gone for a few minutes."

"Only a few minutes." He sighed and shook his head.

~ ☾ ~

"Only a few minutes. He can't afford that, and neither can you. Don't you see? All you have, all anyone has, is just a few minutes. Every second is precious."

The words touched her, she wanted to give in to them, but she fought on. "Leave us alone. We're none of your business."

The coal in his eyes ignited. "And that's just what you want. To be left alone, even if it murders what is human in Jozey. All because you're too proud or too stupid to accept help."

She slapped him before she knew it. His cheek gleamed pink and she could see the marks of her fingers on his skin. She went to touch his face, as if she could take it back. "I'm sorry. I'm so sorry."

He brushed her aside, moving quickly across the parking lot.

She tripped after him. "Chael, please, I'm sorry. Come back. Please."

It was like she had crossed an invisible line and she wanted to jump back on the safe side of things, where she could control herself, where life made sense, where she wasn't such a monster.

He was moving quickly, but he wasn't running. Still, she couldn't catch up to him. She was stopped at the sidewalk when she realized people were pointing, and they would think the wrong thing. Trying to be casual, Lena walked back to her truck, got in, and drove down the street, searching for him. But as always, he had disappeared. This time, though, she knew where he was going. No way could he beat her to the Cherubim on foot.

In such a small town, there weren't many places to hide, and Lena drove slow but saw no sign of the dark boy. There was only one way to get to Jozey's daycare center and that was the highway. It was empty.

In the parking lot of the Cherubim, Lena stopped and watched the wisps of clouds swirl over the silver cold of

~ ☾ ~

the lake.

"Okay, Lena," she said to herself, touching up her make-up in the mirror. "You are going to kill him with kindness. If he is gunning for you and Jozey, you need to show him you're not completely psychotic." And she wondered how much of what he had told her was the truth, growing up an orphan, sleeping with pigs. She wanted to believe he was lying, but the way he had said it, she knew he was telling her the truth.

She left her truck to wait for him inside because, obviously, he couldn't have walked faster than she drove. Yet, Chael was already there on the floor with Jozey on his lap, looking at a book.

Lena watched them through a window, half-hidden by cartoon dinosaurs. The two fit, like two lost puzzle pieces that curved perfectly together. The sight brought tears to her eyes. She didn't want anyone to be as special to Jozey as she was. Chael had been right. She just wanted the world to be her and her brother. Anyone else was an intruder.

Lena blinked back tears.

She wanted her family back, just her, Jozey, and Mom and Dad, in their house, a normal family, a normal life.

Should we stop?

"No, Mom, we shouldn't."

If Lena went in there now, she knew she could end up slapping him again. She retreated to the parking lot and tried to hold onto something like sanity. Inside the cloud, all she could see was dry dirt and little pebbles and the remnants of broken glass scattered over the crumbling asphalt.

So tired, so hungry, she wanted to curl up in the cold and go to sleep under the truck. But it was freezing. Chael had said at least it was warm with the pigs.

"Okay, Lena. Okay."

She walked back inside and ignored the savage

~ ☾ ~

jealousy of seeing Chael holding Jozey. The two were building houses by stacking books.

"You got here quick," Lena said, her smile a mask.

Chael shrugged, the specter of the slap still on his cheek.

"Hi, Weni," Jozey said.

She was no big deal. She wasn't Chael. The children stared at them, expecting another war.

Lena let out a long breath, avoiding their eyes, and focused on her brother. "Hi, Jozey. Wanna go see Auntie Deirdre?"

"Can Chael come?"

Both her brother and Chael watched her carefully. Of course Chael couldn't come. Deirdre had labeled him an Untouchable. But Lena couldn't say that. "Chael has to work, sweetie," Lena said. "And he probably wouldn't want to come."

"There's less kids than usual, so I think I can get off early," he said. "And I'd like to come."

Jozey threw his arms around Chael. "Hurray! Chael gets to come! Hurray! Hurray!"

Lena smiled through her dread.

Chael's face was serene, mysterious, but kind. So different from his usual glaring. It was as if he had taken off a blindfold and now saw everything with a new understanding.

That scared her more than anything.

~ ☾ ~

V
(chael and dodson)

Deirdre lived in one of the uppermost houses of the Lakeview estates, lots of open space, pine trees, and rocky outcroppings with homes nestled in perfectly.

But "For Sale" signs littered the lawns like tombstones.

Lena couldn't believe Chael was in her truck, couldn't believe he would want to come after she'd slapped him. And all the while, he had that calm look on his face. Patient. Eternally patient. What had happened to change him so dramatically? Maybe he needed a good slap. She hid her smile inside, but the quiet was killing her. Even Jozey had stopped chattering, so Lena had to say something. "We lived up here before the accident."

She hated calling it that. It wasn't an accident. What the driver of the car had done to her and her family had been intentional, but accident was the easiest word to use.

"They're nice," Chael said.

"Our apartment now is nicer," Jozey called out. "I can see my nightlight from my bed. It's cozy."

She shook her head. "I guess you could call it cozy, Jozey."

Her brother giggled at the rhyme.

Chael smiled at the laughter, but his mind was elsewhere. "These houses are nice. Your parents must have worked hard to afford one."

"Mommy and Daddy are in heaven with God," Jozey said. "Have you ever been to heaven, Chael?"

Lena was embarrassed by her brother's question. "No,

~ ☽ ~

Jozey, Chael is still alive."

"I don't know anything about God or heaven, Jozey," Chael said. "I bet you know more about it than me."

"God loves us and He lives in heaven with His angels," Jozey said expertly.

"I wish I could believe that," Chael said in a low voice, his face turned toward the window.

Lena opened her mouth to defend Jozey's faith, but her brother was quicker.

"I believe lots and lots and for everyone," he said and grabbed Chael's hand.

"Most of these houses are in foreclosure," Lena said, desperate for a subject change. The few houses with Halloween decorations didn't look scary. They looked worn out and sad.

Chael nodded. "Deirdre's dad is big into real estate, right? He must be hurting with so much for sale."

"He has this idea of ski condos, but I don't know how that's going to work."

"Neither does he," Chael said.

How would he know? He had been in town two days. But at least he wasn't acting like he was the head prosecutor at her trial. She had to keep him in a good mood for Deirdre, so Lena kept her angry questions to herself.

The Dodson house was alone in a sea of empty houses, so there was plenty of parking. Getting out of the truck, they walked by plastic skeletons reaching up for them from the grass and witches dangling from trees. On the front porch was a leering devil all horns, tail and grinning teeth.

When Lena rang the doorbell, Mr. Dodson opened the door. He was tall and handsome, with gray hair going white. With his youthful features, it was striking. As always, he was in a tie, a dress shirt, and a suit coat. From behind him drifted oldies with poppy, do-wop

~ ☾ ~

lyrics and catchy guitar riffs.

"Lena, so good to see you," Dodson said, then eyed her guest. "And you are?"

"I'm Chael. Lena's friend."

Lena went to protest that Chael wasn't her friend. At present, he was her best enemy.

But Jozey yelled, "And my friend!" then rushed to hug Dodson.

"Hi, Mr. Dodson. How's business?" Lena asked.

"Pray for snow. We need snow and investors."

"What's an investor?" Jozey asked.

Chael answered. "People with money. Doesn't matter where the money comes from, only that they have money to spend."

Dodson appraised Chael with a smile and cool, calculating eyes. "Sure, that's what an investor is. But dirty money spends just as easily as clean money does."

"If I had dirty money, I would clean it," Jozey said loudly.

Dodson nodded, nearly laughing. "Better watch your brother, Lena. Don't want him to get into the money laundering business."

"Some money can't be cleaned," Chael said.

Lena sighed and pushed them all through the door. "Anyway! Is Deirdre around?"

"On the phone, as always." Dodson went to turn away. "I have to make a few calls myself, but help yourselves to anything."

"Calls about the ski condos?" Chael asked.

"Glad even the new people in town know about it. It's going to be the future around here." Dodson's voice sounded like he was daring Chael to disagree.

"Sounds like it," Chael said easily. "I hope it all works out for everyone. Most people think it's pretty risky."

"Life's a risk," Dodson returned.

Chael nodded. "Life's a risk when you do risky things.

~ ☾ ~

Otherwise, life is just life. It is what it is."

"Life is what we make it," Dodson insisted.

"You're right about that, but sometimes when we think we're trying to make life better, we're really hurting the people around us." Chael paused, his eyes never wavering. "Like with parents. The choices they make can break their children. But in the end, you're right, we can choose not to be broken. Wouldn't it be nice if our parents made it easy for us to do the right thing, though?"

Lena wanted to throttle him. At least Chael was an arrogant pain-in-the-ass to everyone and not just her.

Dodson laughed through half-closed eyes. "Quite a friend you have there, Lena. He should join a debating society." He retreated up the stairs and into his office.

"I'm coming!" Deirdre called down.

In that moment, Lena frowned, brow furrowed, hoping she could make her point without slapping him again. "You have to be nice to my friends. You're my guest."

Chael gave her an innocent look.

Why was he here? Just to torture and embarrass her?

Jozey took off and ran through the living room, through the dining room, through the kitchen, and back to them. He knocked over a lamp, but Lena caught it before it fell.

"Jozey, no running. Remember? There's a lot of stuff that can break. Let's go out to the deck and see if we can see the lake through the clouds."

"The clouds is like heaven!" Jozey yelled happily.

The house was professionally decorated, most of the furniture and knick-knacks coming from boutiques in Denver. Lena's Lakeview home had been nice, but Deirdre's was palatial. The back of the house was mostly windows. Trees were ghosts in the clouds and the lake was hidden in the mist.

~ ☾ ~

The minute they were through the patio doors, Jozey shot down the steps of the deck, calling for Ariel, Deirdre's dog.

"You can see Camlann Lake usually," Lena said to Chael. "And there's a great view of Ablach Peak from Deirdre's room, but of course, the clouds are ruining everything."

Around them, the patio furniture was covered in dusty cloth like mourners, the black grill like a preacher.

Chael stood in the cold, nodding. "Ablach, like apples. Eve in the garden of Eden and all that."

"Yeah," Lena said, "blame the woman for everything."

"No, not just women." Chael sighed. "There's enough blame for everyone to have their fair share."

Lena unleashed her questions. "What are you doing here? Why on earth would you want to come with me?"

Before he could answer, Deirdre stepped out onto the deck. "Lena, shame, shame, you should have called first if you wanted to bring a friend. Such a sad thing, the state of etiquette in today's world."

She smiled at Chael, as if she were a lioness and Lena had brought her a bleeding gazelle.

"Hello, Deirdre," Chael said.

And the battle began.

~ ☾ ~

vi
(chael and deirdre)

"Jozey loves him," Lena said quickly. "He wanted you to meet him."

Deirdre cocked her head. "Of course." She turned back to the dark boy. "And how do you know who I am? And what was your name again? Something unusual, I believe."

"Everyone knows who you are," Chael said. "You make sure of that."

"His name is Chael," Lena whispered weakly.

"Odd name," Deirdre said. "Never heard of it before."

"It's a Hebrew name," Chael said in an even, patient voice, "but my parents were Basque."

Lena expected his hating, critical, viciousness, Rottweiler-mean, but here he was, a nice golden retriever.

"Let's go inside," Deirdre said, motioning to the open patio door. "We can just as well chat where it's warm."

Lena called down to her brother, "We're going inside, Jozey. If you need anything, we'll be upstairs."

"Okay, Weni! I love Ariel!"

Lena hurried back in, not wanting to miss a punch.

"What's your last name?" Deirdre was asking. She had a coffee mug in her hands, using it like a judge uses his gavel.

"I'm not sure," the dark boy said. "I remembered my first name. I figured that was good enough."

"Rough flight in?" Deirdre asked. "Jet lag can be such a monster, but making you forget your own last name?"

He shrugged. "You would know. Your mom is in

~ ☾ ~

Switzerland, I think. Is that right?"

There was a flicker of annoyance on Deirdre's face, just the shadow of discomfort, before she could collect herself again. "Yes, Geneva. She loves the mountains. She grew up in Avalon."

"A very different Colorado, though," Chael said. "Back then, things were far more simple. I would imagine she's seeking that same feeling in Geneva, a mountain city by the lake, unspoiled and untouched by tragedy, greed, and corruption. Geneva is anything but that, but there are worse places to be."

Lena interrupted, trying to protect her friend. "Yeah, Deirdre, your dad said Chael should join speech and debate. He likes to argue." Chael, as if by magic, had found Deirdre's only weak spot. Her mother.

"I like to argue," Deirdre said, but her coffee mug had become a shield and something like fear was in her eyes. "No last name? Where are your Mummy and Daddy, Chael?"

"Dead," he said. "For a long, long time."

"An orphan without a last name," Deirdre said dismissively. "Can I pour you both some coffee?"

"I don't drink coffee," he said in his weary patient tone with just a hint of arrogance. "But Lena does. It's the caffeine that keeps her together."

"It's not," Lena protested.

"Why don't you drink coffee?" Deirdre asked.

"I don't like how it makes me feel."

"How does it make you feel?"

"Crazy. Like your mother."

Lena felt all of her breath leave her body. The tension in the kitchen made inhaling impossible.

Deirdre was at the cupboard, getting a mug, and she stopped. She slowly turned. "What did you say?"

Chael leveled his eyes at her and there was hellfire burning there. "It makes me feel crazy. Your mother

~ ☾ ~

doesn't like caffeine either."

"How would you know such a thing?" Deirdre asked. She was a rusty spring, pressed down too tight.

Chael shrugged. "People talk. It's a small town."

"Yes," Deirdre said in a whisper. "Small towns suck when it comes to that. She's getting better, you know. Tell all the idiots who can't keep their idiot mouths shut that she's getting better."

"She loves you," Chael said softly. "She loves Geneva, but she misses you. She aches, she misses you so much."

"Get out," Deirdre whispered. Her eyes sparkled. Not from tears, from something else. "Get out and don't come back. And at school, don't talk to me, don't look at me. Do you understand?"

Chael's whole face fell. "I'm sorry. I didn't mean to hurt you." It was like someone else had taken over Chael's body. He looked as hurt and shocked as Deirdre. "I'm sorry. I'd forgotten…"

"Get out."

Chael nodded. "Yeah, one more mistake. It was so much easier before." He turned to Lena. "Tell Jozey I said goodbye." He paused. "And tell him that tomorrow night we'll have a lot of time together. Hours and hours."

Without another word, he walked through the rooms full of happy oldies-but-goodies music and closed the front door behind him.

"Why did you bring him here?" Deirdre asked. She was seconds from either bawling or scratching Lena's eyes out. "Why would you unleash him on me like that?"

"I didn't know," Lena said. "It all just kind of happened. Jozey invited him, and I tried to say—"

"Do you want to sit by yourself?" Deirdre asked, uncoiled. "Do you want to become a Heretic for real? I can make that happen, you know. Parker Lee would love to see you fall."

Lena's voice died in her throat. The whole scene

~ ☾ ~

seemed so unreal, as if she were in a T.V. show and everything Deirdre had been saying was scripted and rehearsed.

"Oh, we know, poor Lena, so tragic. We let you be miserable, we let you go ghetto with Santiago, but we're getting tired of the drama. And then you call and want me to get involved in your drug thing? Please! Why would I risk my house and my father's reputation to help you? You need to wake up, Lena, wake up and decide, once and for all, do you want to be a Paladin, or do you want to be a Heretic?"

It was Chael's calm patience that filled her. Lena knew it. Somehow, Chael hadn't left, and he was there with her. Her skin shivered into goose bumps. "I want to be me," Lena said. "I'm sorry for what Chael said. He's an ass, but I'm your friend. Well, maybe I was once. Now, I'm not so sure I can be if you're going to threaten me like that."

Deirdre turned away. She was crying, and Lena knew no one was allowed to witness such a thing. "You can go too, Lena. I want to be alone now."

Lena couldn't go. She had known Deirdre all her life. "D, I'm sorry. What he said, about your mom, she does love you."

"Leave. Now."

Lena collected Jozey who was happily playing with the dog. Her brother's face was bright red, his nose ran like a faucet, and his little fingers were colorless. But you can forget all of that when you're playing with a friendly dog.

Lena picked up Jozey and suddenly she was crying.

"What's wrong, Weni? What's wrong?"

Everything. She couldn't say it. All she could do was cry and hold her brother as she walked around the side of the house back to her truck.

Everything was wrong.

Everything. Everything. Everything.

~ ☾ ~

Chael was nowhere to be seen, so it was just her and Jozey for the drive back home.

That night, with Jozey asleep, Lena carefully took off her make-up, put antibiotic cream on her arm, and tried once again to do the impossible. Homework.

No time to gather Jozey's Halloween costume, no energy. She had promised him she would figure out a Halloween costume tomorrow. But it would have to be cheap and easy, and those things never went together.

With the textbook words blurring, Johnny Beels buzzed her cell phone.

"Hey, Johnny," she said. A little spark inside of her fluttered alive.

"Call me Beels, Leni, 'cause everyone else will. Hey, I wanted to let ya in on a little secret. Santiago is coming back to school tomorrow, and I didn't know if that would throw ya."

Of all the things going on, Santiago was just a distraction. "No, it's okay."

"He won't mess with us and our red purses. Me and him had us a little talk, and once it's safe, he's gonna give me all the rest of them red purses he's been collectin' over the past month. And Halloween night, I'm gonna sell the whole stash, and then I'm gettin' out of the racket. Probably better ways to make cash, and if there's not, money's not everything."

"Unless you don't have any," she said. "When my parents were alive, I didn't care at all about money. Now, it's all I think about."

Beels clicked his tongue. "Leni, cash is just cash. No big deal. Just like the old song, money can't buy ya love, darlin'."

"No, but it can pay your rent," Lena said. It was late. "I gotta go, Johnny." She winced. She had forgotten already.

"Call me Beels, Leni. You sleep tight."

~ ☾ ~

She clicked the phone off.

She wondered when they were going to search her for the drugs. She wondered when CPS would come to investigate them. She wondered if she should sit with the Paladins in the morning. Would Deirdre let her?

Her worrying mind kept her up late, and Jozey was up early with his questions and crying.

Once again, she hadn't gotten enough sleep and her mind felt poisoned. She knew every minute of the next day was going to hurt.

~ ☾ ~

THURSDAY'S KISS

i
(the talk with pockets)

Thursday morning, Lena sat in her truck in the cloudy high school parking lot thinking about Halloween with Jozey. If only Wal-Mart wasn't so far away, she could just buy an angel costume, or at least wings. Luther Pem's store in town might have something, but it would be pricey.

Taking care of her brother and doing her life was hard enough. Throw in a holiday and it felt impossible. Never mind the fact she hadn't even considered what costume she would wear, or if she could get Aunt Mercedes to babysit. Maybe she could have Emma sculpt a dress for her. Go as a post-goth vampire princess or something.

The castle-like walls of the school rose up above her. Inside, the Paladin girls would be at their table at the top tier of the cafeteria, gossiping. Even though it was vapid and tiresome, Lena missed the normalcy and high schoolishness of it all, missed Deirdre. Their friendship had survived the nervous breakdown of Deirdre's mother, the death of Lena's parents, Lena's slide into the Heretics, but it might not survive Chael.

Lena didn't know how much damage she had done the previous night to her standing with Deirdre and the Paladins. Better to let it all blow over and give Deirdre time to collect herself. And with Santiago back, Lena could eat lunch with the Heretics, so she wouldn't be alone. Except that with the Heretics, she felt alone. She didn't quite fit in with them.

But she didn't fit in with the Paladins anymore either. She thought of the outcast clique that had congregated

~ ☾ ~

around Chael, Remy the broken-hearted football player, Tubitha, and weird Pockets with his yelling and muttering.

What did they all talk about so intently? Lena couldn't even begin to guess.

She was getting out of her truck when she saw Pockets walking across the parking lot in his green army jacket, mouth moving. He was small and thin, with straw-blond hair sticking out all over his head. His lips were pale and blue from some heart condition that living at high elevation probably didn't help.

Without realizing it, Lena found herself charging over to the boy, barely feeling the cold. He might be able to give her some answers.

"Hey, Paulie," she called out, wondering if that was still his name, or if it was Paul now.

He turned around. "Me?" Surprise showed on his face.

"Yeah, you," she said, moving up to him.

His eyes darted around in his head, frog-like. "You want to talk to me?"

She shrugged. "Yeah, why is that so weird?"

"Isn't there a law against such a thing? I mean, some statute dictating that all Paladin girls must remain fifty yards away from me? I guess that would be a restraining order." His face twisted up in discomfort. "Not that I've ever had a restraining order, or I had to register as a sex offender or anything." He shook his head, laughing. "Funny, that was funny. Only I shouldn't have said all those things. How about we start over?"

But after all that, Lena didn't know where to start over. No wonder Paulie had sat alone for most of his school career. He didn't make it easy for people to talk to him. And she'd completely forgotten why she'd chased him down in the first place.

"So, Lena, last time we talked, I think it was the third grade and we were doing something with Play-doh. How

~ ☾ ~

is the sculpting going? I've moved on to clay, but I did like the Play-doh as a medium." When she didn't answer, he threw up his hands and backed away. "Yeah, this is why there should be a law against Paladin girls talking to me. I have said every possible wrong thing I could say, so I'm just going to slink away and leave your royaltyness in peace."

He started off, but Lena stopped him. "No, wait. Paulie, give me a chance."

"No," he said, half-laughing, "you gave me a chance, and I messed it up. Back to being an Untouchable, I guess."

"I want to talk to you about Chael."

He cocked his head. "What about him?"

"How come you started sitting together?" Lena asked. The question was direct and blunt, like throwing a bone to a pack of dogs.

"He helped my dad and me with our shed." He winced. "Oh, right, I can't talk about my dad. Since I'm sixteen, I'm supposed to hate him. You know, I try to keep up on teen rules but nothing sticks."

Lena waded through the words. "Chael helped you with your shed?"

"Yeah, Monday night, we had to get the roof part on and it was just the two of us. No way we could have done it by ourselves. Chael comes walking right up, we hammer it on, booya, we chat and he didn't run away when I opened my mouth. Then Tabitha came over because Chael talked to her, and then Remy, and now we just sit together. No big deal. The end."

"What do you guys talk about?" Another direct question.

He grinned. "We talk about the meaning of life, mostly. But we also talk about the social structure at school, the universe, string theory, you know, just normal stuff. Why are you so curious? I mean, we've

~ ☾ ~

talked about you because other than us, you're the one who is the most fluid when it comes to cliques. Best friends with Deirdre and boyfriend/girlfriend with Santiago? You defy the social norms, which is why I'm even attempting to talk to you."

"So if Deirdre came over like this?" Lena couldn't help but smile at the idea.

"Deirdre? I wouldn't talk to Deirdre. She's not human, you know. She's a Barbie doll with the soul of Mephistopheles. She's where plastic meets evil. She's—"

"My friend," Lena interrupted.

"Yeah, well, no accounting for taste." His mouth squeezed tight. "Oh, shouldn't have said that. I gotta fix my editor. I don't know, you may see something I don't, but she's the one who named me, and until I blow out of Avalon, I'm stuck with it. And it's not the type of nickname I'm going to cherish when I'm forty, you know?"

Lena nodded. "Yeah, I understand."

He shook his head. "No, you don't. A million bucks says you call me Pockets when you're up there hobnobbing with the elite. Damn editor." He knocked his head softly with his fist. "I gotta get to class. I'm on a streak, never had a tardy, never had an absence. I'm hoping for a gold watch when I graduate."

He walked off, leaving her there with questions hanging.

Like with everyone else, Chael had shown up right when Paulie needed him. Like her with the cop, and Mrs. Weyland when Miss Terri quit.

Maybe she should ask the dark boy about an angel costume for her brother.

~ ☾ ~

ii
(santiago overcome and undone)

On only four hours of sleep, Lena was drinking Diet Cranksta energy drinks every ten minutes whether she needed them or not. The caffeine buzzed through her body like a chainsaw about to throw a chain.

She was counting down the hours until the red purse would be gone, safely away from her in the hands of Johnny Beels. But she had to get through the school day first.

In her classes, she kept to herself, sitting alone. As did Johnny Beels, though he kept smiling at everyone, not even trying to pay attention. Chael and the Untouchables had a place up front, listening and taking notes. Paladins in the center, Heretics in the back, but Santiago wasn't there in the morning. He tip-toed in just before lunch, looking whipped.

Reticent to test her standing with the Paladins, Lena sat with the Heretics in their usual place outside the lunchroom by the principal's office. Like most of them, she didn't have anything to eat. For some, it was by choice. For others, it was a matter of money. Poverty eats the poor belly first.

When Santiago came up, eyes low, Bruise screamed and hugged him. "Santiago! What's up, man? What happened? What the hell?"

Santiago grinned, shrugged, before dropping his gaze to the floor. His voice was a low whisper. "Nothing, man. Just got picked up. Gonna have to chill for a while. That's all."

Bruise cocked his head back. "That's it?"

Santiago shrugged. "That's it."

Dane Bramage grunted and scratched the stubble on his head like a hound ridding fleas. He had the backpack again, flat and empty. What was he not carrying around in it?

"You have been touched by the authorities. They have marked you." Bramage's voice came out in a deep rasp. "You shall not be saved. You have thrown in your lot with the Pharisees and you will burn as happily as everyone else. No stone untouched. No soul unscorched. Apocalypse now."

Santiago started to protest when Johnny Beels strutted out of the cafeteria, his cowboy boots gunning down the hall. In his hand was a plate of oozing nachos, covered in jalapeno peppers. He was slipping chips into his mouth like they were peyote.

"Yeah, marked," Beels said, "but ease on down there, Bramage. Let Jimmy tell us all the rest of the story."

Emma's stare locked onto Beels, like iron to a magnet. That day, she was wearing a yellow bridesmaid dress, tore up short to show ripped black nylons. In the fabric of the frayed thrift store dress, she had woven rusted bicycle chains.

Bruise's face fell into a slack grin. "Who's Jimmy?"

Beels threw Lena a smile, and she threw one back. He was something to see.

"Jimmy? Why, that's Santiago here. Ya see, Santiago is really Saint Iago, which is Saint James, and that makes him a Jimmy, any ol' way ya look at it."

"Who're you?" Bruise asked in a growl.

"Johnny Beels. But y'all can call me Beels, 'cause everyone else will. I'm the new kid in town, new connection, and I sure like Lena's red purse. She don't have it on her right as of now, but I'm a sucker for

sequins. Spent some time in Vegas, seein' the sights.
Love that town." He sucked cheese off his fingers with a
smack. "Wanna nacho, pardner?" He held them up to
Bruise.

Bruise took a chip.

"Johnny Beels." Bramage said the name as if he was
trying to remember a dream.

"He's my replacement," Santiago said quietly.

Beels offered the nachos to Emma. "Yeah, Jimmy, yer
replacement, on account of ya goin' away and leavin' the
red purse racket far behind."

"What's he talking about?" Bruise asked and went for
another chip.

"Nothing," Santiago insisted.

Lena wanted her kind-of boyfriend to be as arrogant
and proud as Beels, for Santiago to sing Bertoglio and be
like he had been just two days before when he and Avery
almost went at it. But Santiago kept shaking his head,
grinning and shrugging.

"Why, Jimmy is going off to treatment. Gonna get
hisself a sponsor and clean up. Which is a good thing,
right?" Beels glanced around at the shocked Heretics.
"Right? I mean, if y'all wanna party, ya should, but if ya
don't, ya should get help. Now, that just makes good
sense."

Wordless, Bruise turned to his friend.

Beels kept talking, passing the plate around. "And he
held his mud, so there won't be no repercussions from
other parties less congenial than ma'self. I take up
swinging red purses and Santiago goes to swing low,
sweet chariot." Beels sang the last part, just like Santiago
would have done.

"Good voice," Santiago said.

Beels' ice-blue eyes twinkled. "Oh, you know it. But
Lena tells me ya got the pipes too. Let's hear it."

"Not today," Santiago said and looked away to find

~ ☾ ~

Lena watching him. He nodded at her. "Hey Lena, can I talk to you outside?"

Beels held up the last bit of food on the plate. "Don't go, Leni. I saved the last nacho for ya. It's spicy good."

"No, thanks, but they look tasty." Lena smiled at Beels and then stood up, losing the smile when Santiago took her hand. They went out the door into the cold cloud and found a corner in the courtyard.

Seeing Santiago without his song hurt her, made her want a cigarette. She could bum one and add the nicotine to the caffeine soup inside of her. But Santiago had probably given up cigarettes as well. He was distant, as wintry as the mist around them.

"It's true," Santiago said. "I'm going to get clean."

"Because you talked with Chael. And let me guess, he showed up right when you needed something, like he was saving the day."

He shook his head. "No, nothing like that. I was thinking about cleaning up before. When the cops grabbed me, it seemed like the time. He did say I should turn in all the dope to the cops, but the guys we're dealing with would have killed me if I had done that."

She nodded and wished for a Diet Cranksta to go along with the cigarette. Something other than a heart-to-heart with the boyfriend.

"Listen, Lena, it's a twenty-eight day program, and you and I haven't been that close. I just didn't want you to wait around for me."

He was so sincere, so ardent, it made Lena laugh. "But I want to wait."

"What?" He was all shock.

She waved a hand. "I'm kidding. We were pretty much broken up anyway."

"You have to get out of the game, Lena."

She wrapped her arms around herself. "The other day, you said you had no choice. Well, I guess you did after

~ ☾ ~

all. But I'm still right where I was. I need the money."

"Dealing isn't the only way to make money. You could go legit."

She stepped away from him. "You go get clean. I never did the stuff, so no preaching, no pushing. I'll live my own life, thank you. You go and live yours."

Santiago caught her hand in his. "Get out of the game before you get caught. We all know Chael is with the police. He's going to turn you in if he hasn't done that already."

"We're done, Santiago. I'm off your leash." And she walked into the cloud away from him.

"I loved you, Lena."

She turned around. He was almost invisible in the freezing fog. Like a ghost fading. No words for the ex-boyfriend, just a smile and then a last, little wave.

All afternoon she thought about her time with Santiago, how he had lost his own father when he was little, and the mutual grief had brought them together. How he would hold her in his arms, his mouth kissing her while his music caressed her. They had some good times, but it wasn't meant to last.

After school, as she was walking out of her final class, her cell phone rang with Beels on the other end.

"You a free woman? Jimmy had that breakin-up-is-hard-to-do look about him when he led ya out."

She sighed. "Yeah, free at last."

"What's it about y'all that creates such a stir among us po' boys?"

Lena reddened, loving the flutter Beels put in her. "Oh, Johnny. The things you say. But what about my red purse?"

"Call me, Beels, baby. Hey, I'm gonna have a party tonight. I could examine your fashion accessories of the crimson nature either before or after. Either way, girl, I want ya by my side."

~ ☽ ~

She was speechless, an excited chill aching through
her.

"We'll be talkin'," Beels said in an easy, easy voice.

"Yes, we will," Lena said, finding her breath. She shut
the phone and wandered to a window. She couldn't see
any of the town, nothing of Mount Cadmus, Ablach Peak,
nothing, just the swirl of the cloud.

She'd told Beels she was free, but if that were the case,
how come she felt so caged?

And the cage was about to close even further.

Bruise ran up to her, gasping.

"Lena, they're here for you. They got warrants and
everything. You better get out of here."

Footsteps echoed off the walls, and Lena turned to see
Lancing walking up the stairs.

~ ☾ ~

iii
(return to hell)

Lena fled down the back hallways, every breath catching. She smelled something raw and metallic and realized it was her. Panic or adrenaline or madness or all of it at once.

Her heart echoed the clatter of her shoes on the steps.

They would be watching her truck, of course. Everyone knew what it looked like. But would they break into it to search? If they did, the red purse would be easy enough to find.

Small town. They knew she would either be at the school, picking up her brother, or at home. Which meant she couldn't get her brother, but Aunt Mercedes had to work her shift at the Gas 'n Sip. There was no one else.

What would happen to Jozey if she were caught? And the Halloween costume? And carving pumpkins? Their first Halloween since the accident would be ruined.

Down hallways and through doorways to the back of the school and the back doors. She was startled to see the dark boy turn the corner, his white hoodie glowing, his coat so black it looked like midnight cut into cloth.

It was a *déjà vu* of Tuesday night: her running from the police and Chael disappearing down into the basement.

Chael had said he and Jozey would be spending hours and hours together that night. Those were the words he had used. Hours and hours. The words came back to Lena and her fear turned into anger. The only way Chael could have known that is if he had orchestrated everything with the police.

~ ☾ ~

She marched down the steps after him, her jaws
clenched, her hands fisted. She had warned him, and he
had crossed the line.

Like before, the basement was hellishly hot and crypt-
dark.

Like before, Chael was searching for something.

"You leave us alone!" she screamed. It was a feral
sound, and she was surprised something like that had
come from her. The screech left claw marks in her throat.

Chael slowly turned around. Like a gunslinger
reaching for his pistol.

Lena found herself in slapping distance. "Why do you
hate me? You help everyone else but me!"

His face was passive in the heat and gloom. "I don't
hate you, and I am trying to help you."

"Like you helped Deirdre last night? Like you helped
Santiago? I can't imagine what you're doing to Pockets
and Tubitha." Her make-up ran down the wash of sweat
on her face.

"Paulie and Tabitha, those are their names," he shot
back. "Some people need to be beaten to wake them up.
Some have been beaten enough."

She was close to snarling. "So I suppose I need to be
beaten? And Deirdre, you beat her for sure. Who gave
you the right to decide all this? Who died and made you
God?"

Chael didn't say anything. He just stood there, and
Lena couldn't read him, but his silence felt like he was
laughing at her. She couldn't take that. She fell into him,
wanting to scratch and bite him until he was nothing but
rags.

He caught both of her hands in his and pulled her
close. She felt the breath leave her in a hiss. His touch
was scalding water.

"I haven't called anyone," he said, "and I'm not a cop.
I'm not God. I'm just me."

~ ☾ ~

"You're a liar." But she knew he was telling the truth. It seemed Chael could only tell the truth, no matter how brutal, no matter how stark.

His eyes were dark, like the char of paper eaten away by flame. But there wasn't fury there, there was anguish. "You don't see it, but I do. It's all so fragile. We're all so fragile. And the world is so broken. All of our prayers so uncertain."

In the Cherubim, that first day, she had seen him break down and she had felt a connection to him. It was like that now, in the basement, with the furnaces roaring. Her anger melted right out of her just as she melted into him, like two candles burning down together on a cold night.

"Maybe what I did to Deirdre and her father was wrong," he said. "And maybe with you I'm wrong. For all of those things, I'm sorry, but I don't know how to make it right. I made the biggest mistake of anyone, but I blamed everyone else."

"What did you do?" she asked in a whisper.

"I couldn't let the police arrest you," he said, closing his eyes. "I couldn't let that happen to you or to Jozey. I couldn't take one more lost soul, not with what you both had already been through. So I answered the prayer you couldn't speak."

His touch, his sorrow, seemed to complete something inside of her. She lifted her face to him. The magnetic draw of a closed connection pulled her up to kiss him.

He stopped her. "Lena, let me take the drugs to the police. I'll say I was working with Santiago and they'll stop looking. You'll be safe. Will you let me help you?"

He was flushed in the light of the furnace, trembling, burning. On his cheeks were either tears or sweat. She couldn't tell. Before she could answer, the cell phone rang.

"Don't," he whispered. "We both know who it is."

~ ☾ ~

But she had already answered it.

"Hey, Leni. Hope I caught y'all sinnin'. Can ya talk?"

"No," she said to both Beels and Chael. She couldn't let Chael take the fall for her. And she didn't want to talk to Beels right then.

She turned away from the dark boy, covering her eyes. His touch lingered, making everything fuzzy and hot like pink cotton candy melting inside her.

"I betcha know the cops are everywhere and you are one in demand little girl. Why don't y'all come up and see me in the usual place, and we can talk about what's going on?"

Beels' charm cut her the wrong way just then. "I can't. I'm with..."

But she wasn't with anyone. She was alone. It was the same dance with Chael, over and over again, and he always left her alone and feeling ashamed.

Time to find a new boy to dance with.

~ ☾ ~

iv
(the hard kiss of desire)

Lena sneaked up into the corridors of the school and hid in a bathroom to touch up her make-up and calm the demons rattling around in her heart. She had almost kissed Chael.

What was she thinking?

And yet, the memory of his touch, his skin, left her feeling weak and woozy. Like getting off a carnival ride with the world spinning, every muscle, every cell, dazed.

"Bad time for this," she whispered at herself in the mirror. "You're officially running from the cops. Save the lovey-dovey stuff for later."

Lancing could be anywhere. She had to focus, get to Beels in room seven, give him the red purse and run to get Jozey before Mrs. Weyland called Aunt Mercedes. If she didn't have the red purse, the police could question her all they wanted.

And almost kissing Chael could be chalked up to temporary insanity brought on by stress. End of story.

The hallways were empty as she made her way to the third floor, unlocked the gate with Beels' master key, and walked through the dust to the blond boy's empty library.

Beels was by the windows filled with clouds. He was eating one of Gramma Scar's hand-made cannolis.

"Hey girl." He licked sweet off his thumb as he smiled at her. "Wanna bite?"

Lena shook her head, but seeing his tongue caressing the creamy pastry tempted her. Here she was, off one roller coaster and right on to another. Better to talk only

~ ☾ ~

business. "I have to give you the red purse and go pick up my brother."

"Wine, then?"

She stood there, awkward, wondering if he had heard her.

"Cigarette?"

"Sure," she said too quickly. Before thinking about it. Which was the way addictions worked.

He finished off the cannoli, popped a smoke out of his pack, and tossed it to her.

She caught it but wasn't sure she really wanted it. Quitting had been hell, and there was Aunt Mercedes' cough to consider.

He moved closer, like a lion on the savannah, so smooth and graceful, his blond hair like a mane.

"The red purse is in yer truck, right?"

She nodded.

"Well, then..." He reached out and touched her cheek with cold fingers.

"What's your story, Johnny Beels?" Lena asked. "You a vampire?" She put up her tough girl mask, but inside, she was chocolate pudding, shaking and quaking.

"I got me cold hands, but I assure ya, my heart is warm and sunny."

"And you said you couldn't handle Avalon High School politics. Seems like everyone likes you."

He nodded and moved closer. His blue-eyed gaze gripped her. "Yeah, 'cause I'm a boy who brings the parties, and everyone always loves the party."

She felt ensorcelled, snared, like a rabbit in a trap. "But you're more than just a party boy."

He nodded but said the opposite. "Nope. That's all I am, but it's been okay, all these years."

"What about my purse?" Lena asked. Every syllable quivered.

"First, a little kiss, if y'all don't mind. Then we can talk

~ ☾ ~

bidness."

Lena felt the world disappear into his eyes and she wanted to throw herself into him, but she couldn't move. "You're a vampire. Definitely."

"I do like to eat," he murmured and put his cold hands on her hips.

His breath felt just as cold on her skin. His thin lips barely moved as he whispered, "Y'all're hotter than a carnival candy apple, Leni. Ya know that?"

She stopped thinking, stopped moving, stopped feeling anything except his breath on her face and the pound of her heart.

There was only a snowflake distance between their lips, but Beels continued to murmur. "Funny, we do all this craziness not for the kiss itself but for the second before the kiss. Whole world is in the second before the kiss. Whole world. Ya wonderin' what it's gonna be like, huh?"

Eyes closed, she nodded slightly. Lightning fired every part of her body. It hurt. Bad.

"Well, girlie," he whispered, "let's wait a little longer. Let's live in the second before the kiss—" he brushed his lips across her cheek, "—just…a…little…while…longer."

He stepped back.

She was shaking. Anger and sadness were jumbled up inside of her, making her want to slap him, kiss him, or just curl up and cry in his arms. She did none of those things. She just held up the cigarette, trying to be cool even as she shattered.

"I quit," she said. "I don't want to go back."

"Yeah, me, too." He took the smoke from her, lit it with an ivory Zippo lighter, and inhaled deeply. "Me, too." He handed it back to her.

Lena took a drag. It was a door closing.

"Ah, Leni, the world certainly is an interestin' place, idn't it?" From his pocket, Beels took out a wad of dollar

~ ☾ ~

bills and pushed them into her hands. "Here's the money for the pick-up. Now, about the red purse. Thing about mulin' is, y'all get paid to take the risk until the drop. Ain't time for the drop just yet."

"Please. Just take it from me now."

Beels squinched up his face, like her pain hurt him. "Sorry. It just ain't time yet. Cops're everywhere, and I got a lot of irons in the fire, what with securin' Santiago's stash before Halloween and all. Tonight at the party we'll do the drop. Just a few more hours, girl. Then I take it away, and we get our kiss. Y'all want the kiss, yeah?"

Lena smiled. "Maybe. Maybe now I feel like you're messing with me."

He put a pale hand to the white of his shirt. "Me? Ah no. Johnny Beels don't never mess around. Trust me. I want that kiss more than y'all could ever know."

She sighed and handed him the cigarette. Her mouth tasted like a fireplace after burning skunks. "Fine. At seven o'clock, I'll be in the parking lot behind Gramma Scar's. Pick me up then, okay?"

"And I get that kiss?" he asked hopefully.

She shrugged. "Maybe I'll mess with you."

But she was still shaking when she left the cold room.

~ ☾ ~

v
(good deeds done)

Back in a bathroom, Lena glanced at her watch. She knew she should stay where she was, hiding, but she knew she couldn't just sit on a toilet doing nothing. The wait would kill her, if not the smell. It was a quarter to four, but she couldn't pick up Jozey. The cops would be at the Cherubim, definitely.

But that's where Chael was, with Jozey, taking care of him. Instead of hate, she felt grateful to Chael for being there when she couldn't. And he'd apologized for what he'd done to Deirdre and her dad. And even offered to take the red purse from her. All the while touching her with his inferno hands and caressing her with the understanding in his sad, black eyes.

"Jozey will be okay," she said to the mirror. At six o'clock, Mrs. Weyland would call Aunt Mercedes, and her aunt would have to leave work early to pick him up. Not a big deal. They had two days until Halloween to work on the angel costume. Saturday they would carve pumpkins.

Chael's face broke into her mind. All his words echoed through her. This *was* a big deal. The world was fragile. Everyone was given only so many minutes to live. Every second was precious.

"Shut up," she told him, herself, everyone.

She needed to get the purse out of the truck but had no idea how to make that happen. Maybe at seven o'clock, she and Beels could drive by and pick it up. But he might not want that, and she'd have to spend another miserable day hiding from the police.

~ ☾ ~

No, she had to get the purse, but more importantly, she needed to disappear until seven o'clock. And that was a lot of time. Three hours in a small town was forever.

She thought about calling Deirdre, but now that was impossible. And the police would be watching the Heretics, of course, which meant no one could help her.

There was only one place to go. La Rosa Calda. Gramma Scar's restaurant, where she would be meeting Beels anyway.

A flash of Jozey crying for her knifed through her. She felt the tears come but forced herself to freeze them away. He would be fine, just like the other night.

In front of the sink in the bathroom, she counted Beels' money. Three hundred dollars. She could give Auntie a hundred and then save the rest for when Aunt Mercedes asked for more. After that, she didn't know.

It was unfair. Her whole life was unfair. If only they hadn't stopped to help that car, that stranger, that drunk with a gun. Her eyes went to the half-moon wounds on her arm where she had hurt herself.

Should we stop?

She fled from the bathroom and into the deserted hallways, but her dead mother's question followed.

Footsteps in the hall, reverberating off the walls. At first, she thought they were hers, but there was another set approaching, coming toward her from around the corner. The school wasn't as deserted as she had thought.

Of course it would be Lancing and he would haul her away. She would lose Jozey. Lena knew Chael was done saving her.

The footsteps shuffled toward her.

She needed to run but couldn't. Too afraid, or too tired.

Remy Bach rounded the corner, smiling. No one had

~ ☾ ~

seen him smile for a long time, not since football had
been shut down.

Lena pretended to hunt for something in her purse as
he came up to her. He was tall, big, with a wide face and
hair chopped close to his scalp. He was wearing his letter
jacket and black Nike sweats.

His voice came out deep and low. "Hey, I know I ain't
talked to you or any of the other Paladins for months,
but I got news, and I gotta tell someone."

"Okay." Lena felt the walls tumbling down on her. She
had no idea why Remy was talking to her on the most
terrifying and confusing day of her life.

"You know that new kid, Chael?"

"Sure." She dropped the one word and hoped he
would get to the point. Prayed it had nothing to do with
her.

"Well, we were talking. I have no idea why I didn't
think of this before. I mean, dang, it was all so clear once
I heard his idea."

Her stomach twisted. "About what?"

His smile broadened. "About football. What else? You
see, I called Lake County High School in Leadville and I
talked to a coach there. He knew about me. Somehow.
Anyway, I can play there. Getting over to Leadville is
going to be rough, but man, I'll fly if I have to."

She let out a long sigh. "That's great. Finally, someone
has some good news."

"Chael probably called the coach. That guy is cool.
God, I can't believe I get to play football again."

He hugged her then danced down the hall. "I get to
play football!"

Lena had to smile. Ever since he had fallen out with
the Paladins, Remy had just been a ghost, but now he
looked like he really could fly to Leadville.

At the back door, Lena checked in the parking lot. No
sign of Lancing's SUV or any other police cars, but she

~ ☾ ~

couldn't see far in the twisting mist. Cautiously, she started down the street, taking the long way to Gramma Scar, which led to a little park of ragged, yellow grass that appeared white in the weak light. The temperature had plummeted. When Lena breathed in through her nose, she could feel the skin freezing inside. It was probably around zero, if not below.

At least the clouds hid her. She was on her way to the swing set, when a figure materialized out of the fog, walking toward her.

It was Tabitha.

Lena kept her eyes low, expecting the big girl to move on by.

Instead, Tabitha stopped her. "Hey Lena..."

First Paulie, then Remy, now Tabitha. In one day, she had touched all the Untouchables, each one of them. But what on earth could she talk to Tabitha about? They came from two different worlds.

At least Lena could be nice. "Hi, Tabitha. It's pretty cold, huh?"

Tabitha wasn't going to talk about the weather. "I know we don't know each other. I mean, we've gone to school together forever, but we've never really talked." The girl's voice was shaking and she was trembling, like a scared dog wanting to bolt but held there by an invisible leash.

At the same time, the awkwardness was killing Lena.

Tabitha kept talking in a shivering voice. "It's Chael. I've seen you talking with him. He's worried about you."

"Yeah, Chael, my guardian angel who hates me." It was too late to get the words back into her mouth, and she thought about Paulie and his editor. Lena tried to back up. "I didn't mean that. It's just—"

Tabitha cut her off. "He challenged me. He told me I should start doing all the things I'm afraid of so that's why I'm talking to you."

~ ☾ ~

Lena pulled her coat around her tighter. "You shouldn't be afraid to talk to me. I'm just a person."

Tabitha shrugged. Her coat whispered in the hush. "You're a Paladin and a Heretic. I'm nobody."

An Untouchable according to Deirdre, but right then Lena would have given her soul to be a nobody for a day. Anonymous and free. "Tabitha, the stupid cliques don't mean anything."

"Unless you're not in one," the outcast girl said. "Just be careful. I know the police are looking for you. I don't know what kind of trouble you're in but be careful. I've always known you were different than the rest. No way would I try to talk to Deirdre like this."

Lena smiled. "No, Deirdre probably wouldn't take this very well."

Tabitha moved away from her. "I have to get going, but it was nice talking to you."

The idea struck Lena like a sledge hammer bashing her in the head. She shouldn't ask Tabitha for help, but what else could she do?

Chael had told her she was stupid for thinking she could go through life without asking anyone for help, and if there was ever a day she needed some assistance...

"Tabitha, wait."

The girl turned around. Lena walked over, afraid of what the outcast girl might say. Asking for help was taking a chance, but then, so was offering help. Lena knew that better than anyone.

"Tabitha, I need a favor. It's a huge favor, and you could get into trouble."

The girl smiled. She had a nice smile. "I've never been in trouble before. How can I help?"

"I need to get a red purse out of my truck." Filled with guilt, Lena shared her crazy, crazy plan with Tabitha.

~ ☾ ~

vi
(tabitha and the red purse)

The two girls walked back toward the school as Lena explained the plan. "Are you sure you want to do this?" she asked. A part of her wanted Tabitha to say no. Another part of her was terrified she might.

Tabitha was breathing hard and sweating and it wasn't from the walking. "No, I don't want to do this at all, but it's funny, we were all talking the other day, with Chael. And he said it was easy to find people who needed help. He said we could just go outside, walk around, and someone would need us. We all thought he was crazy."

"Well, the world isn't getting any saner," Lena said. "You don't have to do this. It's not like helping me get a kitten out of a tree. It's illegal."

"No," Tabitha said, determined. "Chael said to do things that scare us. This is scaring me to death."

"Yeah, I know how you feel," Lena said. She could feel her own sweat dripping down her sides. And she loathed asking for help. It felt like trying to speak Chinese. "Listen, what can I do to pay you back?"

"Deirdre still calls me Tubitha, right?" the girl asked.

Lena couldn't lie. "Yeah."

"Next time she says it, you tell her to shut the hell up."

They hid in the weeds of an abandoned house across the street from the school's parking lot. Only a few cars could be seen through the clouds, while the school itself, all that stone, was completely hidden.

Tabitha flattened herself against the peeled paint of the house. "Okay, so I'm going to take the purse out of the truck and put it by the light pole, then drive off. I'll

~ ☾ ~

park in front of your apartment on Mountain, then keep the keys 'til tomorrow."

Lena nodded. How could she be asking Tabitha to do this?

"And if the police stop me, I'll make up some story."

"Any story." Lena gazed at the chubby girl, truly seeing her for the first time. "Are you sure you want to do this?"

Tabitha nodded. She had a hand over her heart. "Yeah. Let me just catch my breath. You do this kind of thing a lot?"

Lena shook her head. "No. Never."

"Good. I'm not sure I could ever do this again." Without another word, Tabitha walked through the yard, into the street, and disappeared into the cloud.

Lena knew she should wait, but she couldn't. She followed almost immediately, but stopped when she got to one of the trashed cars at the edge of the lot.

Minutes ticked away. Her heart thrummed.

When Lena heard her truck fire up, she dashed across the dirt. Panic felt like rats in her chest, chewing down into her stomach.

Police sirens yelped at the edge of the lot. Cherry red lights flashed in the mist. Lena scooped up her purse where Tabitha had set it on the light post, then ran back to the school and crouched by dumpsters near the cafeteria.

The red lights continued to flash. There was the murmur of voices. She heard Tabitha laughing, and it was as nervous and as panicky as Lena felt.

Who knew Tabitha could do that? Who knew Lena would ever need the outcast girl's help?

Thanking God for the clouds, Lena edged down the side of the building, sneaked across the street, and took the longest route possible to Gramma Scar's restaurant.

When she got there, she was freezing, exhausted, and

~ ☾ ~

done. The darkness of the night was complete, as if any sort of dawn was impossible. Like the sun was gone forever, and Lena would die in darkness and cold.

~ ☾ ~

vii
(gramma scar's husbands)

Gramma Scar extended a plump hand, fingers squeezed by rings. "Can I take your purse, my beauty?"

Lena clutched the red bag and shook her head. "No, it's okay. Is it all right if I stay here and do some homework tonight? I'm so behind, taking care of Jozey and all."

"Sure. Can I get you something to eat?"

"Okay," Lena said, suddenly hungry.

How long had it been since she last ate? When had Beels come in with the nachos? Yesterday? Lena didn't know. Lots of caffeine. No food.

Lena sat down at a checkered table cloth and let the window paint a picture of the street outside. Just clouds, no police cars, no cops.

She spread papers around and opened books, then just sat and watched the ink blur into nonsense. Dizziness took her, and she rode it like a drug. She shouldn't eat. She should just drink more caffeine and see how buzzed she could get on chemicals and exhaustion.

And forget everything. The tragedy of her parents. Being mean to her aunt. Leaving Jozey behind. Closing the door on Santiago. Chael's softness. Beels' almost kiss. Asking Tabitha for help. The police cars. The drugs. The dog men.

Gramma Scar brought out the saucy meatballs and noodles and waited for Lena to clear her homework before sliding a plate in front of her.

Saliva washed into Lena's mouth.

~ ☾ ~

"What to drink, my precious beauty?" Gramma Scar asked.

"Coffee?"

The old woman frowned. "You don't need coffee! Next you'll be asking me for one of those energy drinks. I heard on the radio that they're poisonous..."

She continued to chatter as she walked back to the kitchen but all the words turned to static as the food hit Lena's system.

Gramma Scar came back and set a glass of milk down at the table. As always, the old Italian woman's flowery dress was just a little too tight, her wig a little askew, and she wore a little too much make-up.

"So, tell me, precious Lena, where are you sleeping tonight?"

"What do you mean?" Lena asked.

The old woman's brown eyes were warm above plump, chipmunk cheeks. "Oh, this isn't the first time I've aided and abetted. This ain't Denver, you know. Small town like Avalon, no hiding here."

"But who told you?"

Gramma Scar smiled kindly. "There's the new boy. And then there's your aunt. And then Lancing came by, but we don't like each other too much."

Lena picked at the meatballs, now as appealing as rotten meat. "You have to turn me in, right?"

"Who says? I was just going to talk to you and see how I can help. Whatever is happening must be horrible, terrible because you're a good girl, and I've known my fair share of bad. Some even family."

Lena knew she was talking about Santiago's mom.

"This is the thing," Gramma Scar continued. "I turn you over to the law, and then the state of Colorado gets in your business and things generally turn nasty. Maybe with Santiago it will be different. I hope so. The real question here, my good girl, my precious beauty, is this.

~ ☾ ~

Do you think the police can help you?"

Lena dropped the fork, her appetite gone. All she wanted was a Diet Cranksta and a LeMac cigarette. The craving increased as she weighed Gramma Scar's words. The new boy. Chael. Turning her in. Santiago had warned her. Her aunt calling meant Mrs. Weyland hadn't waited until 6 o'clock. Probably because of Chael again. And Lancing, sniffing around for the red purse.

Could the cops help her?

"I don't know," Lena whispered. "It's only for a few more hours. After that, I'm out of it, I promise."

"Promises can be as flimsy as an overcooked lasagna noodle. I've said it before, you make all the wrong choices for all the right reasons. How can I know you'll keep your promise?" She sat down in the booth across from Lena.

"Teddy, was my..." Gramma Scar tabulated on her chubby digits. "My third husband. Yes, third. One day, Teddy comes in with a lot of money. Not just a little. A lot. We were in East Denver then, a hundred years ago, before your parents were even born, God rest their souls. Teddy gives me money. He says, 'This is the last time. Just hide it.' So I hid it. A week later, he comes in with more money. Same song and dance. Don't think your men will change, my precious, they won't. Might as well think Mount Calibum will turn into donuts to think a man will change just 'cause you want him to. With Teddy, he ran out of time. The police were chasing him, like they're chasing you, and they found him in a dumpster shot to death by bad men. One of whom I think I married. That was Rico. Number four. A real criminal, but by then, I was used to all that."

Gramma Scar paused to get a cup of decaf coffee. She came back with packets of Splenda and a cookie. "So Rico. He's very funny, and he treats me well. But same story. Well, this time I think I'll do the right thing. When

~ ☾ ~

the police start looking real hard for Rico, I turn him in
right away. Better he's in jail than dead, right? Poor Rico
hangs himself, and I lose him anyway."

The old woman smiled. "Why am I telling you all this?
Well, I did nothing with Teddy, and he died. And I did
my best with Rico, and he died. So I don't know anything
about anything. But I do know this." She paused to
nibble her cookie and sip her decaf. "This is what I would
do, if I were you. I would give me whatever you got, then
you go to Lancing, and ask him why he's harassing you.
That is what I would do if I were a girl looking for help."

The bell on the door jingled, bringing in travelers.
They smiled politely at Lena, her spread of homework,
and Gramma Scar.

"Just sit anywhere, folks. I'll be with you in just a
moment." Then back to Lena. "I don't feel so bad about
Rico. He brought all that trouble on himself then took
the easy way out. But with Teddy, I feel bad about what I
didn't do. I know I'm not to blame for what happened to
him, but sometimes I feel like I am."

The old woman used the table to lift herself off her
chair and moved away to hostess and cook, leaving Lena
alone.

Over and over, she thought of Chael, offering to take
the purse, telling her she was stupid for not letting
anyone help her. Chael telling Tabitha to do the things
she was afraid to do. Tabitha helping Lena even when
the outcast girl probably knew she was just being used.

And suddenly it was six-thirty.

"Okay," Lena said. She stood up, lifted the bulk of her
red purse, and walked over to the counter where Gramma
Scar was sitting. Lena held the purse out, so heavy, so
wretched. "Okay, Gramma, I'll let you help me."

The door opened again. The bells didn't just jingle,
they boomed, as if they should have been hanging in a
cathedral.

~ ☾ ~

viii
(in the wanting car)

Gramma Scar scowled at the door, at the bells, and at who came in.

Lena expected Lancing, but it was Johnny Beels in a shiny new ski coat, icy white and sky blue.

"Gamma, that cannoli was fine, just fine, but now I think I'm in the mood for a big ol' sausage sammich. Can ya whip one up real quick like?" His sunshine smile fell on Lena. "Why, Leni, it's such a pleasure to see ya and in such good company."

His frigid hand on Lena's arm made her shiver. She remembered the almost kiss and felt herself floating.

"Sure, Johnny, I'll make you a sandwich," Gramma Scar said in a weary voice, all of her usual energy gone. She adjusted her wig as she disappeared into the kitchen.

"Gamma, call me Beels, 'cause everyone else will. Such a nice place, Avalon. I could stay here forever."

The way he said "forever" struck Lena wrong. But then he pulled her close and whispered into her ear. "I came early, Lena, 'cause I do enjoy sequins. Once I get my sammich, I'll take it, and you, far away, off to the party and more fun than a barrel of swamp rats swimmin' in nacho cheese."

As his breath brushed her ear, she felt as if she was standing naked in a lightning storm. She wanted that kiss, now more than ever.

"Once I give you my purse, I should get home to be with my brother," she said.

He shrugged. "Shoulds kill us long before the Reaper gets us. When's the last time ya got a night off?"

~ ☾ ~

"Well, earlier this week. Kind of."

"Kind of? Kind of doesn't mean a night off!" Beels smiled a devilish little smirk. "I mean a night of freedom, for howlin' at the moon, for being crazy, for feelin' yer oats and sowin' some wild ones."

"Not for a long time," she said and collapsed against Beels, relaxing into his body.

Gramma Scar pushed her way between them, then shoved the bag into Beels' pale hand. "Here you go, Johnny."

"Beels," he corrected with a grin.

"Johnny," Gramma Scar insisted, then turned to Lena. "Offer is still open, Lena."

"I think I'll be okay now," Lena said.

"Yeah, she will," Beels said. "'Cause I'm all about the okay. Johnny Beels has a magic for making everything okay."

Gramma Scar barked a little laugh. "Johnny, you and okay parted company a long time ago."

He laughed. "Oh Gamma, I won't argue with ya a lick. But tonight, okay and me are real good friends. And call me Beels."

"Lena, please," the old woman said.

But Lena allowed herself to be led outside.

Night and cloud hid them from the spectral light of the passing cars on Mountain Avenue. In front of her was a powder blue Camaro, rusted underneath, with gleaming mag wheels that glowed despite the damaged moonlight.

Beels saw her staring. "Yeah, my car is old, but she certainly is majestic."

"Majestic is not quite the word I would use." She had to force herself to shake off Gramma Scar's last plea, had to forget about her aunt and her brother, just for that night, just to see where Beels would take her.

Plenty of time for the angel costume and Halloween

~ ☾ ~

pumpkins later. The damage had already been done. She had missed picking her brother up, and Aunt Mercedes had already been called.

Beels threw her a Las Vegas key chain with only two keys on it.

"You drive while I eat," he said.

"Are you sure?" she asked.

But he was already in the passenger seat. Lena walked around the front and slid in behind the wheel. She put the red purse in the back seat and thought the drop was complete.

Inside, the ragged leather seats were soft and white, but cold, oh so cold. Had he been driving with the heat off? The engine rumbled as if there were four hundred dragons under the hood, breathing fire. In seconds, they were roaring down the street.

Beels dug into his sloppy sandwich like he was digging for gold, all the while preaching. "Here's the deal about this crazy world, Leni. It's like our kiss. The wantin' is the good part. Pure desire is like a polished diamond. The trick is to stretch out the wantin' by wantin' things you can never, ever have." He slurped sauce from his fingers and ate some more.

"Where am I going?" Lena asked.

"Just drive west, baby. Avalon don't have many roads and nobody, and I mean nobody, knows this is my car, so we are as safe as chickens in roost. Head toward the old Climax Mine. Ah, mining, now that's good wantin' right there. Dirty and gritty and desperate."

"What about being happy with what you have?" Lena asked.

Beels reached back and grabbed a pack of LeMac cigarettes and a four pack of Crankstas. He cracked two open and slid one between Lena's legs.

She gripped the wheel tighter when he touched her.

Still eating his sandwich, he fired up two cigarettes

~ ☾ ~

and put one to her lips.

Even though she knew it was disastrous, she accepted it. The smoke, the smell of the sausage, the idea of the energy drink, it was all grinding madness into her belly. She should be home with Jozey. He would be crying. Her aunt would be pissed, but then Aunt Mercedes' anger was a lot like her despair, only quieter and deeper. Lena knew she should at least call.

At the party. She would call Aunt Mercedes at the party.

Beels took a long drink from his Cranksta, dragged smoke from his cigarette, and finished it off with the sandwich. "Like right now. Everybody, Paladins, Heretics, all of the school, is waiting for a call from me about where the party is. See, that's so the cops can't track us there. If I told everyone where the party was this morning, Lancing would have heard about it and there goes our fun. This way, cops won't know until after the fact." He sighed happily.

"I can almost feel it," Beels continued. "All yer friends, all on edge. They want the party. Don't know if it's gonna be bad or good, and that's what's nice about wantin' things ya ain't got. The future is all open, it's all possible. Could get love, could get into a fight, could just get drunk and stupid. But ya don't know. When ya got what ya got, that's all ya got."

Lena smiled, smoked, and her stomach boiled. "I don't know, Beels. I think what you're talking about is a hard way to go. If you're only happy wanting, then what's the point of life?"

"To eat, honey, to eat and keep on eating and never, ever stop."

At the mine, they pulled over on the highway while he made the calls. He told everyone about the old church, long since abandoned, hidden away down a dirt road.

Her head spun from the nicotine, caffeine, and the

~ ☾ ~

other Cranksta chemicals. She felt like Beels had hijacked her life and was holding her hostage. It was odd, scary, but nice, knowing she wasn't in charge. She wasn't responsible.

It didn't feel like there was enough time to call Aunt Mercedes, so Lena just let it go.

When he was done phoning, he smiled at her.

She touched his cold cheek. "You sure are something, Mr. Johnny Beels."

"You have no idea what though," he whispered with a grin.

But she had the idea that this was the night she was going to find out.

~ ☾ ~

ix
(at the church)

"You sure you want me to drive this car on this road?" Lena's hands were tight on the wheel. The undercarriage scraped rocks on the rough slash of dirt between the pine trees clawing the sides of the Camaro like long-armed, shadowy monsters crouched in the mist.

"Sure, girl, nice thing about having such an old car, ya don't care none about what happens to it. Let's just get there." Beels lit another cigarette off the butt in his mouth. He called it turkey-kissing. With all the smoke, the inside of the car was as cloudy as the outside.

She had to gun it up a steep ravine. At the top, there was a scream of rock on metal and she gritted her teeth against the sound. But then the pine trees receded and they drove into a meadow next to the gray timbers of a dead church. The steeple dropped wood like splintered bone across the gaping holes in the roof. Normally, the place would have been under a couple of feet of snow by the end of October, but Mother Nature wasn't playing nice.

There was a little shack a hundred yards away from the church, leaning like a drunk man against an outcropping of craggy rock, nearly hidden by trees. Inside the shack was the flicker of a light, dancing but dim. A rusted, mustard yellow Ford Bronco was parked as close to the shack as the trees would allow.

"Anyone else know about this?" Lena asked.

Beels raised an eyebrow and a smile. "Maybe." He got out of the car, retrieved a toolbox and a can of gasoline out of the trunk, then glanced at the shack before

~ ☾ ~

striding toward the church. He turned to smile at her, and bathed in the headlights, he looked angelic.

Lena thought distantly she didn't know Beels. He could be leading her inside to rape her. But that didn't feel right. The party would come soon enough. For now, she had him all to herself. She left the lights on and followed him across the frozen ground to the mouth of the church.

The glow from the Camaro's headlights created a mosaic of light and darkness inside the church. Pews lay scattered over a rotted wood floor now mostly dirt, some places weedy, some places mossy. It all led to a wooden altar under the remains of a hacked-up cross. Beels stood by the altar, grinning at the chaos.

"Yeah, nice place for a party," she said. Beels felt right, but the church felt wrong. It made her stomach hurt.

"Just wait, Leni, I'm gonna decorate." The blond boy stripped off his coat and shirt to reveal a tattoo across his chest and stomach. It was a long sword, silvered and scrolling on his white skin, running diagonally from his left shoulder, across his heart, down to his belt on the right side of his stomach.

Gramma Scar's words came flooding back to her. Johnny Beels and okay had parted company a long time ago. What had she meant?

"Nice tattoo," Lena said. "Must have hurt like hell."

"Don't even remember getting it. Don't that just beat all? Ya wake up and suddenly ya got tattoos all over. Funny how life works sometimes. But I reckon I'm an angel, and an angel has to have a sword and wings." Beels laughed. He took a hatchet out of the toolbox and cut pieces of wood off the altar. On his back was another tattoo, this one of wings, but Lena couldn't tell if they were drawn to have feathers or scales.

Lena knew he had to be joking about not remembering getting the tattoos because the intricate

~ ☾ ~

designs on his skin would have taken hours to do. But she let it go.

From the gas can, Beels sloshed fluid across the collection of splinters and then lit it with a match. The flames exploded into heat and light.

"Are you going to burn the cross?" she asked.

He shrugged. "Naw, we got plenty of wood, and I like it up there, looking down on us. Far away. Always so far away." He slipped on his shirt and coat but left them unbuttoned and glided over to her. "Yer a special girl, Leni. Ya know it, right?"

She shook her head and backed up a little. "No, not so special. Johnny, this place is psycho. I think I'm going to wait in the car."

"Call me Beels."

"'Cause everyone else will," she finished, shivering.

Beels threw out a finger and clicked a gunshot. "You got me. I'm a broken record." He stepped closer to her.

The roaring fire wasn't warming her. She felt cold, scared, completely overwhelmed by this Johnny Beels and his charm and beauty. "You're a vampire, not an angel," Lena said, taking another step back.

He nodded, grinning. "Oh yeah, that's exactly what I am. Can I drink yer blood now, Leni? Is it time for our kiss?" He was suddenly against her, his hands in her hair at the back of her neck.

She leaned toward him, the fear disappearing into the melt of his touch, his frigid hands on her skin, his lips brushing her face, drifting toward her mouth.

Then the honking started. The party rained down on them with people, music, and hard liquor from stolen bottles.

Whoever was in the shack stayed hidden.

~ ☾ ~

X
(in the shack)

"Gonna have to wait a little for the kiss." Beels sighed. Skin itching, stomach boiling, Lena felt awful. "Desire. That's really what you are about, huh, Johnny?"

"Beels is my name, wantin' is my game." He laughed and escorted people into the church. "Welcome to the second Sunday of sin. I'm your pastor, Johnny Beels, but you can call me Beels 'cause everyone else will. We'll have communion in a bit. Ah yes, the holy Eucharist."

Only the blade of the sword tattoo could be seen under his shirt. The rest was pale, perfect skin and muscle.

Deirdre noticed it right away. She pulled herself into Lena's face. "Well, you have certainly moved on to far more pleasant pastures. You and Johnny Beels. Very well done."

Lena touched her pockets, searching for cigarettes, the habit so ingrained. Not a habit, she reminded herself, an addiction she had stupidly shaken awake after it had been sleeping so peacefully. "I guess, but I don't know what to make of him."

Deirdre held out a hand and some Paladin girl put a beer into it. "Magdalena, darling, you don't marry the Johnny Beels of this world. You can't live your life on a roller coaster, but you can certainly enjoy the ride." She laughed, and Lena laughed with her.

What had happened the night before seemed completely forgotten.

"We missed you before school today," Deirdre said. "I hope you aren't forsaking the Paladins completely."

Lena shook her head. "No, Santiago broke up with me.

~ ☾ ~

I'm done being a Heretic. You'll just have to put up with me at lunch as well."

"It'll be good to have you back. I'm so glad you made the right decision." Deirdre pressed her cheek against Lena's.

No questions about Santiago, no mention of the drama Chael had brought upon them, just a superficial hug and business as usual.

Deirdre smiled. "I can't believe Beels invited everyone, both Heretic and Paladin. No wonder you like him so much. He has your dream of unity."

Lena somehow found herself holding a beer, and she sipped it, hating it, but she needed something in her. And then it was easy to forget about everything, forget about Jozey and Aunt Mercedes and the past few days of carrying the red purse around.

And Chael. So easy to forget about the dark boy and his vicious judging.

All eyes were on Johnny Beels as the party whirled around him, but his eyes were always on Lena. All the girls saw the staring, and it made Lena feel a little better. She wasn't the damaged girl with dead parents. She had the boy all the girls wanted.

Gramma Scar had been wrong. Johnny Beels and okay danced together every day of his life. But why hadn't he kissed her yet?

Dane Bramage walked up to her with a bottle of homemade whiskey in his fist. He stopped, made the sign of the cross over her, then climbed on top of the altar to sit and drink, looking down on them all, laughing at them all.

It unnerved Lena, so she moved out of the church and into the night.

All the cars had left their headlights on so the trees and the church were lit up like a stadium, making every tendril of mist glow. Even the bonfires scattered around

~ ☽ ~

were eclipsed by the radiance.

Music swelled from stereos. The battered Heretic cars played death metal. The new, shining Paladin SUV's played heavy hip-hop. And as the Heretics turned up their music, the Paladins matched them, until the sounds were as swirled together as the cloud.

Bruise howled at the Paladins. "Turn that rap shit off!"

Avery and Cutler sat on the hood of Avery's car, both drinking beer. Cutler spit dip into the dirt. "Can't hear you, Bruce, not over that noise. You do know your music is stupid, right?"

Bruise's hands curled into fists, his dull eyes getting sharper.

"Where's Santiago?" Avery asked.

"Locked up, the way I hear it." Cutler laughed. "That's where all you Heretic dirtbags belong. Locked up."

Bruise and the other Heretics stormed over, flexing their muscles and bringing out their practiced scowls. Cutler and the other Paladins were ready for them.

But Avery hung back, shaking his head. "Personally, I liked how the music sounded together. Like a mash-up," he said to no one in particular.

Lena was heading over to stop the fight when Beels appeared out of nowhere and pulled her to him. He was carrying the red purse.

"It's time, Lena. They'll just rooster around 'til they get tuckered out."

Lena pushed herself into him, a little buzzed now. The pain in her stomach felt like it belonged to someone else. "How come your hands are always so cold?"

"Vampire. Comes with the territory." He walked her through the party, toward the shack.

Emma gave Lena a secret smile, and Lena smiled back at the Heretic girl.

"Inside is our kiss," Beels whispered.

But wasn't someone else already inside? The someone

~ ☾ ~

who had the mustard Bronco parked in the trees.

Lena felt too electrified to ask any questions. She had the red purse in her hand but didn't remember Beels giving it to her. She wasn't that drunk, or maybe she was, on Beels and his desire.

And all the girls wanted to be her right then. Lena didn't just feel lucky, she felt blessed.

Until Beels opened the door. Until he pushed her inside and closed the door behind them.

Sitting on stumps in the shack, with kerosene lamps hissing around them, were the dog men, with their whiskey bottles, drugs, and dogs. Four big Dobermans eyed Lena like she was raw meat walking.

Like how the dog men eyed her.

"You know Rex, right, Lena?" Beels asked in a cheery voice.

The music outside seemed to fade into silence. It felt like she was back in the Vail condo, waiting for the package, stifled by the dog stink.

"Rex." Lena laughed through her terror. "Sure."

Rex stood up and grinned, his mouth too full of yellow teeth. "Beels said you did a good job. We wanted to congratulate you. A lot of heat on right now."

He was close enough she could smell him, the awful stench of the unwashed and uncaring. She refused to show an ounce of the fear grinding through her like glacial ice. "Yeah, well, I'm out of it. That was my last run." She held out the red purse to him.

"Why would I want that? I gave it to you." Rex leaned in closer, ignoring the purse. "Last run, huh? Well, since you're getting out of the game, we don't need to hold back like we did before. You're gonna bark again for us. You're gonna be barking all night long."

Beels pushed her toward him. "These guys sure love their dogs."

Suddenly, her fear twisted into rage, the cold water in

~ ☾ ~

her blood had turned into molten lead. She slapped Rex with the purse. Sequins sprinkled them both. Spinning, she hit Beels, trying to get to the door.

He shoved her back into the men.

"Why are you doing this?" The question came out of her as a plea.

Beels smiled, unmoved, just his usual self, as if nothing were wrong. "Fear is just like desire, Leni. It's just a different kind of want, that's all. Bitter like. And Johnny Beels likes the bitter as much as the sweet. Maybe even a little more so."

"Jesus," Lena whispered

Johnny Beels laughed. "Ah, that ol' boy ain't been 'round for a couple thousand years, baby. Better ask someone else a little more lively for help."

Rex seized her by the hair, and the other dog men rose, fingers rattling their belt buckles loose. Lena fought them, shrieking for help but knowing the music outside was too loud.

The Dobermans were on their feet, slavering, growling.

Rex drew her close and Lena wasn't sure if he was going to kiss her or bite her. Beels chuckled. It was all just a joke to him, a nice little joke.

He was still chortling when the roof of the shack came down.

There was a sweep of wings, wails of pain, and then Lena felt herself wrapped into strong arms, lifted out of the shack, and taken into the clouds.

~ ☾ ~

xi
(chael in the clouds)

She looked up into Chael's face and then behind him. His huge, black wings flapped lightly. A feather drifted down onto her wrist, where her arms were around his neck.

Just like the feathers Jozey always found.

She should have been freezing, but with his arms around her, she felt like she was next to a roaring fire. Sweat slid down the side of her face onto his dark skin. He was shirtless, and though she couldn't see all of it, she knew Chael had a sword tattoo as well.

She glanced around her, scarcely able to believe this was all really happening. The clouds were a milky ocean beneath them. For the first time in days, she could see the moon and the infinity of stars above.

"How can I be breathing?" she asked. "How come I'm not freezing to death?"

Chael's eyes were warm on her, soft, kind, and understanding. "I don't know, Lena. I've come to realize, I don't know anything."

"You're an angel," she whispered.

"You'd think so, but I'm not so sure."

Chael's body tensed as he whipped around, wings slicing through the air. Emerging from the clouds, Beels rose on white wings, his skin glowing except where the ink of the tattoo spilled across his chest. "Why, Leni, y'all just left the party right when it was gettin' good. Where I come from, thass juss rude."

"Leave her alone," Chael called across the sky to the blond boy.

~ ☾ ~

Beels laughed. "You should have followed yer own advice, Chael. Y'all were the one who started this. I'm just here to eat."

Chael wrapped Lena up into his dark wings and they fell down into the puffball clouds. Lena's face against his chest, his wings a blanket around her, she felt his heart pound beneath her cheek. At the very last instant, his wings opened and they soared across the tops of the pines. With a sweep of his wings, Chael dodged a tall tree and hurtled them back into the clouds.

Beels was there. He kicked Chael in the face with his polished boots. The dark boy grunted, swirled upward, and slammed his palm right into the blond boy's chin. Lena gripped Chael tighter now that he was only holding her with one arm.

Hot blood trickled against her skin. Chael's blood. He went to fly away, but Beels grabbed him by the leg. The demon raised a clawed hand the color of ivory and brought it down on Chael's hamstring, ripping through his flesh.

He cried out, wheeled, and booted Beels in the face.

Beels giggled and snorted through blood and snot. "Good one, Chael. Ya always were a hot one. Feisty. I like that in an angel."

Chael's wings strained but he couldn't pull away. The blond boy's talons dug deeper. All the while, Beels laughed. It sparked such a hate in Lena, she pushed away from Chael and fell down right on top of Beels, feet first. She latched onto the demon to stop her fall.

"Ah, Leni, ya dropped in for our kiss. How sweet."

Arms clutching Beels' neck, she sank her teeth into his ear.

Beels screeched, ripped his talons out of Chael's leg, and shoved her away.

Lena fell. Alone.

Without Chael, the cold snatched away her breath and

~ ☾ ~

froze her skin. Her mouth was soiled with the revolting taste of blood. She had bitten the demon and freed her angel.

It was okay.

A strange peace filled her as she fell through the clouds to her death, the wind roaring, hair sweeping around her face, hands reaching but touching nothing. It was going to be okay. For months, for what felt like forever, she had gripped life with such savagery it had exhausted every bit of her. Now, letting go, she knew it would all be okay. Jozey would grow up, somehow, and find his path. Her aunt would heal. Avalon would go on until it couldn't go on any more. People would move, or die, and it was all okay.

Because the world was okay.

I was stupid.

The thought whispered through her mind, but her heart knew the truth. She wasn't stupid. She was human. That was all. A broken human doing the best she could. Frigid wind was killing her, but it was all just white cloud, the entire universe, just white cloud, and even the shriek of the wind couldn't touch the peace inside her.

I'm tired of the cold and clouds. Take me home, God. Take me home. I'm so tired.

Tree tops appeared out of the mist, tree tops and the brutal ground. Lena closed her eyes.

A flutter of angel wings before hot-coal arms once more cradled her, and they careened through the trees, snapping branches, punching past pine boughs, scratching naked limbs. Chael turned on his side to dash through a stand of aspens. Then they were above the tree line and into more clouds.

Lena wept on Chael's skin.

She was alive. She was safe. She could live a different life now that she had let go.

This time when they swam into the stars above the

~ ☾ ~

clouds, the sky was empty. Beels was gone, and they were alone.

"Are you hurt?" Chael asked.

Being next to him thawed her, made her nerves tingle as feeling returned to her limbs and she could breathe again. But she couldn't answer. She could only cry until there were no more tears.

When she found some more, she cried them too, and it was as if the stars had poured their sorrow into her, each star someone's grief. Then she was crying because for every star of agony, there were two stars of hope.

Chael had saved more than her body. He had saved her soul.

She wanted to thank him, but they were over Avalon, then on her doorstep. On his face were Lena's own tears.

"We can talk inside," he whispered. "I'll tell you everything I know."

~ ☾ ~

xii
(chael overnight)

Even though it was past eleven o'clock, Jozey was not asleep. His howling filled the apartment when Lena opened the door.

The sound cut her. She left Chael in the kitchen to sprint through the little apartment to their bed where Jozey was crying, tossed in sheets wet with his tears. Aunt Mercedes stood next to the bed with dog-tired eyes.

But Lena pushed her aside and clutched Jozey to her. He cried harder.

When he could talk, his words came out in choked breaths. "Weni! Why you no come? Why, Weni, why?"

"I'm here now." Her voice cracked open. "I'm so sorry, Jozey. I'm so, so sorry." "You were deaded, Weni. Why you deaded?"

She brushed a hand through his hair. She was going to argue with him, saying she wasn't dead, but she had been. As dead as her parents. "I'm back alive now, Jozey, and I'll always pick you up, and if I'm not going to be there, I'll let you know ahead of time. I'm so, so sorry."

Aunt Mercedes stood like a hunk of stone above them. "You know the police want to talk to you, right?"

"Why, Weni?"

She squeezed her brother tighter. "They just want to make sure I'm looking after you. I messed up tonight, but I'm better. I'll talk to them tomorrow."

Jozey screamed. "Will they take you to jail?"

"No, baby, 'cause they know you'd miss me too much."

"I lost my job at the Gas 'n Sip," Aunt Mercedes said in a hazy whisper. "I had to pick up Jozey. I had to leave. I

~ ☾ ~

got fired."

Lena rocked Jozey while she tried not to glare at her aunt. "We can figure that out tomorrow. I have some extra money, and it's going to snow. It has to."

"No, it doesn't," her aunt said. "Maybe this is winter. Just clouds and cold and no snow."

"Tomorrow. We can figure this all out tomorrow."

Aunt Mercedes shuffled away into her room and closed the door quietly.

Jozey fell asleep on Lena's chest, his breathing calming both of them. She laid him gently down and put a blanket around him. Kissing his forehead, she whispered against his shut eyes, "I won't let you down again, Jozey. I promise. Things are going to change."

Back out in the hallway, she went into the kitchen and was surprised to see Chael sitting at the table, shirtless. His sword-shaped tattoo spilled across his dark skin. She laughed a little. "I'm surprised you stuck around. You're so good at disappearing." She put a hand up to her mouth.

He peered at her through eyes circled with exhaustion, like ash in the gaunt hollows of his face. He said nothing.

"I'm sorry, Chael. I didn't mean it."

He put up a hand. "No, it's okay. You're right."

Both were quiet for a moment, and the only sound was the plink of his blood dripping onto the floor. "God, I forgot," she gasped. "Beels. The fight. Come on, let's get you into the bathroom. We have to be quiet. My aunt is in her room."

Chael didn't say a word as she led him into the bathroom. The right leg of his jeans was black with smeared blood down to his scuffed-up boots.

"You'll have to take off—," she started, then he fell against her and she had to gently help him into the bathtub.

"Should've eaten more. Should've slept more. I forgot

~ ☾ ~

you can't go without those things."

"You sound like me," she whispered.

He smiled. "I forgot being human is such a chore. That's why I was so hard on you at first. When you're outside of things, you think it's all so simple, but that's not the case. It didn't hit me until you slapped me, how confusing it is here. First, you're hitting me, then we're almost kissing."

"Yeah, well, welcome to my world." She helped him take off his boots and socks. He winced as he pushed his jeans down.

She kept her eyes off his boxers, but the temperature in the bathroom was skyrocketing and her breaths were stifled. Sweat trickled down her nose. "Do you want me to leave while you wash?" she asked in a choked voice.

"I can't do it alone. Too weak. I'm sorry, Lena. I should have told you everything right away. I was so ashamed though. I was so angry. At myself, mostly, but it was easier to hate you."

"No apologies," Lena said. "I should be the one begging for forgiveness." She picked up the removable shower head and started the water running. "Turn around. Let me look at you." She blushed. Everything she said was wrong.

Like Beels, he had wings tattooed on his back. Unlike Beels, his wings were simple and dark, just shadowy smudges on his skin. She looked down over his underwear and farther to where the skin had been clawed through. The long, horrible, wounds oozed blood. "Chael, we have to get you to a hospital."

"How would we pay? What would I tell them when they asked for a last name? You know me. I don't lie very well."

She moved the showerhead over his wounded leg and the bathtub turned pink from his blood. She cleaned the wound, turned off the water, and used a washcloth to

~ ☾ ~

dab at his skin.

"Press hard," he said in a gasp. "We have to stop the bleeding or I'll die."

"Can you die?" she asked.

For a long time, the only sound was the water dripping from the faucet. Then, "Yes. And maybe that would be for the best."

She pressed harder and he hissed in pain. "Why, Chael? What's going on?"

He didn't answer. He was gasping, the tattoos of his wings rising and falling with each breath. "I have to lie down."

She helped him lay down in the bathtub on his stomach and then she shoved the washcloth back onto the wound.

"I don't want to tell you, Lena. I'm so ashamed. Please, don't make me." His face was turned away from her. "It was easier to see everyone else's mistakes and not my own. It was easier for me to be mean to you and Deirdre and her father."

The water on the washcloth was hot, but compared to his skin, it felt chill. She continued to sweat as her head spun. "Beels is a demon," she whispered. "And you're an angel. But this is impossible, right? Things like this don't happen."

"And they shouldn't happen," he said through gritted teeth.

"Did my parents send you?" she asked, though she knew he wasn't going to be able to tell her anything. Like in those movies where someone from the future time-travels to the past and is careful so they don't ruin timelines or break the things they were trying to fix.

He took in a deep breath and let it out slowly. "No, not your parents. I was just on the outside of things, trying to help because the world is so broken."

"Can you at least tell me about God? Or is that against

~ ☾ ~

the rules that angels have to live by?"

His body shook with a suppressed laugh. "There's no rule book, no hierarchy of angels, nothing like that. And I don't know if there is a hell, or a heaven, or limbo. I don't even know if there is a God or not. I wish I could believe in something good watching over the universe. I did before, when I was alive, but now, I don't know. I hope there isn't a God sometimes. I hope we're all just alone and the world is just chance and luck and pushing."

"Before, when you were alive?"

The dark boy sighed. "And I asked you not to talk about this. You're not much of a listener. Can't you let me bleed in peace?"

"There you are. There's the Chael I know and love. How else am I all messed up?" Lena asked, but she didn't feel hurt by his words. Things had changed.

He shook his head. "No, you're right. See? So easy to judge. I was alive in Lapurdum, Basque country, not Spain, not France, just Lapurdum. I was killed. A long time ago. And I couldn't leave, not when there was so much suffering in the world, not after what happened to my sister. You say I'm an angel? Maybe. Never thought I would have wings and a sword. I didn't when I was outside of the world. I was just me and I just pushed at things a little. That's all I could do."

Lena was desperate to understand. "What do you mean? Push?"

He glanced over his shoulder at her, his sweaty hair hanging in his dark eyes. His gaze wrenched her breath away.

Chael went on. "Some souls don't go to wherever most souls go. They stay, like I stayed, drawn to people to help them." He paused. "I kept hiding your red purse, hoping you would take the hint and not get involved with the drug deals. And with Santiago, when he told you he

~ ☾ ~

could send Bruise for the drugs, I whispered that idea to him. And the truck, when it wouldn't start, I wanted to give you some time, so you could think about what you were doing. Just little pushes to help, so you wouldn't do the run, so you wouldn't get caught."

Lena's voice was low. "But with the cop, that night when I first saw you, you didn't just push then, huh?"

He hung his head and the small room was silent except for the drip of water.

"Okay," she said. Her arms were getting tired, but she kept the washcloth on his wound. "We won't talk about that. What about Beels?"

"Like you said, he's a demon. He was whispering for you to turn yourself in when you got pulled over. He wanted you dealing drugs and risking your life. When I give, he takes. I help. He hinders. I push. He pulls from life. As long as I was beyond, so was he. I sensed him around you before, but I didn't know his name. I pushed for Jozey, and he pulled from you."

"So you brought him here?"

His body tensed. "Yes," he whispered. His voice was chewed away by an agony far worse than the pain in his legs. He stood up, breathing hard.

She pulled away the washcloth to see that the wounds had stopped bleeding. Droplets of water dribbled down his skin. Instinctively, she wanted to lick them away from his muscled body. His wet boxer shorts left nothing to the imagination.

She looked away and handed him a towel. "I'll get you some food and clothes. In the medicine cabinet, we have some bandages."

"You'll have to help me. If I start to bleed again, I might die, and I don't know if Beels will leave when I go. I can't take that chance."

She carefully wrapped his leg, then left to get him some clothes. Out in the hallway, Lena found her breath.

~ ☾ ~

But then the possibility of Chael sleeping over took it away from her again.

In her closet, she found her father's box and took out khaki's and a flannel shirt. She opened the bathroom door just enough to push them through. Then she went to clean the blood off the floor with Windex and paper towels.

He came into the kitchen as she put stuffed manicotti leftovers from Gramma Scar into the microwave.

"Your dad was big," he said. He was swimming in the clothes.

"No, he was huge," she said with a smile. "So was my mom. I was always getting on them to eat less."

He limped to the chair and sat down.

"Did your parents really die?" she asked.

He nodded. "Soldiers killed them when I was Jozey's age. I can't remember much about them, just a smell, stories, maybe an image of a smile, but not much. Probably how Jozey will remember your parents. But like him, I had a sister who could be wonderful, like you can be. But who was just as fragile."

Lena didn't know what was okay to ask, but she had to know more. "How long ago was all that?"

He shrugged. "Five hundred years. Maybe six."

"How come you don't speak French?"

"Who says I don't?" He smiled. "When I was alive, I spoke mostly Basque, but also French and Spanish, even some Arabic. When I was beyond, I could speak any language. They're all about the same. I pushed in Africa for a while. Now there is a place that needs angels."

Gramma Scar's leftovers were just as good as a fresh plate, sometimes better. The sauce glued to the noodles had deepened in flavor. The ricotta was rich and hot. She ate with him, the food offering as much comfort as a kiss.

"Now you don't have to just push, though, right?" Lena asked. "I mean, you can actually do things. Like

~ ☾ ~

help Remy play football. What about Tabitha?"

Chael laid his fork down and closed his eyes. "Just talked to her. That's what most people need. Someone to talk to, to understand them. I could never do that before. With Remy, it was so simple. One phone call. How come no one thought of it? None of the coaches, not his parents, no one. When I was beyond, I could see it all so clearly, but I couldn't do anything. Just a hint here, a nudge, a push. That's why I got so caught up and forgot about eating and sleeping. I can do so much now. I can help so many people, and so directly. But with Beels here, it isn't worth it. I should just..."

"What, Chael, what is it?"

Misery painted his face. "I should kill myself, but I can't. I'm just not sure how connected Beels and I are."

In silence, they finished the manicotti. The only sound was their forks on their plates. Lena peeked at the clock. A little after midnight, which meant another night without sleep. Jozey would be up for his routine in only a few hours. Then she noticed Chael's eyes were closed. She put her hand on his and shook him a little.

"I'll go," he mumbled, half opening his eyes.

But she led him back to her room.

He resisted. "Lena, please, you don't have to do this."

Still not trusting herself to speak, she laid down on the bed next to Jozey then drew Chael down next to her. He lay woodenly until she put his arm around her.

And it all fell into place. She held Jozey. He held her. And having someone hold her made her cry again until sleep captured her and her tears dried on her cheeks.

At five, Jozey didn't wake up, but out of habit, Lena's eyes popped open. She felt Chael's fire-hot breath on her neck. She fell back asleep, drifting away in a comfort and warmth she hadn't known in months, years, not since she was Jozey's age, safe in her parent's arms.

As if they would always be there.

~ ☾ ~

As if nothing could ever change.

In the morning, with the sun shrouded in the clouds drowning Avalon, Lena woke and Chael was gone. On the pillow there was a single, black feather.

And there on the door to the bathroom, where she always kept it, was the red purse, full of drugs, glimmering like blood in the morning light.

More of the devil whispering despair.

~ ☾ ~

GOOD FRIDAY

i
(heretics in the morning)

For the first time in a long time, Lena ate breakfast with Jozey. Just an egg and a toaster waffle, but it was something.

"Weni, you pick me up, right?"

That was the question he kept asking. Over and over. And each time, she had to assure him she wouldn't abandon him again.

The door to Aunt Mercedes' room stayed shut. Lena wondered if she should check to see if her aunt was dead. Instead, she just hustled Jozey out the door to tackle another day without sleep.

But she didn't feel tired. Same cloud, different day. With a spare key, she unlocked the truck right where Tabitha had parked it. The truck's heater did little to break through the chill covering her skin like scales, but the cold didn't bother her so much. It was like Chael had left some of his warmth behind.

She stuffed the red purse behind her seat, then belted Jozey into his car seat.

"Weni, you pick me up, right?"

"Oh yes, Jozey, I'll be there."

At the Cherubim, she gave him a kiss, a hug, and more promises.

On the way back across town, Lena thought about the red purse. There was some famous poem about an albatross tied around a sailor's neck. That's how it felt with the red purse. Beels must have snuck it back into her room and didn't mess with her or Jozey because her angel had been sleeping next to her.

~ ☾ ~

Chael. Her guardian angel.

Parking in front of Avalon High School, she slung the red purse over her shoulder and ran through the doors of the cafeteria. The Paladin tables were empty except for Parker Lee who hadn't been at the party the night before.

Lena sat down, and Parker looked up, frowned, then dropped her head back to her books.

"Hey, Parker."

The girl bent further into her studying.

Lena opened up her own homework but any effort seemed useless. She numbly turned pages, wondering how on earth she could avoid failing.

"Did you turn Deirdre's dad in?" Parker asked with spiders in her voice.

Lena felt all of the blood drain out of her face, out of her chest, out of her body. "What?"

"Deirdre's dad got arrested last night. Drugs, I guess. She tried calling you, but you wouldn't answer, so she called me. We both think you did it. The cops were looking everywhere for you, and Deirdre said you left the party early last night."

Lena tore the cell phone out of her leather bag. It was turned off. She turned it back on and sure enough, six messages. During Deirdre's mother's breakdown, Mr. Dodson had held Deirdre together. With her father in jail, what would happen to the queen of the Paladins?

"I didn't do anything," Lena said. "I haven't talked to the police at all."

"But you were dealing," Parker Lee yapped. "You wanted Deirdre to take the drugs so you wouldn't get caught with them. I don't care if your life is all tragic or whatever, but it's so unfair to ask a friend to do such a thing."

Lena's stomach balled up in anger. Here was another perfect Paladin girl with a nice family and an even nicer house in Lakeview talking about Lena's life as if she

~ ☾ ~

understood everything.

"You have no idea what you're saying." Lena tried to keep her voice even, but fury gnawed at every word. "So just shut your bitch mouth."

"Nice." The word sounded toxic the way Parker half-hissed, half-laughed it. "You had more class when your parents were alive."

Lena reached back to slap the color out of Parker Lee's face when a cold hand caught her wrist.

"Now, I likes me a cat fight as much as the next man, but how 'bout we save the fightin' for later, so's I can git my vidya camera? How 'bout it, Leni?" Johnny Beels, with a bandage on his torn ear, let go of her hand to finger out a cheap chocolate donut from a cellophane tube. Behind him were the Heretics, still chemicalled from the night before.

"Don't call me Leni."

Bruise sat down next to Parker and pushed her pencil across the page. "Oops. You're gonna lose points for neatness."

Dane Bramage sat down on the other side. "You, Parker Lee, a part of you yearns for the burn whether you know it or not."

Scowling, she packed up her things.

Beels laughed at her, licked another donut from the package, and winked at Lena. "With Parker there, it's a little fear, a little intolerance, but mostly sweet desire to get away from us. I like it, Parker, I like it a lot. Y'all got a good taste 'bout ya."

The Paladin fled from the Heretics as they took up residence.

"What are you doing?" Lena asked.

Bruise and Bramage exchanged blasted glances. Bruise did the talking. "Beels says we ain't gotta stay out in the hall no more. The Paladins don't own these tables."

~ ☾ ~

The cafeteria filled with noise, all the younger kids in hysterics. Heretics at the top tables? It was sacrilege.

"Cutler and the other basketball players aren't going to take this well," Lena said. "And if Deirdre were here—"

Beels cut her off. "Deirdre is pro'lly not gonna be at school today. Y'all heard about her old man I'll bet. Shockin' how deep the secrets of a small town run." He swooped an arm around Emma. The girl was twilight ashen, wearing a gown far more leather than lace.

"Stay away from him, Emma," Lena warned. "Beels is a demon."

"It's too late," Emma whispered from the haze of the drugs.

"Things are going to change, Lena," Bramage said dreamily. "When the fires come, no one will escape. Cleansed in ice."

"I'm done." Lena threw the red purse at Beels. He didn't catch it, and it fell to the floor.

Beels grinned, showing chocolate-stained teeth. "What's in that purse, darlin'? Y'all wanna share?"

"Drugs," Bruise grunted. "Lena, you're crazy bringing them here."

"I'm done," Lena repeated and leaned into Beels' face. "We're going to get you, Johnny. Chael and I are gonna stop you."

Beels took in a deep breath. "God, I love that hate in ya. It churns and churns, and y'all have no idea how to let go. And call me Beels, Leni, ya know the rules."

"If you keep calling me Leni, I'll keep calling you Johnny." Lena turned to give Emma one last look of supplication, and then left the Paladin tables to sit down with the middle school kids.

The police didn't come for Lena until after the bell rang. By that time, the Paladins had heard about the Heretics sitting at their tables and were preparing for war. But Lena wasn't thinking about that as Mr. Percy,

~ ☾ ~

the principal, led her to his dark, paper-littered office.

Lancing was there with the red purse on his lap. "We pulled this out of your locker," the sheriff said.

~ ☾ ~

ii
(the drugs)

Standing before Lancing, Lena would have run if Mr. Percy hadn't been behind her. Where was that serenity she had felt the night before? Could you only feel that way right before you die?

Chael was right. The world was fragile and peace of mind even more brittle and easily broken.

"It's not mine," Lena said, not even looking at her albatross.

"And yet we found it in your locker," Lancing said in a gentle voice, scratching his beard.

"Because Beels put it there," Lena shot back.

Lancing shook his head. "No, I doubt that."

Principal Percy moved her to a chair and Lena fell into it. "Why do you doubt that?" she asked.

Lancing shrugged. "I know which side Johnny Beels is on."

And it all came slamming into her. Chael hadn't been making phone calls. Chael hadn't turned in Santiago or Dodson, hadn't reported Lena to Child Protective Services. It was all Johnny Beels. Pulling apart the lives of those around him and feeding on the dripping insides.

"Beels is evil," Lena said weakly. "Can't you see that?"

The sheriff shrugged. "Well, if I had to choose an evil one, it would be Chael. Wherever he goes, there's trouble. He was at the Bearly last night, right in the middle of a fight. And then there was a robbery at the Gas 'n Sip and guess who was a witness? Chael. No last name, no parents. At least Johnny Beels has a dad."

"Let me guess. Huge guy with big teeth?" Lena felt

~ ☾ ~

herself collapsing.

Lancing nodded. "Rex Beels."

"Rex is the supplier. He and his friends and their dogs." Lena talked numbly, but every word felt hollow and useless. "They were giving Santiago his drugs. I don't know who the buyer is, but I think he's from Buena Vista. He's coming Halloween night to make a huge deal with Beels."

"You mean Dodson," Lancing said.

"I don't know anything about Dodson," she returned.

Lancing's face was as mild as ever. Like a summer meadow. "You don't have to protect Dodson any more. Or Santiago. He gave you up, you know. That's how we knew the drugs were in your locker."

"You're a liar," Lena said in whispers. "I heard you the other night. You said Santiago didn't give anyone up."

A blush poured over Lancing, and for a moment, Lena felt bad for him.

"Darn," he said, "on T.V. they make that lying look so easy. You got me, Lena. Sorry about that."

She glanced down and realized she had stopped breathing. Whether Lancing was lying or not, he still had the red purse, taken from her locker, where Beels had put it.

Mr. Percy stood by the door. She had forgotten he was there. "So, Art, you're going to have to take her to Leadville, right? We'll have to see if Mercedes can watch Jozey then."

At her brother's name, Lena ripped open. "Please. I have to pick up my brother, I have to. Can you just take me in tomorrow? Or tonight, after I get him?"

"So you admit they're your drugs," Lancing said carefully.

She shook her head. "It doesn't matter what I say. If you're listening to Johnny Beels, we're all in trouble. I just want to take care of my brother."

~ ☾ ~

"This isn't going to look good for the CPS people," the sheriff said.

"No, it's not," she said, drowning.

"You tell us everything you know and maybe..."

Lena tried to wipe a tear but missed with a trembling hand and smeared her eye make-up. "It won't matter. You won't believe me. Just let me pick up my brother."

Lancing stopped, opened the red purse, and looked inside. "You got a lot here, Lena. This is serious, more serious than Santiago. Got him on a possession charge, but you, I can get you for...." He trailed off, frowning. He took a sniff, like a bear snuffling for berries. "Well, I'll be." Lancing again blushed then smiled crookedly at her. "Hell, you must think I'm such a fool. Not my best day for sure. Can't very well bust you for laundry soap."

He showed it to her. In the purse was a ziplock bag full of white powder, but she could smell the soap even from a distance.

"You didn't know about Dodson?" the sheriff asked.

Lena shook her head, but what Chael had said to Deidre's father the other night made a lot more sense.

"And Halloween night?"

"Johnny Beels," Lena repeated. "Tomorrow night, he and Rex are going to have all the drugs ready for the Buena Vista guy."

Lancing leaned back, eyes squinting. "I can't believe that, but anyway, you don't have to worry none. You want your purse back?"

"I never, ever want to see that red purse again," she said.

"Good answer."

A miracle. Chael must have flushed the drugs and replaced them with laundry powder while she was still sleeping next to Jozey. He had saved her once more.

Pushing.

"Stay out of the game," Lancing said.

~ ☾ ~

"I'm out. I promise."

It was too late to go back to class, so she went to the cafeteria, not knowing where she would sit. The Paladins didn't want her and the Heretics were enslaved to a blond demon in polished, black cowbow boots.

And there he sat, Johnny Beels, lounging like the devil he was at the Paladin tables, with a tin-foiled burrito dripping green chili.

"Hey, Leni," he drawled. "I been talkin' a lot with Art Lancing. He's such a nice guy, ain't he? Not much of a lawman, but a helluva guy."

~ ☾ ~

iii
(sitting alone)

"I told him all about you," Lena said. She was alone with Beels in the upper tier of the cafeteria. Their voices echoed.

"Good things, I hope."

"He thinks you're some kind of narc."

"We both know I'm far worse than that," Beels said, eyes twinkling, like he had just eaten Santa Claus for breakfast and his sloppy burrito was dessert. He touched the bandage on his ear where Lena had bitten him. "How'd I taste? Sweet I hope!"

"Awful, but it's not every day a girl gets to bite the vampire back. Let's just pray for a fatal infection so we can end this."

Beels grinned. "Well, that would do it. I die, Chael dies, and oh how y'all would miss him. But anyways, yer girl Deirdre called me. She wants to chat 'bout her daddy, I guess."

"You stay away from her, Johnny."

"Johnny Beels is gonna touch everyone in this town, Leni. Your boy Chael unleashed me, and I ain't going back until I've taken a bite outta everyone just like you bit me." He crammed half of the burrito into his mouth and then talked while he gobbled. "But what I wants to know, lil' girl, is where y'all gonna sit? You a Paladin or Heretic? Today, you gonna have to choose."

Lena retreated back into the hall, away from Beels, his grinning, his questions. She ran into Bruise, Bramage, and the rest of the Heretics.

Bruise seized her. "Come on, Lena. You always eat

~ ☾ ~

lunch with the Heretics, and today we're eating in style."

"Hands off!" She wrestled herself free. "I think my days of heresy are over."

Bruise and Bramage looked at each other and laughed. "Back to being Miss Goody-Two-Shoes," Bruise grunted.

"But the darkness has touched you like it has touched me," Bramage whispered.

From the entryway to the cafeteria, Lena watched the leathered Heretics strut up to Beels just as the Paladin girls, Cutler, and the rest of the basketball players marched over to do battle. Avery, though, was missing, which Lena thought was odd.

Paulie walked up beside Lena to survey the fight. He talked, but not to her, only to himself. "I hate it when the social order gets disrupted like this. And I feel terrible for Deirdre. Bad enough about her dad, but this, this'll probably kill her." He moved on past her and sat down with Tabitha and Remy at the lower tables. Chael and Santiago joined them.

Lena stayed in the hallway, but she could hear everything being said in the upper tier.

"Kick their asses," Parker Lee shouted, and Cutler with the other jocks moved forward to do just that.

Mr. Percy was hurrying toward them from the other side of the cafeteria.

Cutler saw him. "We're going to have this out, once and for all," he said.

"Just name the place," Bruise said.

Cutler didn't. Bramage did. "Halloween night in this very place. The saints and sinners will struggle, but all will be kissed by the ice and flame of my Armageddon. No stone untouched. No soul unscorched. Apocalypse now."

"We'll be here," Cutler spat.

Mr. Percy jogged up in his suit, tie fluttering. His solution: the Heretics and the Paladins would share the

~ ☾ ~

upper tier. The principal stood over the grumbling and mumbling, keeping order.

Johnny Beels chowed on his burrito and smiled until his jaw threatened to snap off.

"He's not eating the food," Lena said to herself. "He's eating the fear and hate. The desire."

Chael caught her eye and motioned for her to sit with them. She knew she should go and thank Chael for saving her life. Again. Thank him for pushing.

But she couldn't move.

Tabitha caught her eye, and Lena looked away. The outcast girl probably wanted to give her the keys back. Parker Lee had said it was unfair for Lena to have asked Deirdre for help, and yet Tabitha had been there for her.

Then it hit Lena. Even if Deirdre were at school, Lena wasn't sure she could sit with the Paladins any more. All of the freedom she felt after the fall, all the joy was gone. Now she had to choose.

Shaking, she walked down the steps to a lower tier and sat by herself. She reached for the archives of undone homework and felt tears in her eyes. If her mom were still alive, she would have told Lena to go and sit with Chael and his friends. Gramma Scar would say the same thing. Her dad would hold her and tell her it would all be okay no matter where she sat.

Lena squeezed her eyes shut, trying to reach past the sadness to the anger that could freeze the tears away. But there was no fire, only sorrow. She had never felt so alone in her life, and it was because she was choosing to be alone. It felt unfair for her to do that to herself. But she couldn't help it. Like she couldn't help being mean to Aunt Mercedes.

A tray banged down next to her, surprising her and forcing a tear down her cheek, black with mascara.

Chael and the rest of the Untouchables had come to rescue her from herself.

~ ☾ ~

iv
(lunch with the untouchables)

As the Untouchables moved their lunches to sit around Lena, Santiago sang something about a lonely flower in the mountain.

"Does he always sing?" Remy asked.

Lena smiled and more tears fell. She couldn't talk. She could only nod.

Paulie shook his head. "You can't even request a song. He just sings the opera over and over."

"I like it," Tabitha said.

"Because you have taste, *signorina*," Santiago said. And sang his Bertoglio love song to Tabitha until she blushed.

Chael slid a napkin in front of Lena, but she had her mirror out to salvage her make-up and touch-up her mascara. She had to laugh. At herself, at Chael, at the Untouchable she had become.

"When are they all gonna battle?" Paulie asked.

"Not my problem," Santiago said with a relaxed smile. "I'll be gone Monday. Treatment."

Lena had never seen him so mellow.

"And any day I'll be transferring to Lake County High School in Leadville," Remy said. He cracked his knuckles like he was itching to get his hands on a football again.

Paulie ate his sandwich by picking it apart like a raccoon. Lena kept expecting him to dip it into his milk. "And for those of us so abandoned? Well, nice thing about being a nobody, nobody really cares about what happens to you, so you don't have to care back."

"Except for your friends," Chael said, eyes on Lena.

~ ☾ ~

He looked better, rested, but there were still circles under his eyes and his cheeks were hollowed dark.

Lena closed her compact slowly. "Someone has to stop Johnny Beels. He's the problem."

"She has a point. My old compadres aren't what you call self-starters. They'll follow Beels to hell if he asks them to," Santiago said, chewing an apple.

It was the first time she had ever seen Santiago actually eating. Lena couldn't believe the change.

At the word hell, Chael dropped his head. "Evil has a way of taking care of itself."

Paulie laughed. "Yeah, like Hitler would have given up the Third Reich to work at a Starbucks. No way, Chael."

"We have to do something," Lena said.

Chael closed his eyes. "No way to stop him. Only to outdo him by pushing. Like always."

"Like you did with the laundry soap," Lena murmured. "Thank you." She turned to Tabitha. "And thank you. For what you did last night."

"What did she do last night?" Paulie asked.

Tabitha didn't answer him but gave Lena back her keys. "It's okay. I was glad to help."

"What did you tell them?" Lena asked.

Tabitha smiled secretly. "That I was thinking about buying your truck and was just test driving it. I don't think they believed me."

"What in the truck happened last night?" Paulie asked again.

Then, from nowhere, Tabitha asked a question of her own. "Do you think God cares about what we do?" Her voice was barely audible over the noise in the cafeteria. "Do you even think there's a God?"

Paulie shook his head. "Great, just ignore me. I'm used to that. So go ahead, drop the heavy conversation on me. I can take it."

Tabitha's question hung in the air, and for some

~ ☾ ~

reason, they all looked at Chael.

"I don't know anything about God, but I do know this. We have to be the angels because heaven is empty."

They were all shocked into silence.

Except Santiago. He sang a snippet from a Scattershot song about the prince of darkness cast out of the light.

"How can you say that?" Lena asked. "You of all people should believe in God."

Chael shrugged. "If there is a God, what is He doing to fix what's so obviously broken?"

Lena dug into the argument. "If there isn't a God, then how come you always show up at the right place at the right time? I heard about you breaking up a fight at the Bearly last night."

"Oh, Lena, he has an answer for that." Paulie motioned for Chael to speak. "Go ahead. Tell her all your gospel-altruism-shake-the-dust-from-your-sandals stuff."

Chael grinned wearily at Paulie. "Fine. Truth is, the world is so damaged, you can find people to help anywhere you go. Just look around, and you'll know what to do."

Old anger bristled through Lena. "Yeah, Chael, whatever. No good deed goes unpunished. I know that for a fact. What's the use in helping anyone when what you do doesn't matter?"

"You guys know the story of the kid and the starfish?" Remy asked. No one did. So Remy went on. "A little kid is walking on the beach and there's all these starfish on the sand, dying. Like a million starfish. And the kid starts throwing them back into the ocean, one at a time. Some old guy comes up and says, 'Kid, what you're doing doesn't matter. You can't get all them starfish back in the water.' And the kid just smiles. 'It matters to this one,' he says and throws it back into the water. 'And this one. And this one. And this one.'"

~ ☾ ~

Chael nodded. "Yes, it's just like that."

"Do you guys always talk like this?" Lena asked.

Paulie laughed again. "Well, we didn't because we were all alone, and then we didn't because we were just sitting together, and then Tabitha started talking and she always asks the deep questions. Which is why we love her."

A scarlet Tabitha dropped her head and turned her attention to her lunch.

Paulie went on. "You got the Paladins and Heretics up there, but right here, you have the Untouchables. Can't touch us because we're so wonderfully, wonderfully awesome."

"And because we're at the bottom of the castes," Tabitha murmured.

"Yeah, well, we make being at the bottom awesome," Paulie countered happily.

"So if there's no God and no heaven, then my parents really are dead." Lena waited to see what everyone would do once she talked about it. The Paladins would have changed the subject. The Heretics would have laughed and screamed about her parents burning in hell.

"There can be an afterlife even if there isn't a God," Tabitha said. "People who believe in souls are called essentialists. You can be an atheist and an essentialist."

Paulie clapped. "You go, girl. Take no prisoners."

"There are souls," Chael said. "I know there are."

"I can't believe my grandmother isn't in heaven," Remy threw in. "Just because people are stupid doesn't mean there's no God. It's all about free will."

"Ugh! The free will thing again?" Paulie yelled, just like the other day. "Can we not talk about God without talking about free will?"

Lena captured Chael with a glance. "What are we going to do about Beels?"

Chael answered her with a steady gaze. "If we go after

~ ☾ ~

him, we'll fall right into his trap. We wait and see what
he does and then undo what he does. Like always."

"Pushing," Lena said.

Chael nodded.

The bell rang and it was back to class, her brain
loaded with too much to think about.

And Santiago laid one more thing on her plate.

~ ☾ ~

V
(santiago after school)

In an empty classroom, Santiago caught her arm.
"Can I talk to you for a minute?"

Lena nodded. She didn't have long. She couldn't be
late to pick up Jozey, not after last night.

"Listen, I didn't know about Deirdre's dad. I only dealt
with the Buena Vista guy," he said.

"Do you think it's true about Mr. Dodson?" she asked.
"Or do you think Beels framed him?"

"No, I think Dodson was probably partnered up with
the Buena Vista guy, so no one local knew he was
involved. Dodson must have been desperate, I mean,
with what's happening around here. Where else was he
going to get enough cash for his condo project?" Santiago
paused. "Don't tell anyone, but Gramma Scar is going to
be putting the Rosa up for sale."

Lena gasped. "You're kidding."

He shook his head. "Wish I was. She had to pay my
legal fees somehow. I begged her not to. She was barely
scraping by as it was. I guess we all knew it would
happen at some point, but one more business closing on
Mountain Avenue, and especially the Rosa? That's going
to kill Avalon for sure."

"You sound like Avery," she murmured. "You teased
him about wanting to save our town."

Santiago was sheepish. "Yeah, because that's what
everyone expected me to say. I was high all the time,
Lena. I mean all the time. I remember, like, about fifteen
minutes of last year."

She glanced at the clock. Not much time. But she

~ ☾ ~

wanted to hear more from Santiago. "How come you're sitting with the Untouchables now? What happened with you and the Heretics?"

He shrugged. "When I told Bruise I was getting clean, he dropped me. I thought we were friends, but I guess not. And you've seen how much Bramage loves Beels."

"Bramage is planning something," she said. "Do you know what it is?"

"No clue, but it can't be good. All that no stone unscorched stuff?"

"Whatever Bramage is planning, Beels is probably behind it." Lena frowned. "It's all Beels, everything bad that's been happening is because of him. He turned you in. He turned in Deirdre's dad. He called CPS on me and Jozey. And now he's trying to get the Heretics and Paladins to kill each other over the stupid upper tables."

Santaigo shrugged. "All that sucks, but I'm not sure me being turned in was bad. I knew it wasn't Chael. We talked about it. And besides, that's not how he works."

Lena found herself grinning. "You like Chael. That's why you were sitting with the Untouchables."

"After Beels took over, I found myself alone this morning, until Chael came calling. Funny how things work out. Next thing we know, he and Deirdre will be all chummy. Knowing Chael that just might happen."

Lena sighed. "If only Lancing liked Chael. He doesn't though. Lancing just loves Johnny Beels. He thinks he's a mole, or a narc, or some kind of double-agent or whatever. But Beels doesn't care about anything. He just feeds on the chaos he creates."

"Yeah," Santiago said, nodding. "I mean, Beels still doesn't have my stash, and it's like he doesn't care. Here I am dying, sitting on half a million dollars of product, and he's just taking his time, like he just loves watching me sweat."

"He did the exact same thing to me," she said.

~ ☾ ~

"What he's doing doesn't make sense. I get busted, he comes in, and first thing he does is call Rex to work with him. If Rex worked directly with Dodson and the Buena Vista guy, it would ruin Beels cut. Can't be a middle man if there's no middle. Speaking of Rex and his guys, I want to show you something."

"I can't." She was already late.

"Real quick. You should know."

Santiago led Lena up to the accordion gates on the third floor, as if he were taking her to Beels' damaged library. But the gates were locked.

"What?" Lena asked.

Santiago shook the metal. There was a soft bark, then the click of nails on wood as four Dobermans trotted up, eyes dark and gleaming. They sat on their haunches and licked their chops with red tongues.

"Rex," Lena whispered.

"Beels brought them in and now Rex and his people can meet directly with the Buena Vista guy. I just don't get it. It will hurt his cut. Maybe it's like what you said, Beels doesn't care about the money. He just wants to screw with people."

Lena reached out and rattled the gate.

"What are you doing?"

"If they bark, maybe Mr. Percy will come to investigate," she said.

But the dogs didn't bark. They looked at her like she was crazy, then wandered back down the hall.

"Let's just go," Santiago whispered.

They walked down the steps to the principal's office, but it was already closed. Friday afternoon.

Santiago shook his head. "They got Percy doing everything, man. Principal, teacher, coaching. You know why Chael and Beels could get into our school so easily? It's because Percy gets paid per student by the State. He's just trying to do the best he can, which isn't good 'cause

~ ☾ ~

he's trying to do too much."

Lena smiled. "Are you really the same guy I dated?"

"No, Lena, I'm not," Santiago said, a sad smile on his face. "Getting busted, that wasn't any big deal. But Gramma Scar paying all my legal fees and for treatment and everything else. It hurt her." He grunted discomfort. "Last thing in the world I wanted was to hurt her. So I don't know who I am anymore, but that old Santiago is dead. And to tell you the truth..." He backed down the hall away from her. "I'm glad he's gone, Lena. I'll call you tonight. I promise."

He left singing his old Bertoglio song about being a poor man in a rich man's world.

In her truck, Lena raced across town to pick up her brother. Along the way, she used the cell phone to call Lancing. She still had the card he had given her Tuesday night, which now felt like forever ago. When he answered, Lena told him about Beels and the dog men setting up camp on the third floor.

Lancing chuckled. "I chase you everywhere last night and tonight you call me. Can't believe you roped Tabitha Martin into helping you. Anyway, we know about Beels and his dad. Rex is doing some construction work there, if you must know. And if you think you can pin anything on Beels, I'm telling you, you're wasting your time."

Lena hung up. The police weren't going to be helping her. Not unless she had proof.

A plan settled down into her like it had been sent from heaven. The Buena Vista guy was coming with the money to buy the drugs from Beels. If only she could get the police there to catch them, then Beels would get locked away. And at the same time, if she could steal the money, she could save Gramma Scar's restaurant.

She was at a traffic light, swimming in the idea, when the light turned green. The car behind her honked to get her attention.

~ ☾ ~

"I'm being stupid again," she said to herself. But she couldn't let Gramma Scar lose her restaurant. She had to do something. Even if the something was illegal, dangerous, and idiotic. Even if she had to do it by herself.

At the Cherubim, both Jozey and Chael glared at her. Jozey, because she was late. Chael, because he somehow knew about her plans.

~ ☾ ~

vi
(the lake, the clouds, the kiss)

Lena moved slowly into the room where Chael and Jozey sat on a padded bench next to a big window. She went to pick up her brother, but he clung to Chael.

"It's okay, Jozey," Lena said. "I'll wait until you're ready to go. We're in no hurry."

"Really?" Jozey looked at his sister like she had just spoken Chinese.

"Yep," she said.

Chael's eyes were soft on her, but his tone was still stern. "You can't be serious."

She tried to play innocent. "I have no idea what you are talking about."

"You want to get Beels. You want to get the money. You want to fix everything."

Lena crouched down and ran a matchbox car over Jozey's foot. He took it from her in his fist and drove it through the air, then wandered over to where Mrs. Weyland was reading stories to a circle of children.

Leaving Lena alone with the dark boy. "What I want," she said, "is to feel like I felt with you last night. I felt so connected to everything, so at peace. Where did that go?"

Chael didn't answer but let out a long breath, taking her hand in his. She was used to his heat now. The burn of his skin felt like sleeping in a warm place.

"Sometimes it's best to just let things be," he said. "Sometimes we can't stop tragedy, like what happened to your parents."

Lena pulled her hand away. "This is nothing like that."

"No one could have stopped what happened to your

~ ☾ ~

family."

Her eyes filled with tears, she couldn't breathe, and suddenly she was taken back to that night. The crimson cat eyes of the car stopped by the side of the road. The thwack of the windshield wipers. The wet spring snow crusting to the sides of the window.

Should we stop?

Lena tripped over her feet to get away from him. He wanted her to talk about the murder of her parents, and it was too soon. Was seven months too soon? Maybe after seven years. Or seven lifetimes.

Outside, she was lost in the cloud, but only for a moment, until Chael found her.

"His name was Kyle," he went on. "Do you know what he thought when you pulled up behind him?"

"I don't want to talk about it!" Once again, she was running from him. She had come with hope for her town, and now he wanted to crumble her soul between his fingers. It was unfair.

He followed her to the edge of the asphalt, leaving her no choice but to flee onto the banks of the lake. The stiletto points of her boots sank into the murk.

But he kept walking toward her. She was trapped.

"Do you know what he was thinking when your parents stopped?" Chael asked again.

"You can't know."

But he could.

Lena found herself calf-deep in the freezing water but not feeling anything. She thought she was alone until Chael appeared out of the mist, swishing toward her through the lake.

"He thought you were the cops," he said. "One more DUI and Kyle would have been locked up for life. He was drunk and desperate and the minute your dad stepped out of the car, Kyle just started shooting."

She could hear the bullets hitting the windshield. Her

~ ☾ ~

mother screaming. Her brother screaming. Her dad had dropped to the ground, as if he had slipped. But he hadn't slipped. He had been shot and killed right in front of her. And Lena's mother had been shot in the head.

"He didn't realize his mistake until he heard Jozey crying."

The sobs were a mountain thunderstorm, hitting her before she knew it. She put up her hands to hide her face as the tears fell into the lake.

Chael kept on talking. "Kyle Jackson. Jozey's crying sobered him up. Then he realized what he had done. He had shot up a family. And he was so sure you were cops. Who else would stop? His drunk car was always breaking down. That's what he called it because when he was sober, he could afford a better car, but not when he was drinking."

She wanted him to shut up, wanted him to go away, wished he had never come to rain such trouble down upon them. But all she could do was sob. This was the deeper pain. These were the tears she would only have to cry once.

"And Kyle James Jackson, named after both his grandfathers, he couldn't live with what he had done. He reloaded and stuck his gun in his mouth." Chael's voice dropped. "He could smell the gun oil Grandpa James had used to clean his guns. It was a good smell. It was a being-with-his-grandpa smell. Jozey screaming for his dead parents was too much for Kyle, and he pulled the trigger."

Lena fell into Chael and he held her until the sobs stopped.

When the storm passed, the only sound was Chael's heart, his breathing, and the water of the cold lake around them.

His voice whispered over her, soft and loving. "I came too late to stop Kyle from shooting your family, too late

~ ☾ ~

to stop him from killing himself. Jozey cried like I cried when the soldiers murdered my family. And I cried with you both because the world is so hard and life is fragile. I started pushing for you. For Aunt Mercedes to take you in so you wouldn't live in foster care. For her to get that good job at the ski resort. For Mrs. Weyland to drop the price for Jozey even though she couldn't afford it. And I would go to Kyle's kids who missed their dad because he wasn't always a mean drunk. The sober Kyle loved his family so much it felt better than any whiskey or any drug, but then he'd forget and fall back into the bottle. Kyle wasn't evil, just forgetful."

The water should have been freezing her, but it wasn't because Chael was there, and she wanted to stay in his burning arms forever. In the arms of her angel, lost in the clouds.

Not her angel. She knew that now. He belonged to Jozey, not her.

But he had saved her, over and over, so maybe they could share him.

She pulled away, feeling the tacky, mascara-heavy tears on her face. She was through with make-up. It was expensive and she didn't need the armor any more. She had no one to impress now that she was no longer a Paladin.

"Sometimes you can't push," Chael said. "Sometimes, all you can do is let go and let the world be broken and hold on to the people you love."

"What can we do to help Gramma Scar?" Lena asked in a whisper. "How can we stop Johnny Beels?"

"We can't," Chael said. He closed his eyes. "But you can. You'll do what must be done when the time comes. You'll make an impossible choice and I'll love you for it, Lena." He opened his eyes and they were midnight velvet on her. "And I've come to love you so much already."

He bent and kissed her hair, kissed her ear, kissed her

~ ☾ ~

cheek, then found her lips. Kissing him was coming home, a feast after starving, cold water seconds before dying of thirst. He pulled her close, she clung to him, and the kiss deepened. She didn't forget about her sorrow, it was still there, would always be there, but his touch, his heat, his breath gave her hope. Hope that she could live with the sorrow. That she could feel love. That she could heal. At long last, hope that she could heal.

~ ☾ ~

vii
(pushing)

They walked out of Camlann Lake and back to her truck where Chael stopped, his face troubled.

"Do you want to go with me?" he asked in a feathery voice.

"Okay, but what are you talking about?"

He smiled. "Sorry. Want to go for a drive with me? Jozey'll be all right, and Mrs. Weyland doesn't need me anymore. Five more kids moved away. Let's just go, really quick."

Lena unlocked the truck. When she let go of Chael, she felt the cold slime of the lake mud in her boots. "Are you sure Jozey is going to be all right? He was so upset when I wasn't there last night."

"But you were here tonight. And I talked with him. I thought something like this was going to happen."

"Pushing," Lena whispered.

"Yeah, and it's important."

Lena smiled. "What? Is your spidey-sense tingling?"

He shook his head, jaws tight. "No, nothing like that. Or maybe it is. Let's just drive west. I'll tell you where to turn. Or if you feel it, you turn."

She fired up the truck and they took off down Highway 77 toward Highway 91. "I have an angel costume to make for Jozey for Halloween. Can you help with that?"

He didn't answer. He was focused on the road, the clouds spilling across the asphalt, the trees flashing by.

Lena's hands were sweat-slippery on the steering wheel. She wiped them off one at a time on the seat as

~ ☾ ~

she spoke. "Today at lunch, you said all you had to do was walk around and find someone to help. This isn't like that. You can feel when people need help, but no one else can."

"No, everyone can, but they keep themselves too busy to listen." He stopped talking for a moment. "And yeah, angel costume, I should be able to come up with something."

They drove down the highway, Lena's head spinning, but then she saw a dirt road and knew it was the one they were supposed to take. "It's that one," she said.

He nodded.

She slowed down and turned onto the barely maintained road. The trees pressed into the truck and the clouds grew murkier.

"What you're feeling now, is this what it's like when you're on the outside?" she asked.

He nodded. "But I can get there quicker. Just a thought and I would be there, but then I wouldn't be able to do much. Now, that's changed."

She shifted into four-wheel-drive to climb over a ridge, the brakes squealing as they inched down the other side.

Chael's voice came out strained. "When we stop, call Lancing. Tell him to meet us at mile marker one sixty-four on seventy-seven."

"What are the lottery numbers for tomorrow?" Lena asked nervously.

"It's not like that," Chael said. He was pale and trembling. "This place is going to be bad. I don't know why I brought you. If anything happens to you…"

"Nothing is going to happen to me," Lena said, her anxiety so keen she couldn't help but joke. "You're a bad-ass angel. You can just fly us away."

"I don't feel like a bad-ass angel," he said, "but maybe you're right." He slipped off his coat and pulled the white

~ ☾ ~

hoodie and t-shirt over his head.

The road dropped down into a hidden, narrow, crack of a valley, thick with trees and rocks, littered with trash. Blown, yellow newspapers clung to branches and moldering magazines were piled waist-high next to the corpses of rusted cars. Ruined, blackened kitchen appliances were scattered about: a refrigerator here, a sink there, microwave ovens with the doors smashed open, and toilets shot to pieces with large caliber rifles.

"Well, looks like they're all decorated for Halloween." Her voice cracked.

"Stop here," Chael said.

She braked too hard and they were both thrown forward. "Sorry," she said. "First time pushing."

He didn't laugh but sprang out of the truck, slammed the door shut, and charged toward the house.

Lena followed, but then remembered she had to call Lancing. She flipped open the phone, found the sheriff's number, but had to leave a message. "Mile marker one sixty-four. Get here quick."

She winced when the wind found the wet in her boots.

"This is crazy," she whispered. But what if someone had sensed that her family needed help five minutes before they stopped behind Kyle James Jackson in his drunk car? What if someone had pushed right then?

Chael was nowhere to be seen. She walked over to an old truck without wheels, rusting away. In the back was baby stuff, a crib eaten away by time and weather, a filthy doll with cracked glass eyes, a mattress yellowed and moldy. Strewn across everything were cell phones and wires, and the juxtaposition of ruined baby furniture and pieces of technology made her want to flee.

A newspaper caught by a breeze floated through the air like the pieces of a ripped-up ghost.

"Chael?" she called out.

A stick broke behind her. She spun around to face an

~ ☾ ~

emaciated woman cradling a hunting rifle in her arms.

"What you want?" the woman asked. Her face was ravaged with acne scars, her hair razored down to the scalp, and she wore orange hunting clothes, the glow covered by grime.

"We're here to help someone," Lena whispered.

"No one here needs help." The hunter woman's eyes weren't right. Like something inside her had been turned off. "Get off my property."

Lena was going to run back to her truck and honk the horn until Chael came. That was the plan, but it didn't work out that way.

"I'm gonna kill us all!" a voice screamed from somewhere. It was shrill, followed by the shattering of glass, and a howl.

"Christ on a crutch!" The hunter woman streaked away toward the scream.

Lena ran after her, following an impulse deeper than thought, deeper than feeling. It was the next thing to do, no matter how much it scared her.

She ran through the trash until the whiskey bottles started, leading like bread crumbs up to the house. Not really a house, more like a series of shacks stacked on top of one another, gray wood and plastic covered windows, and a slack-jawed door hanging open.

The hunter woman ran inside, and Lena went in behind her, right into the smell. Kerosene, liquor, urine, the dank, growling stench of human excrement. In a room with the remnants of carpet bleeding backing, there was a girl a little older than Lena but so scratched up by time and life in the garbage heap that she looked forty. She had a kitchen knife raised.

"Jenny!" the hunter woman howled. "Put that knife down! Now!"

Chael was in the room standing next to a mattress. In his arms was a thin girl, maybe ten-years-old, but so

~ ☾ ~

scrawny it was hard to tell her age.

"He's gonna take Maddy!" Jenny screamed. "He's gonna take her away."

The hunter woman turned the gun on Chael. "You give me back my daughter."

"Jenny was going to hurt her," the dark boy said. "Kill Maddy, then kill herself. I'm taking her."

The hunter woman squinted at him. "I'll shoot her myself, you think to take her away. This don't concern you."

Chael was unshaken. "Maddy's life is more important than your pride. You need to get back to meetings. You know it, and I know it. And what you are doing to Jenny is killing both of you. She's not your slave."

Lena was behind the hunter woman, between her and the door. And there was Chael, being Chael. Not even the abyss of a gun barrel could ruffle him.

"You don't know nothing!" the hunter woman howled.

A shock of movement, Jenny leapt at Chael, the hunter woman brought up the rifle to shoot.

Time seemed to slow, and Lena knew exactly what to do.

From behind the hunter woman, Lena snatched the rifle's butt out of her hands and ran outside toward her truck, following the whiskey bottles.

She threw the rifle into a pile of rain-crumpled magazines, flung herself into the truck, and twisted the key. The engine roared. She floored the gas pedal, ripping across the trash toward the house. The hunter woman and Jenny were on the front porch, furious and screaming.

Lena knew Chael wasn't coming out the front door. He wasn't dead, she could feel it, but she also knew what she needed to do.

Knew it deeper than thought, deeper than feeling.

She skidded the truck around, barely missed a tree,

~ ☾ ~

bashed through a pile of trash, and headed for the road.

Behind her, she heard something hit the truck bed. In the rearview mirror, she saw Chael, wings out wide, with the girl, Maddy, glued to his skin.

Lena sped up the road, bouncing around on the rocks, barely missing a graveyard of boulders crouched between ragged trees. On a rock ledge above the road was Bramage, of all people, sitting there. He waved at her. He was doing something with cell phones and wires and long metal cylinders all stacked around him.

She didn't wave back, just drove the truck out of the cursed valley and then down the long dirt road to the highway. Once they hit asphalt, Lena stopped while Chael got out.

Lancing's police SUV hurtled toward them down Highway 77. He had gotten the message.

Chael wrapped the girl gently in a blanket, then laid her down on the soft pine needles next to the highway. Back in the cab, he shook his head. "I feel bad just leaving her," he whispered, "but Lancing already doesn't think too much of me. He'll help her, though. He's a good man."

Lena drove away just as the sheriff pulled up.

"She'll be safe now," Chael said, letting out a long breath.

"So that's pushing." She breathed out along with him.

~ ☾ ~

viii
(three times born)

Lena stopped at the Gas 'N Sip where Highway 77 hit Highway 91, the place where Aunt Mercedes used to work. Her heart continued to hammer.

"Tell me it's not always like that," she said.

"No, most times it's really easy."

She thought about how perfect it had been, pulling the gun out of the hunter woman's arms. "What if we hadn't been there?"

"Jenny would have hurt her cousin Maddy. Maybe not killed her, but it was bad. It may still not turn out right, but we had to do something."

She turned on him. "So how come you got all mad at me for trying to stop Johnny Beels and save Gramma Scar's restaurant? God, Chael, look what we just did. It's not like my thing would have been more dangerous."

He seemed to ignore her question. "Pat used to go to AA. She was better back then, back when Dane's parents were still around."

"Who's Pat?" Lena asked. "The woman with the rifle?"

He nodded. "Yeah, she's Maddy's mother. She took Jenny and Dane in when their parents were taken away."

"What does Pat do to Jenny?" Lena asked, not sure if she really wanted to know.

Chael closed his eyes. "I don't know all the details, but Pat dominates her. Knocked her down and kept her there, under her control, not letting Jenny go to the bathroom without her consent. Same with Maddy. Dane, though, Dane can come and go as he pleases. Because he's a boy."

~ ☾ ~

"I always wondered about Bramage's home life. Now I know. God, I thought I had problems. So how come we can't go after Beels, but we can rescue little girls?"

Chael wiped the sweat off his face. "In AA, there's a prayer, the Serenity Prayer I think it's called."

Lena knew it. "Yeah, serenity to accept the things you can't change, courage to change the things you can, and the wisdom to know the difference."

"You need more of the wisdom part," he said simply. "We could save Maddy. That we could change. Other things, we can't."

"You need more of the wisdom part," she fired back at him. "I'm not the one who brought a demon into our world."

"I do need more wisdom," he said. "Most people just die and go away, but I stayed because I didn't have that wisdom. Maybe if I had let go, I'd be with God and my sister right now."

"That's what I don't get!" She was trying not to yell, but found herself yelling. "When do you let go, and when do you push?"

"The wisdom to know the difference," he whispered.

"There has to be a God," she said. "There has to be because all of this is too hard for us to be here alone." She reached out and touched the hot skin of his arm. "I'm sorry for what I said, about you bringing Beels along with you. You did it to save me, so really, I'm to blame."

"It doesn't matter now. We can stop pointing fingers at the guilty because we're all guilty of something." He leaned his head against the window and closed his eyes.

It took the whole drive to the Cherubim for Lena to calm down, and once inside the daycare center, all she wanted was to hold Jozey and never let go. Her brother had been fine during their time away, and he was squawking happily at the idea that both Lena and Chael would be in the truck with him for the drive home,

~ ☾ ~

together, like a family.

With Jozey car-seated between them, Lena asked Chael, "So you knew what was going to happen. How? I mean, how does that feel?"

"Intuition is like poetry," he said. "It doesn't make sense, until it does. I can't predict the future. I just know some things. Like Dane has hidden something bad at the school. Like you'll get arrested and Jozey will go to foster care."

"But how?" she insisted.

"What's foster care?" Jozey asked.

"You won't have to worry about that, Jozey," she said quickly.

"When I was on the outside of things," Chael said, "I was so connected to everything, I just knew. Like electricity flowing through a current of people. That's how I knew so much about Kyle, and the cop that pulled you over, and Deirdre's family. It's all connected. Here, it's harder. I have to listen, really listen, to know the next right thing to do."

In the silence that followed, Lena made the decision. "I'm not going to go after Beels. I can't risk Jozey."

"No, Lena, don't risk me," her brother said very seriously.

She laughed away some of the tension. "I won't, sweetie."

They pulled up in front of Aunt Mercedes' apartment and swam through the clouds, into the apartment where it was warm and full of light.

Chael didn't come in. "I'm going to check the school again. Dane's been hiding stuff in the basement, but I can't find it."

"I saw him working on something," Lena said and told him about the wires, cell phones, metal cylinders.

"Blasting caps," Chael said. "And with all the mining around here, he could have found dynamite. This feels

~ ☾ ~

right. It fits what he's been saying. No stone untouched.
No soul unscorched."

Jozey ran back into their bedroom to play with his
toys, but Lena stood in the doorway, not wanting to let
Chael go.

"Why would he blow up the school?" she asked.
"What's wrong with him?"

"I was like him for a while," he said. "Dane's dead,
walking around like he's alive. I don't know what
changed in me, but something did. Maybe that's what
they mean by the resurrection. That which was dead,
lives again. I was his age when I was reborn. I took in
orphans like me. There were so many because of the
wars and plagues. We begged money for the most part,
stole from priests when we couldn't get enough food, but
we were a family. It was good."

"How did you die?" Lena asked, then laughed and
shook her head at the question.

His face went loose with the memory. "There was a
war. Soldiers came and took our crops and burned our
fields and killed my parents. And hurt Darlita, my sister.
She never got over the hurt. She hurt herself more and
said it was to feed us. She sold herself to soldiers, maybe
the same ones who took her that first time."

He winced at the memory. "She grew thin. She drank
wine and never ate. She would get angry with me and
beat me when I begged her to stop, and then she went
out one night and never came back." He touched his
chest, where the sword tattoo crossed his heart. "Years
later, after I took in the orphans, we went to a bigger city
to look for better begging places. One night, we broke
into a church to steal bread and sleep. The priests called
soldiers to remove us. An arrow hit me in the back while
I was running away. I remember feeling death on me,
and I remember I wouldn't leave my friends. I wouldn't
leave anyone, until there was no more suffering, until

~ ☾ ~

there were no more orphans, even if it took the rest of time. I never prayed for the serenity to accept the things I couldn't change. Ever. I pushed for my family of orphans, for their grandchildren and great grandchildren, and then I moved on and pushed all over the world, life after life, until I met you and Jozey. And we know the rest."

Lena was shivering, but she didn't want to move, and she knew if she invited Chael in, he would refuse and leave. She needed to hear the rest of it.

Jozey called to her. "Weni, it's cold. Why you no shut the door?"

Lena stepped outside and closed the door. Above her, she could hear the Mexican music the Torres family listened to, but it was only a murmur. A few cars slid by on Mountain Avenue, but it was quiet. The Rosa was open, though, the bell jingling happily over the voices of a crowd down the street.

"How did you...get a body?" Lena asked. "How did you know you could cross over again?"

"My third birth?" Chael said shyly. "I didn't know I could. I saw you in trouble and knew what would happen to Jozey if you were arrested. So I stepped into the ashes and dust and had a body and clothes, right there. Courage to change the things I can. From ashes to flesh. From dust to life."

"But the wings? The sword?"

Chael nodded. "Yeah, I know. I don't understand why I have them. But I think maybe others have done what I did, and that's how we see angels, people with wings and a sword, doing God's will. If there is a God."

"Or the devil's will. When you crossed back over, Johnny Beels got the same deal, huh?"

"Yes," Chael said. "Beels saw me. He was around because of you, I think."

"Me?"

~ ☾ ~

He nodded. "Just like I was drawn to Jozey, Beels was drawn to you."

"Why?"

"I don't know." Chael reached out and held her for a moment, and she was no longer cold. "But before this ends, you'll know why. We'll all get our answers, I think."

He stepped away from her and was gone.

"I don't want answers. I want you," Lena said to the angel, lost in the cloud. She touched her forehead wearily. She had forgotten to remind him about the angel costume for Jozey.

Hungry, Lena knocked on Aunt Mercedes' door. "Auntie, I was going to get some food from Gramma Scar. Should I get you anything?"

Just the mutter of the T.V. And then a whisper from the other side of the door. "No. Take Jozey with you. I'm too tired to watch him tonight."

Lena shook her head, teeth tight. Jozey was easy. He played so well by himself. And why was her aunt tired? She didn't do anything but smoke now that she had lost her job.

But that thought made Lena relax her mouth. Her aunt had lost her job because of her. "Okay, Auntie, but can I come in?" Lena asked.

"Sure."

Lena opened the door and from her pocket held up the three hundred dollars Beels had given her. "I know with losing your job this isn't much, but maybe it's a start."

Her aunt's glazed eyes looked at the money and then closed. "No more money from you, Lena. No more. I can't bear it."

Lena laid the money on her aunt's dresser. "I know. I'm out. I'll look for a real job and things will get better."

Her aunt sighed and shook her head.

Lena couldn't take the sorrow she saw and slowly closed the door. She found Jozey in their room playing

~ ☾ ~

and made herself smile at him. "Wanna go to the Rosa?"

"The Rosa! Yeah, Gramma Scar!"

Walking through the cloud, carrying Jozey, Lena found the little restaurant packed with people, which was good. Since it was the last night it would be open.

~ ☾ ~

ix
(untouchables at la rosa calda)

Lena read the sign drawn hurriedly in magic marker announcing Gramma Scar was going out of business. Everything half-priced 'til the fridge was empty.

"What's it say, Weni?"

She had to swallow hard several times in order to answer. "Gramma Scar is going away."

Jozey sighed like he was an old man. "Everybody always goes away always."

"It sure feels like that sometimes." Jerking open the door, Lena crowded herself into the restaurant. It was packed. Gramma Scar was slinging food with Santiago and his mother helping.

When she saw Lena and Jozey, Gramma Scar marched over in her "If you loved me you would eat more" apron. She squeezed them until Jozey cried out.

"I'm so glad you came," Gramma Scar shouted above the noise. "I kept asking Santiago to call you, but we've been so busy. The only other time I cooked this much was for my fifth wedding. That was Phil. He died of natural causes. It was true love. Fifth time is a charm. What can I make you? Name it and it's yours. It's all going tonight. I'll stuff you, your aunt, Jozey. You'll never need to eat again!"

Santiago started to sing Bertoglio but his mother slapped him. "Quit singing, dammit!"

Gramma Scar threw up her hands and yelled at her daughter-in-law. "Theresa, let the boy sing! Tonight is a party!"

Lena hugged the old woman. "I'm so sorry you have to

~ ☾ ~

close. I'm so, so sorry."

"Oh, my precious beauty, such is life. We'll move to Denver, and I'll find some sort of job. I have a third cousin who runs a nice deli in Wheat Ridge, and he'll give me work. But tonight let's eat. Let's be happy right now."

Lena glanced around. To her surprise, the Untouchables were there, Remy, Tabitha and Paulie. Tabitha caught her looking but glanced away. As did Lena. Which was silly, but why would they want her to sit with them? They had eaten lunch together once. That didn't make them friends.

"I'll make you the stuffed manicotti! I know how you love it," Gramma Scar shouted and then she was back in the kitchen, yelling and cooking and laughing.

There was no place for Lena to sit. Bill Cutler, Rob's father, pushed into her and muttered a very unsorry sorry. Like father, like son.

"Hey, Lena, don't just stand there! Come and sit with us!" Paulie yelled.

She maneuvered Jozey through the crowd and found a place to sit next to Tabitha on the edge, Jozey on her lap. Santiago brought over paper and crayons, and Jozey got busy coloring.

"So, Lena, what's up?" Paulie asked.

"Oh, nothing," she said, only she had just saved Bramage's little cousin from being murdered by his sister. No big deal. Just another day in the drama.

Santiago slid a plate of rigatoni and meatballs in front of Remy who dug right in. He was a boy who could eat. In seconds, half his plate was gone. Santiago disappeared back into the kitchen, singing, until his mother yelled at him again, and his grandmother yelled back.

None of the Untouchables said anything. It was just as awkward as Lena had feared.

Tabitha's hand inched over and touched a purple

~ ☾ ~

crayon, then withdrew. Jozey watched her carefully. Again, Tabitha's fingers moved over the table.

Jozey giggled. "You can help color."

"Did you know with purple crayons you can draw anything and it will come to life?" Tabitha asked quietly.

"Your name has to be Harold though," Paulie said. "Is your name Harold?"

"My name's Jozey. I'm Lena's brother."

"You like football?" Remy asked.

"I love the Broncos," Jozey said, "and my dad loves them, too."

"Of course. Is there any other team?"

Paulie cut him off. "No football. You and Santiago nearly killed us with football speak earlier today. You watch football, Lena?"

She shook her head.

"Good. So no football talk," Paulie said. "We were surprised to see you here, Lena. Are you a La Rosa Calda freak?"

"I guess," she said.

"Best food around is right in that kitchen," Remy said. "I guess we'll have to start eating more at the Perkins down the highway."

Paulie leaned back his head. "Pukins. Ugh. It won't be the same, man. Gramma Scar has a gift."

Santiago came up and gave Tabitha and Paulie their food, then disappeared back into the crowd.

In the pause of conversation, Lena couldn't stop herself from asking, "Paulie, we would see you sitting by yourself, talking and laughing like you were crazy. What was that all about?"

"Was that when you were slumming with the Paladins?" he asked.

Lena nodded.

Paulie laughed. "Well, Lena. Here's the thing. As you well know, since you're friends with the ice queen, I got

~ ☾ ~

branded with a nickname, which the ice queen gave me. My chances of any real happiness at Avalon High School are nil, but that doesn't matter because this is all temporary. It's four frakkin' years of my life, then I'll get to leave and this will all have been just an unpleasant dream. I'll never have to be Pockets again."

"You were weird," Tabitha said. "Which is why I never sat with you. What were you doing talking to yourself?"

"Were weird?" Paulie asked. "I am weird. Okay, so I knew you all were laughing and talking about me. So one day, I decided I was going to laugh and talk about you right back. Who cares I was alone? I'm a funny guy. I like my jokes. Since Avalon High School life doesn't matter, I was going to really give you all something to talk about."

Remy laughed. "That's funny. That's cool."

Paulie saluted him with his fork. "Thank you. Don't get me wrong, being alone all the time sucked, but one day, I just said frak it."

"What's that word?" Lena asked. "I don't want Jozey saying it."

"It's from *Battlestar Galactica*," Tabitha said.

"Best show ever!" Paulie yelled.

"Best show ever," Remy agreed.

Santiago danced the stuffed manicotti over to Lena along with a plate of Jozey's favorite, old-fashioned spaghetti and meatballs with garlic bread.

"*Bon appetit, mia bella,*" he sang before vanishing into the crowd again.

"Since we're asking questions," Tabitha said, "what happened with you and the Paladins, Remy? How come you started sitting with us?"

Remy leaned back. His mound of food was gone and he was smiling. "Got tired of Cutler. Got tired of not being able to say what I wanted. And when they cut football, I got tired of life. I was like Paulie. I knew I would leave eventually, so who I sat with, what I said,

~ ☾ ~

didn't matter. With the Untouchables, I don't have to act a certain way. I can just be me. And Paulie is funny. And Tabitha is deep. And *Battlestar Galactica* is the best show ever. I couldn't talk Battlestar with the Paladins."

Lena knew about the landmine conversations with the popular crowd. Every word had to be so carefully chosen.

Remy went on. "But really, I wouldn't have given Paulie or Tabitha a chance if it hadn't been for Chael."

"To Chael!" Paulie said, raising his glass.

"To Chael," Tabitha echoed.

They toasted Chael, talked, ate, and watched as the Rosa filled and emptied, filled and emptied, like breathing, until Jozey was yawning and it was time to go.

"Thanks for letting me sit with you," Lena said finally.

Paulie laughed. "Next stop, Twilight Zone. Lena Marquez sits with us, and then thanks us. We all knew you were different, but I never, ever would've thought you would be cool."

Lena blushed. "I'm not cool. I'm just me."

"Which is why I'm an Untouchable," Remy said. "I can be just me."

Santiago waved as he washed dishes, and Gramma Scar gave her a last hug and kiss. "Oh, my precious beauty. I'm so glad you could say goodbye to the old girl. I'll still be around for awhile, so visit me, okay?"

Lena nodded.

She was getting Jozey ready for bed when the doorbell rang.

Chael was there, holding a pair of plastic angel wings, a halo, and a robe. And a little plastic sword in a gold-painted scabbard. "Happy Halloween," he said.

~ ☽ ~

X
(together, alone)

Lena grabbed Chael, kissed him, and led him back into the basement apartment where Jozey exploded with happiness and excitement. After putting on the costume and battling all the hosts of hell, it took another half an hour of books to calm him down. Chael sat on the mattress and read in an even, lovely voice as Jozey's eyes lowered, then closed, and all the while Lena cleaned and organized the chaos of the room, embarrassed but buzzing inside at what might happen next.

She found Jozey's old baby monitor, plugged in the base, and tested the receiver. It still worked.

Chael rose from the bed and went to Lena. "He's asleep."

Lena was breathless, but life was too short not to say exactly what she wanted. "I want us to be together."

Chael touched her face with a shaky, scalding hand. "I know," he said smiling shyly. "It's part of the reason I came back." He stooped and picked up an old quilt from the bed, took her hand, and led her out the front door.

"Where can we go?" Lena asked. She held up the baby monitor for him to see. "I'm not sure how far this will work."

Chael pulled off the white hoodie and his t-shirt, but Lena stopped him. "I want to see," she said and turned him around.

She watched as the tattoo ink of the wings on his back grew more distinct and then feather by feather, they pulled from his skin, becoming larger, until he was standing in front of her, a boy with wings.

~ ☾ ~

"God, that's amazing," she whispered.

He took her in his arms and the cold was gone. Then they were flying, but they didn't go far, only up to the roof of the Torres' house. Next to the warm chimney, on a slope of shingles littered with the debris from autumn, Lena found herself wrapped in the quilt, touching Chael, lost in a kiss that melted every part of her into honey.

He was tentative at first, and Lena had the idea this was his first time, ever, but she shushed him when he went to speak and slowly drew her hand across the fire in his skin, feeling the hard life in every muscle. She should have been freezing, but being so close to Chael, she was sweating as much as he was. His smell, her smell, mingled across their slick skin, and she ached to have him touch her everywhere with his burning hands. She kissed him harder, tasting his mouth as he tasted hers, with their hands in each others hair, warm and wet between their fingers. Minutes melted away, meaningless, as they touched, kissed, and built a heaven for themselves in the clouds.

After the fire, he held her, and she never wanted to leave his arms because they were strong, certain, and just. But the time came for him to leave. She could feel it. Wordless, he flew her to her door, kissed her a last time, and flew off into the night.

He was going to search the school some more, probably sleep in the basement, an exile from the outside of things, an angel with black wings and a black sword tattooed on his skin. Given to him by a God he didn't believe in.

At peace with the universe, Lena took a long shower and slowly washed the wounds on her left arm where she had hurt herself. The girl who had done that seemed to be long dead, and Lena was glad. Let her rest in peace. Clean, she slipped into bed next to Jozey, missing her angel.

~ ☾ ~

She was nearly asleep when her cell phone buzzed. It was a text message from Deirdre. *Beels turned in Dad, not Chael. Mtg Beels at school. He's gonna pay.*

~ ☾ ~

xi
(gathering santiago)

Lena blinked at the words on the phone. They seemed to grow bigger, more evil. Deirdre would be walking into the lair of a demon with no idea of the danger. Rex, his men, his dogs, would be there waiting for her.

Lena dialed Deirdre, but the phone just rang until the voicemail prompt came on. She left a short, panicked message. "Don't go after Beels. Call me."

Cell phones in the Rockies were iffy. But Avalon had coverage. Maybe Deirdre was coming in from Leadville?

Lena found Lancing's number in her phone's history. At least he could get them for trespassing. But no, supposedly they were doing some sort of construction work. Lancing wouldn't help. He loved Johnny Beels too much.

Instead of the police, she called Santiago.

He answered right away. "Lena, you call to save me? Being clean on a Friday night feels like I'm walking upside-down on Mars. I was just thinking I probably shouldn't have broken up with you until after I went into treatment." His words rambled on and on.

She cut him off. "Deirdre's gone to get even with Johnny Beels at the school. They'll kill her, or worse. We've got to do something."

"Have you talked to Chael?" Santiago asked, serious now.

"I don't know how to get a hold of him, but he'll probably be at the school. He'll need our help."

After a long pause, Santiago said, "God, forgive me for what I'm about to say, but what about Lancing?"

~ ☾ ~

She explained why that wouldn't work.

"I'll pick you up," he said. "I know this is crazy, but do you think the Untouchables would help us?"

"To help Deirdre? No way," she said, but still had to ask the question. "Do you have their phone numbers?"

"Yeah, Lena, weird enough, I do. I'll come and pick you up. Maybe if things turn south, we'll call them."

Lena clicked off the phone and found Jozey staring at her, wide awake.

"Why aren't you sleeping?" she asked.

He shrugged.

"Look, Jozey, I have to go out tonight, but Aunt Mercedes will be here, okay?"

He wrestled up and kissed her softly. "Sure, Weni. It's okay. Chael loves you."

She cocked her head. "What's that?"

"Chael loves you. And you love Chael."

"I guess I do love him." The memories of his words and their time up on the roof in the clouds made her feel weepy.

"Then it's okay," Jozey said. Like love was ever enough.

Lena ran and knocked on her aunt's door. Aunt Mercedes came out slowly, a snail from her shell. Inside the shell, the T.V. was on, but the sound was turned off.

"Deirdre might be in trouble at school," Lena said. "Could you watch Jozey?"

Her aunt nodded.

"I'll be back as soon as I can. Or I'll call."

Another nod. Eyes distant.

"Are you okay?" Lena asked.

"I was sleeping, maybe. I was dreaming. There was an angel flying over Avalon. And then he turned into snow. Lots of snow. It fell all around, and I was so happy."

There were tears in her aunt's eyes. It was the first time Lena saw anything other than darkness inside

~ ☾ ~

there. It scared her, how broken her aunt was, how crushed by sorrow.

A knock on the front door. Santiago.

"I have to go," Lena said quickly.

She stopped to blow a kiss to Jozey on their bed, a little boy lost in the laundry.

His voice was quiet. "Bye, Weni. I love you. I miss you."

No time to ask what he meant, but the words would haunt her later. The door closed like a prison cell slamming shut.

~ ☾ ~

xii
(saving deirdre)

Santiago's Ford Explorer was from the 80's and the heater had stopped working around that time. Inside was a landfill. He drove it in a full coat, hat, and gloves. Had to.

But Lena's eyes somehow made out a duffle bag under the garbage and blankets. "What's that?" she asked.

Santiago shrugged. "Lots and lots and lots of drugs. Beels called right after you did. He said if I gave him everything, he'd let Deirdre go without messing with her."

Up until then, the adrenaline and fear inside Lena had been a hot water feeling, like her insides were boiling under her skin. But now a dread hardened everything into rusted iron. Something wasn't right.

"But if we are bringing him drugs, it means we can't call Lancing."

"Yeah." Santiago wasn't singing.

"I have a key to the back door," Lena said. "We can go in and just look around. If we get into trouble, we'll call Lancing. Did you bring your gun?"

Santiago closed one eye in a wince. "Sorry. My lawyer told me to get rid of Roscoe."

"This is bad," she whispered.

"It ain't good," he agreed.

It only took a few minutes to get to the school. The building rose up into the clouds like a castle, daring them to lay siege to it.

"Chael will be in the basement I bet," she said. "He'll help us."

~ ☾ ~

"Chael is cool," Santiago said, "but with four guys and Beels, what's he going to do?"

Lena got out of the vehicle before she said something about Chael's powers. He hadn't told her not to say anything, but it still felt like a secret best kept. And who would believe her?

Santiago ran after her with the duffle bag on his shoulder. Their breath puffed out like they were smoking. They made it into the dumpster smell by the back doors, and Lena grimaced against it. It was all too familiar.

"Okay, we'll go the back way to the third floor," she said. "I'm getting used to going that way."

He nodded. "Right, room seven, Beels said."

"Should have been room six-six-six," she whispered and slid the demon's key into the lock. She opened the door and stepped into the arms of the dog men. Rex flung Santiago to the floor and kicked him in the ribs. When he tried to get up, Rex kicked him in the face.

Then Rex turned on her, bristling with teeth and laughter. "Johnny Beels sure has your number."

"Where's Deirdre?" Lena asked in a quaking voice.

"Oh, you mean the bait? Well, Beels got her cell phone, but she's still in Leadville with her daddy. Probably be there all weekend, which means Dodson'll miss the big deal he's been brokering. But tonight, this party was just for you. You want for us to get the dogs so they can watch?"

Santiago tried to get up but was kicked down again.

"I bet there's medication for this dog thing you have." Lena laughed jaggedly. She couldn't run, couldn't fight them, but she could hurl insults.

Rex drove a fist into her stomach. She collapsed, wheezing against the pain, her lungs slamming shut.

"I love to hit girls," Rex growled. "Now, where were we? I think you was about to start barking for us."

~ ☾ ~

Lena was on all fours, trying to get a breath in. A hand grabbed her hair, mashing her face against the crotch of one of the men. Hands went to rip off her jeans.

Footsteps from the basement.

All eyes turned to see Chael stroll out into the hallway. "Oh goody," Rex rumbled, "another ass for us to kick."

Chael stormed toward them, his eyes blazing with fury and hellfire. In his fist was what looked like a sword made completely of darkness.

That darkness fell on them all, vomiting strips of impossible shadows and dim arcs of light. Rex swung wildly, then was taken to his knees, face bleeding. Another dog man fell and then all light vanished.

Lena couldn't see, but she finally gasped in a breath.

Chael's voice rang out in the pitch black hallway. "Run, Santiago! Run!"

Howls of pain and screams from the dog men, and then Chael had her in his arms. He was burning, filled with so much heat, she could smell the ends of her hair sizzle. He ran with her until the beat of his wings took them off their feet and they were flying, soaring through the halls, up staircases, past lockers and classrooms, going so fast, it felt like a dream. They dashed down steps and then past the principal's office and into the cafeteria.

Beels was on the upper Paladin tables with a lasso in his hands. He howled a yee-haw before he threw the rope. It curled around Chael's already wounded leg.

Chael yelped in pain and pushed Lena to the floor before he crashed down onto the cafeteria tables, right into the angles, wood, and unyielding metal.

Lena slid across the hardwood floor on her hands, burning her palms, bashing her knees, but she couldn't breathe to scream. Again her diaphragm spasmed uselessly.

Leaping down onto his prey, Beels tied Chael's hands

~ ☾ ~

behind his back and bound his feet. All the while, talking so quickly and happily, with such a Southern drawl, it sounded like nonsense. "Ah, Leni, y'all'er too easy. Led yer boyfriend right to me, and I betcha Santiago'll be here any minute. Hmm, hmm, hmm, Leni, you's all fear and want. I want my brother. I want my mommy. I want my daddy. I wanna be popular and pretty. You's fine eatin', Leni. Mighty fine eatin'. You an' my sister would have gotten along like a pair of lil' ol' princesses, I'll tell ya what."

Lena crawled across the floor, trying to get to Chael.

Santiago burst out from the other side, the duffle bag over his shoulder. Behind him were the dog men, bloodied, bruised, beaten. Infuriated. Before Santiago could stop, Beels tripped him. Santiago hit the tables and landed next to Chael.

The edges of Lena's vision were darkening. She could hear Beels laughing and laughing.

"Oh, just leave a lil' drugs, boys," he was saying. "Won't take much to ruin 'em both. And we got the big deal tomorrow night, yeah? Ah, tomorrow night's gonna be sweet. What does my homie say? Ah, yeah. No stone untouched. No soul unscorched. A lil' ol' apocalypse now."

She felt Rex on her, touching her everywhere. He bent down to smother her face with wet kisses and licks. His smell was rank, animal, dog.

Sirens.

Lancing.

The dog man jerked away from her. "Cops! What the hell?"

Beels giggled. "Oh, yeah, I called 'em. I mean, we was 'bout done, yeah?"

"No, you promised we could have her. What the hell?"

"Y'all 'll get it, Rexie, and won't it be sweeter for the wantin'?"

~ ☾ ~

That was Beels. That was what the demon wanted everyone to feel. Forever wanting, forever hungry, forever seeking satisfaction. And forever failing.

"Christ!" Rex yelled.

"Now, Rexie, I didn't take ya for a Christian!" Beels was still laughing, but his voice was fading into the distance.

Lena looked up. She could breathe again.

There was Lancing and two state patrol guys, eyes wide.

Beels, Chael, Rex and the dog men, all of them were gone. The duffle bag, splattered with blood, lay next to Santiago on the table, open and ransacked, but far from empty.

~ ☾ ~

xiii
(taken away)

Lena sat in Lancing's SUV screaming. "You can't take Jozey away from me! You can't do this!"

Santiago and the duffle bag of drugs were in a state trooper's car. Lancing had insisted he drive her to Leadville. But he hadn't figured she would hear his call to Child Protective Services to pick up Jozey.

Handcuffed in the back of the police car, Lena bit and hissed and yelled through the steel mesh until it felt like her lungs were bleeding.

"You can't take Jozey into foster care. He should stay with Aunt Mercedes. You can't do this. It'll kill him. It'll kill all of us. Lancing, please!"

Avalon's sheriff just kept nodding, whispering, talking more to himself than to her. "Had to do it. Your aunt wasn't right. What she had to do to her sister broke something in her. Wasn't my choice, Lena. You have to believe me. The CPS people were already checking out your case. Wasn't my choice. Terrible thing, two kids taken into foster care on the same day. Poor Maddy. She was about starved to death. What a world we live in. What a world."

Her life before, even with Jozey waking up every morning begging for their dead parents, seemed like heaven now. Chael's prophecy had come true. She was arrested for intent to sell. Jozey was taken away to foster parents in Vail. Her life had been shattered and now lay in wrecked pieces around her.

And she had let go. She hadn't tried to trick Beels and get his drug money. She had tried to do the right thing

~ ☾ ~

and save Deirdre.

Once again, life didn't care if you wanted to be good or not. It just wanted to hurt you, over and over and over, kick you down every time you tried to stand up.

Chael killed for stealing bread from a church.

Where was he? What was Beels doing to him?

She slumped down against the leather of the backseats. She could smell urine and hoped she hadn't wet herself. She hadn't. Must have been from one of the drunks Lancing hauled out of the Bearly Inn.

"Please, God. Please." But heaven was silent.

In the Leadville police station, the lights were fluorescent and buzzing, making everything glow a sickly green. Mug shots, fingerprints, an overweight woman with bags under her eyes and sighs in her heart processed Lena. With her one phone call, she dialed Aunt Mercedes in the apartment, but the phone just rang and rang. Where was she? With Jozey taken away, what would her aunt do? Lena hung up the phone. No one else to call.

She was led to her cell: a bed, a toilet, and cold cinderblock walls. The door was industrial steel with a little meshed window at the top. Lena sat on the bed and wished she had a mirror to look at her face. To see if she was still real.

All the hours spent working on her make-up felt lost to her now. She should have played more with Jozey. She should have held him more. She should have been nicer to her aunt. What Lancing had said was true. Her aunt had been broken, and Lena had hated her for it instead of trying to help. Instead of forgiving her.

"I'm sorry, Chael. You were right. You were right about everything."

She wanted to cry, but the tears were all gone. There was just stone in her heart now. It had happened. What she had wanted since her parents died had happened.

~ ☾ ~

Her chest was filled with nothing.

It felt worse than the worst pain. And Lena sought sleep to escape the empty hole inside of her. To escape the cold as the night froze solid around her.

~ ☽ ~

APOCALYPSE
SATURDAY

i
(taken back)

Lena woke to the clack of the cell door unlocking a little before five. The time Jozey usually woke up. It was too hard to be awake, and so she drifted back into sleep. For how long, she had no idea.

She smelled Gramma Scar's food before she saw the old woman, wig on, face made-up, and her colorful dress too tight.

"Oh, my precious beauty. I'm working to get you and Santiago out. Jozey is okay. He's in Vail, but he won't be there long. Don't lose hope." She set a styrofoam box on Lena's lap. Inside were eggs, sausage, hash browns, and orange slices.

"I'm not hungry," Lena whispered. Jozey would be calling for her. He had never been away from her this long. Calling for his mommy, his daddy, Weni, Weni, Weni.

Gramma Scar grasped her chin. Hard. "Now, listen. The worst has happened, and now it can only get better. Do you understand me?" The old woman's eyes were hard, anchored in the strong, stone depths within her. "Santiago isn't leaving here today, not with his rap sheet. And I talked with him. He's going to take it all on himself. So sit tight. I'll be back, and we'll go home."

The approaching guard outside cleared his throat and Gramma Scar moved away.

The food smelled too good not to try, but Lena ate only a little, each bite tasting more and more like bricks. Like Aunt Mercedes, she was broken now. She put the food aside, dropped her face into her hands and pressed

~ ☾ ~

her fingernails into her skin, not hard, but hard enough.

She thought about flying with Chael, kissing him on the rooftop, the way his wings came out of his skin, feather by feather. She thought of Jozey's last words to her before she left. She thought about her aunt, alone in her room with the T.V. on, the noise off.

More hours past, until, as if by magic, she was in Gramma Scar's car, driving back to Avalon. It was night again. Clouds, cold, and darkness. Lena sat with her forehead against the window, feeling the vibrations of the car moving but feeling nothing else.

She was still numb when Gramma Scar stopped the car and Lena saw the people standing by the door of her aunt's basement apartment.

The Untouchables. And Deirdre was with them.

~ ☾ ~

ii
(deirdre and the untouchables)

Gramma Scar's car trembled beneath Lena, but she didn't move to get out. "What are they doing here?" she asked. Dealing with Deirdre, talking to the Untouchables, it all seemed like too much of a hassle to even bother with. She wanted to crawl into her room, into her bed, and die.

Gramma Scar rubbed her back. "Oh, my precious beauty, maybe you are more loved than you know."

"But they don't know me. I don't think Deirdre even knows me."

"Lena, now is not the time to insist on being alone. You can do that later when we get Jozey back."

Lena got out, wishing she had stayed in the car as it drove off. She walked over, head down, knowing she looked horrible. Her hair was wild, and only a little bruise of make-up remained from the day before. "What are you guys doing here?" she asked.

Deirdre was as gorgeous as ever, from base to blush, every line perfect and pretty. Except her eyes were just a little swollen. "Magdalena, it's the end of the world, obviously. Why wouldn't I want to spend it with my best friend? Especially since you risked your life because you thought you could save me. Gramma Scar told me everything."

A little whisper wept inside Lena, like the sighed word from a soft song. But she crushed it, still numb from the abyss inside of her. She wasn't sure she wanted to let Deirdre into her life again. "What about you three?" she asked.

~ ☾ ~

Remy, Paulie, and Tabitha were clustered together against the house above Lena's dark apartment, eyes hidden.

Remy spoke first. "We wanted to see if you were all right. And if you knew where Chael was? Something is wrong. We can feel it."

Paulie grinned and nodded. "Chael would say we're here to push. Funny, we all had the same thought at the same time. Visit Lena and see about Chael. This is where you invite us in before I lose a toe to frostbite."

Lena shook her head. "I still don't get why you three and Deirdre..."

"Coincidence," Tabitha said.

Deirdre shrugged. "It's not like we're from different planets. We do all go to the same school."

Paulie laughed a bang of wordless sarcasm. "Lena could cross into our circle because she was already all over the place, socially speaking. But you, Deirdre, you can't just ease into our little clique because you're having issues at home."

Tabitha didn't say a word, just had her hands shoved into her coat, staring off into the distance. Remy watched Deirdre carefully. Lena knew the Paladin queen would walk away. Of course she would.

But she didn't. Deirdre's voice cracked as her eyes filled with tears. "I don't want to be a Heretic, but that's probably where I belong now. With my dad in jail, I'm not a Paladin any more. We'll probably move anyway, so I won't be around for much longer. I just want to be Lena's friend. And if you're her friends now, maybe I can sit with you."

This was the Deirdre who Lena loved, an unsure girl, desperate to fit in.

Paulie shook his head. "It really is the end of the world, isn't it? Well, I guess I can say everything I ever wanted to say to you. You're one evil, stuck-up bitch,

~ ☾ ~

Deirdre. Go back to your coffin before we break out the wooden stakes and holy water. No way can you sit with us."

Deirdre dropped her head. "I'll go." She turned and started to walk away.

"Wait." Something was moving inside Lena. Deep in the bedrock of her soul, something was shining and on fire, moving through her, waking every nerve. It was the sun on flowers. A spring rain. Snow for thirsty trees.

Beels had said it. Lena was all fear and want and despair. He'd been feeding on her from the beginning, just like he would be feeding on Paulie in his resentment and on Deirdre in her sorrow.

It was time to push. Lena knew it like she knew nothing else. It was time to starve Johnny Beels.

"She stuck by me when Parker Lee was trying to kick me out of the Paladins," Lena said. "She's been my friend my whole life. She's good. She can be bitchy, but she's good."

Deirdre stood with her back to them, her shoulders shaking.

"Let's forgive her," Tabitha said. "Let's do this really hard thing and forgive her."

"She ain't so bad," Remy joined in. "She's just got that high school princess thing going on, like in *The Breakfast Club*, but Molly Ringwald was okay. Deirdre can be okay too."

All eyes turned to Paulie. "She has to say she's sorry," he said. "I want to hear it. If she says she's sorry, I'll let her in."

Deirdre still had her back to them, motionless in her long, black wool coat, her matching black hat, and her fashionista black shoes.

She wasn't going to do it. How could she? This was Deirdre Dodson. This was the queen of the Paladins. Deirdre begging Paulie for forgiveness was impossible.

~ ☾ ~

The world wouldn't allow it. God wouldn't allow it.

Deirdre turned around, slowly. Her make-up was ruined, and where there had been a queen, now stood a simple girl. "I'm sorry, Lena, for what I said Wednesday night. I'm sorry, Paul, for starting that stupid nickname. Tabitha, I'm sorry. For everything. I'm so sorry for everything."

Lena ran to her and held her friend as they both cried.

"Yeah, end of the world," Paulie said. "If she can do that, she can sit with us. But I want to be prom king. Y'all will vote for me, yeah?"

Remy knocked him. "Shut up, Pockets."

Lena led her friends into the basement apartment and shut the door on the cold. There were dishes everywhere and the place was a mess. She should have heard Jozey running for her, but instead, it was silent.

"Let me check on my aunt," Lena said quickly. "You guys chat. Deirdre, these are the Untouchables. The Untouchables, meet Deirdre."

Deirdre raised a weak hand. "Hi, but first, let me use your bathroom. Oh my God. This has been the worst week of my life."

"I hear you," Lena said. She knocked on her aunt's door as Deirdre fled into the bathroom.

No answer from her aunt. When Lena opened the door, the room was empty. She was gone. But where? Aunt Mercedes never left.

Terror knifed through Lena. Her aunt was going to kill herself. With Jozey gone and Lena in jail, she must have given up all hope.

A knock on the front door echoed through the apartment.

"Please, God, let it be my auntie," Lena prayed.

It wasn't.

~ ☾ ~

iii
(stealing the night)

Santiago pushed past Lena, tripped down the steps, and fell into the hallway, breathing hard, covered in sweat, his face purple from last night's beating. His eyes widened when he saw Deirdre come out of the bathroom. "Deirdre. Wow. Cool. Things are just getting crazier and crazier."

"Santiago! What are you doing here?" Lena helped him into the kitchen and sat him down at the table. "Why aren't you still in jail?"

"Let's just say there are two cops probably still waiting for me to get out of the bathroom. I'm on the lam. A fugitive from the law." And then of course, Bertoglio opera. Something about criminals and roses and love.

"But why?" Lena asked.

"To rescue Chael, of course. You'll need my help. And the Paladins and the Heretics are going to rumble. And Bramage is probably trying to blow up the school. Oh yeah, and if that weren't enough, Johnny Beels has his big drug deal. If I'm going to get locked up forever, heavy on the ever and ever part, I might as well do some actual drug dealing."

"They got you on possession," Deirdre said. "They're charging my dad with everything. Racketeering, intent to sell, criminal conspiracy."

Santiago blinked at her. "Holy cow, Deirdre, is that you or that hot chick on *Law & Order*? And about your dad, I didn't know a thing about him. I just dealt with the Buena Vista guy."

She shook her head. "Doesn't matter. It's okay."

~ ☾ ~

"What are you doing with the great unwashed here?" Santiago asked.

Paulie answered for her. "Deirdre's my new BFF now. She apologized for sixteen years of torment, and we forgave her. It was epic."

"Did I ever torment you?" Santiago asked.

Paulie nodded. "Oh, yeah."

"Sorry about that. I was high. Hey, I think I might have just made an amends. Step nine done. Check." He clicked his tongue.

Paulie grimaced. "That apology sucked. Deirdre did a much better job."

Santiago was too much like his old self for Lena not to ask, "Are you high now?"

"High on life, baby. I ran here from the Bearly. Hitchhiked from Leadville. Such stories I have to tell, but seriously, we have got to get to Chael before Johnny Beels begins the slicing and the dicing." A head tilt to Remy. "You run for the endorphins? Natural high? I like it. I like it."

Remy smiled. "Nope. I run 'cause I can and nobody can catch me. You're just an addict."

Santiago bounced up, hand in the air like a deranged Boy Scout. "Guilty as charged. Now, are we going to save the day or what?"

"Oh yeah, baby," Paulie said. "Untouchables to the rescue! Okay, Beels must have grabbed Chael because he figured out Bramage's evil plan. That Chael is one prescient mofo."

"Nice word," Deirdre said quietly.

"Prescient or mofo?" Paulie asked.

Deirdre shook her head and closed her eyes.

"We laugh," Tabitha said. "It makes him feel better."

"I still have my key to the school's back door." Lena held the key up. "This time, they won't be expecting us."

"Okay, then let's try this one more time," Santiago

~ ☾ ~

said. "We can't get massacred two nights in a row, can we?"

Lena didn't answer.

"Everyone in?" Santiago asked around.

Remy nodded. "For Chael. Anything."

Paulie raised his fist. "Untouchables unite. Maybe if we save everyone's life, we'll get to sit at the Paladin tables."

Tabitha let out a long breath. "Chael told me to do things I was afraid of. This definitely qualifies. What about you, Deirdre?"

Deirdre's face was stripped of make-up and it left her pale. "Since I am prone to peer pressure, I cannot say no. And the school is a nice piece of real estate, too nice for Bramage to blow it up."

Lena drank in every face: the king of the Heretics, the queen of the Paladins, the dregs of the dregs of the outcasts. And her, Lena Marquez, all of them and none of them.

"Let's walk," she said. "The police'll be looking for Santiago and we don't want to give Johnny Beels any warning. Chael will be on the third floor, room seven. If we can get to him, he can stop the rest."

"Why do you say that?" Deirdre asked.

"Because he's an angel," Lena said simply. She got her big, black leather purse and threw things in it, and then they were out in the cold, running through the night.

~ ☾ ~

iv
(chocolate ice cream)

Again, Avalon High School loomed, black stone and dead windows lost in the clouds. Milky light glowed in the cafeteria. Movement inside. The parking lot was deserted, but the streets around the school were lined with cars not normally there.

"Is it me, or is it getting warmer?" Santiago asked.

Paulie laughed. "No, it's called adrenaline. It has an '-ine' sound, so you'll like it. Nicotine, benzedrine, adrenaline."

"On benzedrine you can do anything," Santiago said dreamily. "Benny and the Jets."

"God, you're such an addict," Paulie whispered.

"And I got the scars to prove it."

They followed Lena around to the back door by the dumpsters. She opened the door to peek inside. Just a dimly lit hallway, freshly cleaned by the smell of it. There must have been a lot of blood from the skirmish with the dog men the night before.

From the cafeteria came the murmur of a crowd: the Paladins and the Heretics about to do battle.

"Should we try and stop them?" Tabitha asked.

"No, let's get to Chael so he can help us," Lena said. "There'll be a lot of posturing before the actual fighting starts."

They fell quiet as they followed Lena up her familiar route to the third floor. The gates were locked, but the dogs were there, their eyes furious diamonds in the dark.

A bark, but only one. From her black purse, Lena tossed out frozen Gramma Scar leftovers onto the floor.

~ ☾ ~

Even when she wasn't around, Gramma Scar was helping them, once again, with her food.

The four Dobermans lapped at the icy sausages while Lena unlocked the gate with the key Beels had given her. It sprang open and the six of them started down the hallway. Tools and construction lights were littered about. The big acetylene torches had recently been used. She could feel the heat emanating from the tanks and nozzles. What had they welded? Or had they used them on Chael?

Lena and her friends approached room seven and heard voices inside. In the hallway, it was colder than it had been outside, frigid, because of Johnny Beels.

"We bust in, get Chael, and get out," Santiago whispered. "If we do it fast enough, no one will get hurt. There will be guns. Lots of 'em."

They heard a booming voice.

"That's the Buena Vista guy," Santiago said. "He'll be the huge Russian with the AK-47."

"I feel like I'm in a Martin Scorsese movie," Paulie wheezed under his breath.

"*Goodfellas*," Remy whispered, "or *The Godfather*."

"That wasn't Scorsese, that was Coppola."

"Shut the hell up," Tabitha hissed.

"On three," from Santiago.

Lena closed her eyes, praying she would live to hold Jozey and Chael again. It all came down to this.

Santiago counted down and then threw open the door.

Storming in, Lena and all of her friends stopped suddenly, paralyzed with surprise.

Chael wasn't there.

Although both fireplaces were going, an arctic chill enveloped the room. Rex and the three other dog men were beside one fireplace. On the other side of the room, a giant of a man stood, nearly seven feet tall, easily three hundred pounds, with a machine gun in his hands, the

~ ☾ ~

clip like the fang of a dragon.

Beels laughed at their shock. "Comp'ny! Leni, y'all knowed I don't like unexpected comp'ny. I likes ta want ta see people, not just see 'em." He was getting harder to understand, his words slurring into a parody of some nonsensical Southern accent no one had ever actually spoken.

The demon sat in the middle of the room, shirtless, with his feet up on a desk, eating a tub of chocolate ice cream with a salad serving spoon. He smiled at them and chocolate goo dripped from his teeth and onto his chest next to his sword tattoo. The bandage was off his ear, revealing a jagged, red wound, obviously infected.

Despite her terror, Lena took some satisfaction in that.

"Who are they?" the giant asked in a thick, Russian accent. The barrel of his gun turned toward them.

"Y'all don't pay 'em any mind. They's just here to watch."

The dog men also had guns in their hand, pistols and shotguns, all pointed at Lena and her friends.

"Sit your asses down," Rex ordered, then grinned at Lena. "Tonight. You and me. I got your boyfriend all strung up like Christ on the cross, so he won't be around to bother us no more."

Lena was trembling uncontrollably as she sat with the others against the wall, close to the door but still so far away. Her heart was grinding away in her chest, so loud she could barely think.

"Now, as I was sayin'," Beels gurgled through ice cream. "I gots the drugs, but there's a wee lil' ol' problem."

The Buena Vista giant grunted. "Always problem with you." Like Santiago had said, the Buena Vista guy was the biggest, baddest man in the room. Except for Beels.

He grinned at the Russian. "Can I get y'all some ice

~ ☾ ~

cream?"

The Buena Vista guy shook his head. "Enough of this. I give you money like you say. Now you give me drugs."

Beels licked his big spoon noisily. "Problem is, the drugs're here, but they're in lockers next to sticks of dynamite. Don't worry, the lockers ain't got no locks on 'em, so y'all can get the drugs, but no telling if you'll live to sell 'em. Or use 'em. Or stick 'em up yer butt, for all I cares."

Rex exploded. "Jesus Christ, Johnny. You don't know who you're dickin' with. I don't know why you had us weld the doors shut, but that's not going to stop his people from getting to us if we don't—"

Beel flung a spoonful of ice cream at Rex. "You'll call me Beels, Rexie, 'cause everyone else will and does, and y'all don't get to call me Johnny. Only my sister. So what's my name?"

Rex licked his lips, trembling. "Beels. Your name is Beels."

Lena saw the fear in the dog man. He knew what Beels was, could feel the evil at the core of the blond boy. Her jaws ached from clenching them.

Beels stood, strutting around in his black boots. "Good. Now, Buena Vista Guy, I want to know, how does it feel? He ain't jokin'. We welded the doors shut tight. Except for one. So yer trapped. I have yer money." He jerked his head back to a black duffle bag near more sweating tubs of ice cream. "But y'all ain't got yer drugs."

"I kill," the giant said. "I kill them, I don't get my drugs. And I pull off your fingers until you tell me which door to use to go away, then I kill you."

Lena touched Deirdre's hand and squeezed it. Both their palms were slimy with sweat.

Rex erupted. "God in heaven, Beels! Don't you care about anything?"

Beels smiled pretty, pretty. "Oh, I cares. I love what

~ ☾ ~

Buena Vista Guy is feeling right now. I cares about that, and what yer feeling, and them kids over there. Oh yeah, so much fear." He shivered. "Gives a feller goose-bumps it does." He wheeled on the giant, voice raging. "For the love of Pete, I ain't givin' you yer drugs. Why aren't you shootin' already?"

The thunder of the gunfire made Lena run. It was too loud for her to do anything else. The dog men and the Buena Vista Russian were only aiming for each other, not caring about the spectators.

Lena and her friends fled from the Armageddon in the room, past the dogs who were barking and howling over the fate of their masters, down the steps and into the cafeteria.

Cutler and the Paladins were face to face with Bruise and the Heretics, but their fight had been broken up by the hellish noise above them. Parker Lee and the Paladin girls, Emma and the Heretic girls, glanced around, faces shining with sweat.

"Where's Santiago?" Remy asked Lena.

He wasn't with them.

From the top of the Paladin section, Dane Bramage stood up on the highest table and screamed out in the panicked silence, freezing everyone in place. "No stone untouched! No soul unscorched! Apocalypse now!"

Cutler yelled at him. "What in the hell is going on?"

"Dynamite in the lockers," Deirdre shouted to the people clustered in the cafeteria. "Bramage and Beels put dynamite in empty lockers, and he's going to blow us all up. The doors are all sealed except for one—"

The people broke apart with fear, eyes wide, mouths moving, cutting Deirdre off. Lena wanted Chael there, wanted him to fly in on those dark wings and rescue them all, but she knew that wasn't going to happen. Where Chael was, he couldn't push things better.

They would have to do it themselves.

~ ☾ ~

v
(apocalypse now)

"Why are you doing this?" Lena shouted her question above the din. She and her friends stood by at the mouth of the cafeteria, afraid to move. The crowd fell quiet to hear the answer.

Bramage laughed, standing on a Paladin table, his face showing his sickness. "Lena, you know as well as I do these people are all insects. They worry about their tables, and they worry about their pathetic little lives, but none of that matters. This is the reckoning. Now they will know what's important."

"When is it all rigged to go off?" Cutler asked. His eyes had turned rabbit-scared.

Bramage held up a cell phone. "Beels helped me with that part. In each locker, there's a cell phone. I can send out one text message and all the phones will set off the dynamite. I just hit one button and it's the apocalypse. Now."

Lena's fists tightened. Out of one hell and into another.

Bruise's mouth dropped open. "You would kill me? But we're friends."

"You don't care about me." Bramage's eyes looked like they were melting inside his skull. "We just got high together. Santiago got clean, and you dropped him. You would have done the same thing to me. We ain't friends." He turned to everyone else and raised his voice. "And you all, you've known me all my life, but all you ever did was ignore me or laugh at me. You have sinned against me and against heaven. You will pay."

~ ☾ ~

"I'm going to shove that phone up your ass," Cutler howled and hurled himself forward. But Bruise stopped him.

Bramage held up the phone. "You are chaff, Cutler. You will burn."

Deirdre approached Bramage, too quick for Lena to stop her.

"You think a Deirdre apology is going to fix that psycho?" Paulie asked. "She got to me, but I have some grip on reality."

"A tentative grip," Tabitha whispered.

"Dane," Deirdre said, moving slowly. "I was the worst of them, right? The other morning, you were pointing at me, Parker Lee, all of us, but I was the worst, right?"

Bramage grinned. It looked skeletal. "Yeah, you are the worst. You come up here to beg for your life? I will hear your confession. I will shreve you before the flame comes. Perhaps, in the end, you are wheat. That would surprise me."

Deirdre was right next to him. Lena felt frozen. Deirdre had become someone else. She seemed strong now, like a serene goddess.

"I probably deserve to die," Deirdre said. "I was a bitch to you, to everyone. But what about Tabitha and Paulie? What did they ever do to you? What about Lena?"

Bramage glanced over. "They weren't supposed to be here. They aren't Paladins or Heretics."

"But they are here."

"No soul unscorched." Bramage wiped sweat from his face with a trembling hand. "I'm sorry, but I have to do it. Even if I don't, Beels will."

"When my dad got arrested, no one called me," Deirdre said. "Only Lena, and that's because she thought I was in trouble. She's a friend. The rest of them dropped me, just like you got dropped. Lena is good. Don't kill

~ ☾ ~

her."

Remy moved up to Lena. "I'm going for the phone," he whispered. "I'm going to run up there and get that phone."

"Are you sure?" Lena whispered back.

He nodded. "I'm fast. I can do it. Nothing that Deirdre is going to say is going to stop him. And we both know Chael isn't going to save the day this time."

And this was life, Lena thought. When do you push? When do you let go?

Deirdre was in front of Bramage, but Lena could still see his face. She watched as the light in Bramage's eyes went out, like a snuffed candle. "Poor, poor Deirde. You think you're like me just because you didn't get your pony? The sins of your father are being visited upon you. As it should be. You think you are like me? No one is like me."

Paulie laughed loudly. He moved up as Remy inched forward.

"Dude," Paulie called out. "You think you had it bad? My nickname is Pockets. I would trade lives with you in a minute. And yeah, honestly, I thought about going Columbine on everyone, but come on. It's like what you said. This is petty high school bullshit. We're all going to graduate, God willing, and in ten years, who is going to care what Deirdre Dodson thought of them?"

"I will take away your pain," Bramage said to Paulie.

"But I want to live," Tabitha spoke up suddenly. "Paulie wants to live. You won't be taking away our pain. You'll be taking away our chance to be happy. And this isn't about Armageddon. This is about you feeling bad. Killing us would just be selfish and stupid."

Bramage closed his eyes. "You weren't supposed to be here!"

"No soul unscorched. I'm a soul," Tabitha said.

~ ☾ ~

Remy took off. It was so sudden, so unbelievably fast, Lena thought she had imagined it. He streaked up the stairs, leapt on to a table, then on to another one, and he was just a table away when Bramage opened his eyes.

But by then, Remy dove, snatched away the cell phone, rolled across a table and dropped down to the hardwood floor, back on his feet. He held up the phone triumphantly. "Now, how could Percy drop football when I can do that?"

"Now we kick his ass," Cutler screamed.

Paulie pushed him back. "Knock it off, Rob. You really are a moron, aren't you?"

"Oh yeah. I'd say he was a special stupid kind of dumb." Beels walked into the cafeteria, still shirtless. He had his tub of ice cream clutched to him, face and chest stained with sticky chocolate. "And I gots myself a cell phone. The monkey might've gotten the phone from Bramage over there, but I can guarantee y'all that I'm a whole lot faster. And I won't be moved by no pretty words. That I can also guarantee y'all."

Bramage ran off down the hall, ripping down Halloween decorations as he went, bellowing, gnashing, frothing. But now no longer a threat.

Beels stood eating his ice cream, not saying a thing.

Cutler wiped sweat off his forehead with his arm and grinned. "He don't have a cell phone."

Paulie shook his head. "Moron."

"Y'all want to know somethin' interestin'?" Beels asked suddenly, like a clever idea had just popped into his head.

Emma and Parker Lee burst into tears. The tension had been bad with Bramage, but with Beels, it was intolerable.

"The interestin' thing is that with y'all locked in here, no one can get in to help, and no one can get out. Oh,

~ ☾ ~

what a pickle y'all are in."

"Why are you doing this?" Parker Lee shrieked the question in hysterics, echoing the question Lena had asked Bramage.

But with Beels, Lena knew the answer.

The demon took a huge bite of ice cream. "I likes to eat. That's the only reason why anyone does anythin'." He paused. "There is one door that's not welded shut, but it sure is locked. Now, we're going to play a little game. Them Untouchables, they die. Who cares about 'em, right? But now, if yer a Heretic or a Paladin, y'all have a chance. One group is gonna get out of here. Whoever gets the key first, their group gets to live, and the group that don't get the key, they's all gonna die. Then come Monday, whatever table they wants, they get. Well, won't be a table here 'cause here it's all gonna be rubble. Like what Bramage was always sayin'. Stones, souls, blah, blah, blah."

Bruise and Cutler were eyeing each other. They would go down slavering at each other's jugulars.

"One other thing," Beels said. "I took all the money from the drug deal, wow, I guess it's sittin' pert near three hundred grand, and I spread it around and put it in all them lockers, right next to the drugs and dynamite. Enough to save Gramma Scar's fry pit. Maybe even enough to seed condos to save this ol' dog-tired town."

"Where's the key?" Lena asked.

"Why, in yer very own pocket, Leni. You didn't know?"

Every eye was on her. Every hope. Every fear. They would kill each other, kill her, to get the key. There would be no mercy, no pity, and Beels would lap up every bite, every punch, every scream, every hate, every fear.

"I'll give y'all ten minutes," Beels said. "Then, boom, y'all die. Like jumpin' up and down on an anthill."

~ ☾ ~

Cutler darted forward, but Bruise pulled him down and punched him until another Paladin kicked him away. Then it was a horror as they shredded each other to get to Lena. She escaped down the hallway, Beels' key a cold lump in her pocket.

~ ☾ ~

vi
(crucified)

"Get out of my way!" It was Cutler, or Bruise, shouting at someone. Was it Remy who got in their way? Was it Paulie? Tabitha?

Footsteps behind Lena. Running up to the second floor, she sped past lockers and wondered which ones held the money. Money for Gramma Scar, but it would be impossible to get to it.

She stopped when she rounded a corner and fell against the windowed walls of the courtyard at the center of the school, the trees like supplicating hands reaching up to a closed sky.

She wasn't sure what to do. Should she go to the third floor to look for Santiago or Chael? Maybe down to the back door to make sure the key worked? It was the back door Beels had locked, that's the door Lena and her friends had used to come inside. The dog men wouldn't have had enough time to weld it shut and get back to room seven, but Beels could have locked it on his way to the cafeteria.

Something moved on the other side of the courtyard. Not something, someone. Chael. He was crucified on the windows across from her in the courtyard, hanging like Christ on the cross, exactly what Rex had said.

Lena circled around the smashed windows to get to him.

"I see her!"

She turned. Cutler was across the courtyard from her, face dribbling blood, and behind him, Bruise, the Heretics, more Paladins, and the Untouchables.

~ ☾ ~

She didn't have much time.

Chael hung by his arms on the welded hooks at the top of the window and his feet were tied to a ragged piece of metal burned and twisted. Blood ran down his dark skin from too many wounds to count.

"Chael, please, God, please."

She climbed up to him, touching his skin now so cold, whipped, slashed, riddled with glass. She thought the worst, but he turned his face to her.

"Lena. You have to leave. Dynamite in the lockers."

"How can we get you down?"

"No, Lena, you have to get out."

Cutler tore her off the window sill. "We need that key. Where is it?"

Cutler was knocked away, but Bruise was just as bad, grunting and wheezing as he scratched at her clothes. Then he, too, was battered back.

Deirdre, her face scratched, helped Lena up. Deirdre was the one who had blocked them to give Lena time to run.

Lena gave the key to her friend. "Here, take it, and get everyone out. Beels won't know. It's the back doors. You can all get out there."

Cutler saw the key in Deirdre's hand. "Paladins win! We get to live!"

"No," Deirdre whispered. "We all go. Tonight, there are no Paladins or Heretics or Untouchables. Tonight, there's just us."

Lena hugged her. Deirdre, her best, best friend.

Remy was already climbing to get to Chael. Paulie and Tabitha were working the knots to free his feet.

"Follow me," Deirdre said. "We have to get out before Beels knows what happened." There was some muttering and protests, but Deirdre was still queen of the school. "We are all leaving." And she led them away.

The Untouchables stayed behind. And Avery.

~ ☾ ~

"What are you doing?" Lena asked the basketball player.

Avery shrugged. "You guys couldn't find Santiago, and we just can't leave him here. Besides, you'll need help finding the money before Beels blows up everything." He paused. "And you heard what Deirdre said. Tonight, it's just us."

"We could use some help over here, jock boy," Paulie gasped. Between him, Avery and Remy, they eased Chael off the hooks and laid him on the floor.

"I'm thirsty," Chael whispered.

Tabitha ran to a drinking fountain and with a cupped hand, dribbled some water onto his lips. "I wish I had my water bottle."

Beels' voice thundered through the halls. "Leni! Y'all are ruinin' my game! Now, that ain't nice. Johnny Beels needs his games."

"Get out," Lena whispered to the Untouchables. "I'll stay with Chael, but you guys get out. The money isn't worth it. You'll die."

"Do what you are afraid to do," Tabitha said. "We're getting the money. Just keep Beels busy. Paulie thinks the money is in the lockers in multiples of 6."

"Lockers of the beast." Paulie's laugh came out as a frightened choke.

Then the Untouchables fled.

Chael's eyes were on Lena. "The hard part comes next. For you. Help me sit up."

Beels turned the corner, gripping a sword that gleamed as if sunshine was licking the metal. The cold light made Lena squint.

"Y'all still have the key, Leni?" Beels asked.

"Yeah, right here," she answered, tapping her empty pocket.

"Liar, liar." Beels strolled toward them, like a cat tracking prey. "Liar, liar, pants on fire." He stopped,

~ ☾ ~

grinned, his face and chest stained with chocolate ice cream. "Speakin' a hot pants, hey, Chael, I'd like to thank y'all for bringin' me in from the outside of things. Look what I did in just five days! I got Gramma Scar closed down. I got the school wired to blow. I got everyone all in such a state. Gonna head on over to Washington, D.C. and get some real eatin' done. I reckon it'll be nuclear war by Christmas if I play my cards right."

Chael crawled to his feet, wincing. Lena felt a wave of heat boil out from him. In his hands was a sword of darkness, as black and dim and hot as Beels' was cold and incandescent.

"You've done your work, Beels," the dark boy said, "and I've done mine. Remy, Tabitha and Paulie are no longer alone. Santiago has changed. Deirdre has changed. Avery right now is risking his life. And most important, Lena has let go of her grief. And that galls you the most because she was your favorite meal for a long time."

Beels chuckled. "Yeah, she was good eatin' all right, but everything else y'all talked about is only temporary. Give 'em twenty minutes and all them people you mentioned'll find new ways to torture themselves so's me and my kind can eat. Ya always gonna be on the losin' side, Chael, 'cause the world don't care a lick 'bout compassion and kindness and la, la, la love. All the world wants is ta eat. And I'm gonna gnaw on you and Leni awhile more."

The cold demon sprouted wings, sprouted claws, then dove toward them with his sword a super nova of light.

Chael didn't move. He was going to let Beels kill him.

~ ☾ ~

vii
(stones and souls)

Beels' sword stopped a kiss away from Chael's skull. The blond demon giggled. "Oh, y'all're good, Chael. Okay, I can't kill ya, so's I reckon I'll just cut off yer arms and legs, and do the same to Leni, and oh what a meal that will be."

Beels swung his sword of light, but Chael bashed it away, then swept his blade around as Beels flew back.

"I see's it. I ain't gonna kill ya, but y'all're gonna try and do me in. But then, no more a Leni's kisses."

Wings unfurled, Chael soared into Beels. The demon swung at him, but Chael turned to the side and the blade sank into the floor, biting deep into the hardwood. Beels seized Chael's wings and threw him into the wall. Chael struck the stone then hit the floor face first.

"Yer pretty badly beaten up there, boy. Y'all really think ya got a chance against me? I's was always stronger. We both knowed it, even on the outside a things."

Beels chopped at Chael's legs, but the angel rolled onto his back and sliced Beels across his stomach. Blood dripped onto the floor.

Beels howled. "Y'all're crazy! Y'all may not wanna live, but I ain't never goin' back." Beels retreated. And caught Lena's eyes. "Ya nearly gutted me, Chaely, but now I'm gonna quadriplegic yer girlfriend."

Beels flung his sword, but Lena leapt away. It struck where she had been seconds before, blade first, the handle quivering.

Blurred by heat, Chael soared through the hall. Lena

~ ☾ ~

felt the hot wind hit her and then Chael smashed into Beels. The demon latched onto the angel's sword hand as they both struggled for the weapon.

"Why y'all fightin' so hard to kill us? Oh, I's see's it. Lena didn't put out none, so ya gotta stay 'round to get a lil' from her. Funny, with me, she was dyin' for it."

Chael's face was grim. His teeth clenched.

Beels spun and threw Chael to the floor. In the demon's hand was the sword of darkness. "Ya know what yer problem is, angel boy? Y'all want the world to be a kiddie's playground. Ain't never gonna be. When I came out of the trash dump, I took a breath and I loved the stink. But not y'all. Y'all pro'lly thought to kill yerself to get rid of me but were too chicken to do it. And that tortured ya. Hmm, hmm, fallen angels is always such good eatin'."

Beels dropped down, sword first, but Chael darted up and rammed Beels into the ceiling, smashing him into the drywall and insulation, wedging him between the studs.

The sword of darkness dropped to the ground. Chael snatched it up to stab Beels, but the demon flew away and retrieved his own glowing sword.

Lena could see ice in the drywall from Beels' skin.

Sword in one hand, Beels held up a cell phone in the other. "Now, how's 'bout some more fun? Right now them Untouchables are tryin' to get the money, so I won't blow up all my pretty bombs at once. I'll just do one. A little Russian roulette, Avalon High School style. Maybe I'll get lucky and get the fatty. Well, now, that brings up a question. Who's worth more points? The druggy, the jocky, the fatty, the darkie, or the nerdy?"

"No!" Lena and Chael cried out at the same time.

Beels pressed the button. A locker down the hall exploded into a cloud of debris, dust, and shrapnel. Lena couldn't breathe through the detritus.

~ ☾ ~

"Dang it all!" Beels yelled, lost in the fog of concrete dust. "I get another chance. No fair blowin' one when I knowed I's didn't score no points."

Another explosion, distantly.

"There we go!" the demon yowled. "I's wonder which one I killed that time? Let's do another one."

The building shook from another blast. From the mist of destruction came the squeal of steel on steel, but Lena couldn't see a thing through the boiling clouds of dust. Glass breaking, more clangs, and then silence. Beels and Chael had taken their fight outside, into the air of the courtyard, probably heading for the roof.

Lena kept low, trying to breathe, running for the third floor and roof access, knowing what she had to do.

Afraid of the impossible thing she had to do.

~ ☾ ~

viii
(sissy)

In the third floor hallway, only one of the Dobermans had remained behind, and he looked at Lena with soft, whipped eyes. Lena bent and scratched the short fur on his head. "It's okay, boy, but you better get out of here. It's not safe."

The last dog clicked away down the steps and disappeared.

Lena hurried past room seven, but couldn't stop herself from looking inside. The smell of the gunfire lingered over the bloody corpses and empty shell casings scattered on the floor to mix with the melt of Johnny Beels' ice cream. Rex and the dog men were dead, as was the Buena Vista Russian. The black duffle bag of money and Santiago were nowhere to be seen.

But Santiago was still alive. Beels in his ranting had mentioned the druggy, and he must have meant Santiago, going from locker to locker, searching for the money.

Turning a corner, Lena found where the other bomb had gone off. She crept through the mist of rock dust and over the debris littering the floor. She had to maneuver around a twist of destroyed locker doors to get to the other side. The sound of sirens spun out distantly.

But right next to her, Beels, saying her name. "Leni."

She froze.

"Chael went down hard. Only took a minute for me to cut off his hands and feet. That took the fight right out of him, I'll tell ya what."

Her soul shrank. She crouched low. Fear trampled her

~ ☾ ~

heart.

He was lying. He had to be.

"Yeah, poor Chael. I kinda liked him. But I liked y'all more."

His footsteps crunched on the floor, coming closer. If she ran, Beels would hear her for sure, hear her and catch her.

"Ah, Leni, know why I liked y'all? It's 'cause you reminded me of my sister. It was Louisiana, but it might not have been called that back then, ya know. It was a long time ago. Daddy drank. Mommy ran 'round. Left me alone with Sissy."

Lena closed her eyes. All the things Chael and Beels had been talking about during their battle raged through her mind. The rules of the game they were playing.

"Sissy was real nice to me fer a while. Just like y'all were nice to Jozey. That's why I came to ya 'cause a young girl is full of desire. And it wasn't no thang for me to guide ya to Santiago. Wasn't no thang for me to get y'all runnin' red purses for him. For y'all to hate him, hate yerself, hate everybody. Just like Sissy. And in time, y'all'd have started doin' them drugs, just like Sissy drank. And then the real feedin' coulda started."

Lena stood up. She was going to leap on Beels, get his sword, and kill him with it.

"I's just a little boy back then, and Daddy gone, and Momma gone, and even Sissy gone. What's left but eatin'? Nothin'. So I ate up everything I could when I's was alive, and when I got dead? I didn't want no heaven. I wanted to keep on eatin'. And I did. It never fills me up, not like it should, but it's better than anything else I ever did find. The wantin' is a wonderful, terrible thing. And I's want everyone to feel the exact same thing I've felt fer hundreds and hundreds of years."

The mist of dust drifted away, suddenly dispersed by the wind. Beels appeared right in front of her. His sword

~ ☾ ~

was stained with blood. He grinned, held up the cell phone, and pushed another button. This time, no explosion.

He frowned. "Theys must be disconnectin' the bombs. The geek pro'lly knows how to do it, but ah well, now we can talk more, Leni, and I can give ya a kiss. It's gonna be cold. Let me warn y'all right now. My kiss is gonna be real, real cold."

Suddenly, there was a swoosh, the sound of Chael in flight, and Lena felt his heat. He latched onto Beels and dragged him up into the sky.

She scrambled after the pair, climbing up crumbling rock to the roof. Among the exhaust pipes and rooftop machinery, she found them once more hacking and slashing at one another.

But Lena could see them. The clouds were being pushed away by a fierce, warm wind to reveal stars twinkling in the swirling sky.

And she could smell snow.

Chael had been cut, bad, across the chest and leg. He limped, but still he fought, until Beels struck him in the face with the flat of the glowing blade.

The dark boy hit the roof and his shadow sword clattered away from his grip. He was too damaged to keep fighting.

Chael, on his knees, put up an arm to stop the next blow. Beels chopped it off at the elbow.

The screams of the angel matched the sound of the sirens coming. But they would get there too late.

~ ☾ ~

ix
(snowfall)

Lena picked up the sword of shadows. It was warm in her hand as she swept it through the air, as the darkness swirled around her.

Beels chuckled as he fiddled with the cell phone, but there were no more explosions, just the sigh of the wind blowing against them. He tossed the phone away.

"Them Untouchables ruined my bomb game, dang it all. But now you and I can dance, Leni." He did a little jig toward her. "Y'all got fight in ya, Leni. I like that. Y'all woulda lasted longer than Sissy, I reckon. Poor, poor Jozey. He's gone now. Aunt Mercedes is dead. With the dynamite that did go off, I pro'lly killed at least a few of yer Untouchable friends. And y'all think Deirdre is gonna stick around here with her dad locked up? Y'all're alone, Leni. More alone than ever."

Beels' sword shown like a spotlight on top of the castle of Avalon High School making his face a grotesque mask in the light. A demon's leering face.

Chael somehow got to his feet, swaying, clutching his wounded arm to his chest. Lena stood between them, sword in hand.

"Come on, girl. I'll send ya to yer parents. No way y'all can beat me."

Lena felt herself let go. She let go of her parents, of Jozey, of her aunt, the Untouchables, Deirdre. She turned and smiled sadly at Chael. She let go of him. And tears dropped from her eyes.

Sometimes life was pushing. Sometimes life was letting go. And sometimes it was both at once.

~ ☾ ~

It took two steps to get to him. Her face pulled back in grief as she took Chael's sword and slid it home into the dark boy's chest, piercing his heart.

"What are you doing?" Beels screeched. "What in the devil are you doing?"

With his one arm, Chael pulled her close. He was hot as ever, and Lena collapsed into his heat, weeping.

"You did it," Chael whispered. "Look."

Through the blur of tears, she saw Beels take a step toward them. His sword dropped to the ground and shattered into dented, stained license plates and broken computer hard drives. His hand fell to the roof, changing into coffee grounds and used up coffee filters.

"Aw hell no! Johnny Beels can't go out like—" His face melted into curled up orange peels and brown, slick, moldy banana peels, half eaten oatmeal, green lunch meat, fast food wrappers. And little by little, Johnny Beels turned back into the trash heap he had crawled out of.

Chael fell to his knees, and Lena fell with him.

He touched her face. "I'm sorry for making you kill me. He was right, I was too afraid to kill myself."

She shook her head at his words, crying, wanting him to stay. Wanting.

His voice was soft. "I understand now. I see now, like never before." Tears were on his bruised, bloody face. "I wanted a perfect world for you and Jozey. For everyone. I wanted to take away everyone's pain, but this world, this life, all of our lives, it's a struggle and it's meant to be a struggle. If there is a God, He is in the struggle. I see that now, and now I can let go and let the world be as crippled and beautiful as it is. I can let the world be. I can move on."

"Please," Lena whispered. "Don't go." She said the words, but it was she who had killed him.

"Kiss me, Lena," he murmured with a ragged breath.

~ ☾ ~

"Kiss me and send me away."

She pressed her body against his. She pressed her lips against his. There was heat for a moment, then cold, and then he fell from her embrace.

Something brushed her cheek. Like an angel's feather. The world all around her had become feathers, fat, soft, feathers.

Not feathers. Snowflakes.

It was snowing huge, round, dancing snowflakes.

Lena glanced down. There was just highway road dirt and pebbles where Chael had been. He had come out of the ashes to save her, and now he was gone.

Dust to dust.

~ ☾ ~

x
(untouchables on the roof)

A door clicked open and Lena expected to see Art Lancing and the state troopers come busting through.

Instead, Deirdre Dodson ran to her. She had escaped the inferno but had stepped back into hell to find her friend. Deirdre crouched and held Lena as they both wept.

Another swing of the door and the Untouchables and Avery crept out onto the roof in the middle of the snowstorm. Hushed, even Paulie was silent, the four moved carefully around the trash heap that had been Beels and drew together around Lena next to the pile of highway dust.

"Where's Chael?" Remy asked.

Lena put out a bloody, dusty hand and watched as snowflakes collected on her open palm. "He became the snow."

"Where's Santiago?" Deirdre asked.

Before anyone could answer, Lena heard the singing. It was far away and growing more distant. Santiago singing Amazing Grace in his fullest, most wonderful voice.

She looked and saw tears in everyone's eyes.

They had all been, in one way or another, wretches, and they had been saved. The demons would go hungry that night. And maybe for many nights to come.

"We didn't get the money," Tabitha said. "We found the dynamite and drugs and Paulie knew how to unclip the wires to dismantle the bombs, so they didn't all go off, but no money. We think maybe Beels lied about the

~ ☾ ~

whole thing."

"He would do that to eat," Lena said.

"Come on, girlfriend," Deirdre said, lifting her up. "Let's get out of the cold. You can stay with me tonight."

"I have to find Aunt Mercedes," Lena said. "I have something I need to tell her."

Then the police came through the door. Art Lancing led the way, huffing and red-faced from running through the halls. When he saw them, he lost all sense of caution and hugged them all, hugging Lena the longest.

"Thank God you're all alive. Thank God. Thank God. Thank God."

Lena hugged the sheriff back. "Yeah. Thank God." She said the words, but in her heart, she thanked Chael. And she would continue to thank him as the night wore on.

~ ☾ ~

HOLY SUNDAY

i
(the drive to vail)

Through all the questions, Lena and Deirdre held hands at the little police station on Mountain Avenue where Lancing had his little office. Questions and more questions.

Had they seen Santiago?

Where were Bramage, Beels and Chael?

What happened?

Whose idea was it to blow up the school?

And when everyone said it was Beels, over and over, and that Bramage was just his lackey, Lancing sighed like a punctured tire. "Dang, I ain't never been so wrong and dumb in all my life. And I'm not a young man no more."

Lena didn't want to try and explain Chael and Beels to Lancing, not what they really were. She said, like Bramage, they had run off into the night, to take their fight somewhere else. If Chael had let go to find heaven, then her story was a total and complete lie. Otherwise, it might very well have been the truth.

The parents showed up to take their children home, Remy's dad, Tabitha's mom, Paulie's parents, Avery's parents. Lena hugged each of them and thanked them.

"Ain't nothin'," Paulie said. "You guys party like that every Saturday? If so, let me just say right now, I'm in."

Tabitha spoke up right away. "Oh, hell yeah. Me, too."

"You guys are crazy," Remy said shaking his head. "Lena, I'm busy next time. I have to re-arrange my sock drawer."

And then the Untouchables were taken out into the

~ ☾ ~

storm with their parents. Blinding snow slashed down, but no one was going to complain. It had started after the trick-or-treating, and it promised to be three feet at least.

No one was coming for Lena or Deirdre. Mr. Dodson was still in custody and Deirdre's mother was on a plane or in an airport somewhere, trying to get home.

"I need to find my aunt," Lena said. "She wasn't at the apartment, and I'm worried about her."

Lancing protested. "I can't just let you leave without your guardian saying it's okay. It wouldn't be right. And as far as your aunt is concerned, she'll turn up."

"You owe me, Lancing," Lena said. "Just let us go."

The sheriff sighed again. "You've been a step ahead of me all along, so we might as well keep it that way. You're both free to go."

Deirdre and Lena hurried through the blizzard to Lena's apartment, but it was still empty. In her aunt's bedroom, however, next to the silent T.V., Lena found an address in Vail hastily scribbled on a scrap of paper.

"The foster parents in Vail," Lena said her thoughts out loud. "Gramma Scar mentioned something about that. Auntie is going to get Jozey."

Thinking of Jozey made her arms ache to hold him.

Deirdre was already mapquesting it on her phone. "I certainly won't be able to dissuade you from your latest venture into insanity, but I'll come along. However, you shall do the driving." Deirdre smiled at her. "You're used to being sleep deprived, whereas I need my beauty sleep to function."

"But I need to change first." Lena's clothes were ruined, covered with the dust from the school and the blood from Chael's damaged body. She threw on some baggy jeans and one of her mother's sweatshirts and then they were out the door.

Deidre had a four-wheel drive Lexus, and with Lena

~ ☾ ~

behind the wheel, they drove into the storm. Blinded by the ferocity of the blizzard, the two didn't talk as they fought their way through the banking snow, windshield wipers struggling to keep the glass clear.

"Aren't you going to sleep?" Lena asked.

Deirdre clicked her nails together nervously. "Too scared to sleep."

Highway 91 had been plowed, but the snow was falling fast enough that it didn't make much of a difference.

"Are you ever going to tell me what happened with Chael?" Deirdre asked. "I mean, Chael, Beels, that whole thing. They weren't just new boys, were they?"

Lena shook her head. "No. Not just boys. But sure, D, I'll tell you the whole story. You won't believe me, but I'll tell you."

"Not now," Deirdre said, gripping the handle of her door with white knuckles. "You need to focus your attentions on the road."

It took hours to get to I-70. By that time, the sun was coming up, but it was just a smudged glow, lost in the snow.

Deirdre turned on the radio. The Eisenhower Tunnel was closed and there were too many travel advisories to count. Emergency travel only.

"Well, good, because this is an emergency," Lena mumbled.

Another hour over Vail pass and Lena drove by Braille. When she crunched into a snow bank, she would ease the Lexus back onto the highway. The gas gauge dipped into empty.

"We might be walking," Lena said. "Almost out of gas."

Deidre sighed when the fuel light went on. "We need a miracle."

"Or an angel," Lena said. And there must have been one pushing because the Lexus drove into Vail on fumes,

~ ☽ ~

right to a nice little house in a small neighborhood where all of the Halloween decorations were hidden away with snow. Lena thought of the angel costume for Jozey, left unused back in the apartment.

"Next year," she whispered the promise, then saw Aunt Mercedes sitting in her car, wrapped in blankets.

~ ☾ ~

ii
(family)

Lena left Deirdre in the Lexus and trudged through the knee-deep snow to get to Aunt Mercedes. When Lena knocked softly on the window of the passenger side, her aunt looked up with the eyes of a ghost, then unlocked the car.

Once inside, Lena spoke first. "I'm so sorry, Auntie." Her eyes filled with tears because her heart wasn't mud, wasn't stone, wasn't empty. It was full and beating, strong and alive.

"For what?" Mercedes asked in a quiet, nothing voice.

Lena took her aunt's cold hand in hers. "You asked me what we should have done at the hospital with my mom. I didn't say anything. You had to make the choice alone. I'm so sorry. I know how it feels now. I know how it feels to let go of someone even when you have to push them away."

"I never let go," Mercedes whispered. And her voice was thick as tears spilled down her swollen cheeks. "I killed your mother, but I never let go."

Lena moved over the emergency break to hold her aunt. "It's time then. It's time for us both to let go."

For the first time, Lena and Aunt Mercedes grieved together over their time at the hospital, for a mother, for a sister, for letting go.

"Jozey is in there," Mercedes finally said. "I've been here all night. I'm too afraid to go in. It's illegal for me to even be here."

"How did you find him?" Lena asked.

Mercedes smiled, a little smile, and with tears on her

~ ☾ ~

face, she looked wonderfully alive. "Good luck keeping secrets in a small town. And you gotta love Lancing, but he's not much of a policeman."

"Let's go in and see him," Lena said. "It will be okay. I know it will be."

"But it's against the law," Mercedes said.

Lena laughed. "I'm used to breaking laws, and some laws need to be broken. Come on."

The two climbed through the snow to the door and rang the bell. Two jack-o-lanterns grinned at them through masks of snow.

When the door opened, it was Jozey, two black feathers in his hands and a smile on his face. "Auntie! Weni! Chael said you would come. He gave me feathers and said he loved me and said God loved me, and the foster people are okay, but you're more okay."

Jozey gave Lena a feather as she took him in her arms, as Aunt Mercedes held them both. Lena relaxed into the tangle of embraces, closing her eyes. She had a family again.

They had to leave Jozey, but they all knew he would be with the foster people for only a short time. Deirdre paid for the motel in Vail with a credit card, and the three shared a room as Lena told them the story, petting the black feather from Chael.

Monday they drove home and Lena found Santiago's gift. On her kitchen table was the black duffle bag with stacks and stacks of money inside.

On top of the bag, he had left a note.

> Hi Lena,
> I thought I was just a poor, poor man in a rich man's world, but come to find out, I'm also a happy man in a sad, sad world. Who knew?
> Love, Santiago.

~ ☾ ~

DECEMBER'S
DIASPORA

i
(the avalon high school caravan)

A December morning, with snow plowed into towers next to the road, Lena and Jozey had to hurry. They had accidently slept too long, and Lena had to eat breakfast before they could leave.

And just a little make-up. Just a little, because it wasn't her armor any more. Now, it was just fun.

Dropping off Jozey at the Cherubim, she kissed him away and he left smiling, holding up a long, white seagull feather. Since his two weeks in foster care, he always had feathers with him. Where he found them, Lena had no idea, but he found them everywhere. She took it as a sign that God or one of His angels was watching over them.

Lena touched the black feather tied to the rearview mirror of her truck.

She drove back to Gramma Scar's, which now served breakfast, because it was where everyone met before the drive to Leadville. In the clear morning air, Mount Calibum and Ablach Peak guarded Avalon in royal mantles of snow and ice, glistening in the sun.

As dark as Mount Calibum was white, Avalon High School still stood, but it was empty. Out of the dozens of bombs, only three had gone off thanks to the Untouchables and their courage. The civil engineers said the repair work would take months and would be too expensive for the Lake County School District to even consider. But Lena and Deirdre were writing letters. As was Deidre's mom who was back home, now as much of

~ ☾ ~

a mother to Lena as she was to Deirdre.

Some people, like Cutler and Parker Lee, drove to the high school in Fairplay over Igerna Pass, but most went with Lena and Deirdre to Leadville every morning in a long carpool caravan of vehicles, some Heretic old from the miner houses, some Paladin new from the Lakeview estates.

There were buses for the younger kids, but the high schoolers drove themselves.

Inside La Rosa Calda, Gramma Scar was talking to Emma over a bowl of apple cinnamon oatmeal. Emma smiled at Lena. "You're late. Did Jozey sleep in again this morning?"

Lena nodded.

Deirdre came in, hugged Lena, and went over to talk to some other Avalon girls. No Paladins. No Heretics. No Untouchables. Just Avalon. Just us.

Tabitha and Paulie came in holding hands.

Avery, Bruise, and Remy were play fighting outside, pushing each other and laughing. Remy was insisting that heavy metal was just noise, and Avery and Bruise were defending the all mighty glory of the electric guitar.

"When will Santiago get out?" Emma asked.

"Next year," both Gramma Scar and Lena answered at the same time. Both kept in touch.

Avery walked over, red-faced from the cold. "Next year? Are you talking about my dad's condos?"

Lena smiled. "In a sense. We were talking about Santiago. It's a six-month program, but he should be home for Christmas break."

"Cool. I can show him the building site. We won't break ground until spring, but he should see what he helped to create," Avery said.

Gramma Scar shook her head. "Who knew my Santiago had it in him? Who knew?"

"He hit every locker," Tabitha said. "Did Lena tell

~ ☾ ~

you? That night, he hit every locker to find that money."

"Yeah, probably singing opera the whole time," Paulie said, rolling his eyes.

"Not opera," Remy corrected. "Bertoglio."

Bruise made a face. "I miss Santiago, but I don't miss Bertoglio."

"Anyone hear anything about Bramage?" Tabitha asked.

No one said anything.

Tabitha kept talking, fearlessly, despite the awkwardness. "We're all together now, like a family, but he's still alone somewhere. All alone."

"And getting hungry," Lena whispered.

Then Deirdre rounded them up. "Okay, Avalon, are we ready? Day forty-one of the exile has begun. Let's show them Leadville Luddites the quality and wonder that is Avalon."

And like Halloween, Deirdre led them in her Lexus at the very front of the line.

Lena came last, in her father's truck, the feather in the rearview mirror dancing. Most of the time she had passengers but not that morning. That morning, it was just her. With the sun gleaming off the snow, she had to squint to see.

At some point during their short time together, Santiago had made her a mixed tape, his opera, Scattershot, and some rare Sympathies covers, and she was listening to it, at peace, when she saw the teenage boy by the side of the road.

The sun off the snow was so bright she could hardly see, but he was there, walking up the highway in a gray hooded sweatshirt and a blue and white ski jacket, eating Skittles out of a red bag, so red it looked like blood against the snow.

She pulled over suddenly, knowing he needed help, but she hit a patch of ice and skidded into a snow bank.

~ ☾ ~

The engine snapped off. The boy in gray had vanished.

It was bizarre, as strange as the rash on her shoulder that had appeared the night Chael had left. She was considering getting it checked out, but the doctor bills would be steep, and her job at the Cherubim didn't pay much.

"Chael?" She whispered the question, but she knew it couldn't be. Chael was gone, seeking God in a heaven he had denied himself for centuries.

Couldn't be Chael.

"Beels?" She shuddered at the thought.

But the mystery of the boy in gray would have to wait. She had to get to school and keep her grades up. Both Mrs. Dodson and Aunt Mercedes had made that clear.

Her truck started right up and she was able to rejoin the caravan.When they turned left on Highway 91, Lena forgot about the boy in gray. For the first time ever, when she heard her mother's question from that terrible night, she had an answer that felt like balm on a wound.

Should we stop?

"No, Mom," Lena said out loud, "but we did, and now it's time to move on."

She smiled, remembering her drive with Deirdre through the snow. She thought of Jozey and Aunt Mercedes. And she thought of Chael, rising up from the dust and ashes to save her life and then flying away to Avalon on his dark wings. His last words echoed through her.

Chael had stopped pushing.

Though he was gone, Lena knew there were other angels on the outside of things, guiding and nudging, here and there. While the angels pushed, the demons ate. She knew the demons couldn't be killed. Johnny Beels, or someone like him, would always be around with mouths open, tongues wagging, teeth dripping.

You couldn't kill demons, but you could starve them.

~ ☾ ~

"And let them starve," Lena said. Maybe once they got hungry enough, they, too, would move on and find a place to stay, enough to eat. Their hunger finally satisfied by knowing life could be good even in the endless struggle that gives life meaning.

Until it was time to let go and take the short walk home.

All prayers answered.

~ ☾ ~

Acknowledgements

I spent most of my writing career as a solitary monk in the wilderness, toiling in the fields, writing, always writing, but always alone. I didn't get very far. This book is alive and well because my wife, Laura, told me I didn't have to be alone. And that reality wasn't so bad.

On her urging, I found other monks, and the Evergreen One critique group took what I wrote, polished out the rough bits, and made it into something. Thanks to Diane Dodge and Jan Gurney for their many years of reading all my many books. Thanks also to Andrea Stein, Jennifer Herfurt, Andrea Petersen-Leskovar, and NC Weil who joined us. I can't thank them enough, those poor critique group outcasts who made me the writer I am today.

Before there was a book, there was the idea, and my non-writer friends Don Bauman and Bess Vannice helped me with plot and character because they are big idea people, and everyone needs big idea people in their lives.

The Never Prayer actually started as dinner conversation. I was eating with Andrea Brown, of the Andrea Brown Literary Agency, and she said I might think about writing an angel book. Lightning struck, and I returned to my monastery and got straight to work. Big thanks to Andrea Brown and Laura Rennert, who have supported me and encouraged me for years and years.

Books don't get published unless the writer sends out query letters. Without Chris Devlin, *The Never Prayer* would still be languishing on my hard drive.

I liked my book before Crescent Moon Press found

me. However, working with my editor Lin Browne, with her superwoman dedication and loving, red pen, my like turned into love. Thank you Lin, Steph, and Marlene for taking a chance on a lonely, old monk.

Aaron Michael Ritchey

Aaron Michael Ritchey was born with Colorado thunderstorms in his soul. He's sought shelter as a world traveler, an endurance athlete, a story addict, and even gave serious thought to becoming a Roman Catholic priest. After too brief a time in Paris, he moved back to the American West and lives semi-comfortably with three forces of nature: a blonde hurricane, an artistic tornado, and a beautiful, beautiful blizzard.

CPSIA information can be obtained at www.ICGtesting.com
Printed in the USA
BVOW020618050412

286926BV00001B/2/P